The Slayer: Hell Awakens

by

Meg Sechrest

Edited by: Amanda Hardebeck & Meg Sechrest

Printed in the United States of America

First Printing, June 2019

ISBN-13: 978-1-7336817-2-8

To everyone who was ever told to give up on their dreams.

Prologue

Abigail Taylor grew up in the backwoods town of Grundy Hill, West Virginia, which was nothing to speak of, really. A pretty girl—though some would've considered her plain—she stood out in a small town with a population of only 2,098. Her long, caramel brown hair and large brown eyes were enticing to many young men, but her peculiar father kept most men away. Standing at six feet tall with shoulder length black hair and a few days' dark shadow, Arlington Domitius was unkempt and wore a dark, hooded cloak. Everyone knew there was something strange about him, though no one quite knew what it was. Even still, they feared him and stayed away.

The people of Grundy lived a quiet life and liked to be left alone. In fact, most outsiders didn't even know the town existed. That is until they found out about *her*.

It all began the previous year on her 21st birthday …

SEPTEMBER 12, 2017

"Abs!" her mother, Janette, called from their living room as Abigail finished getting ready upstairs.

"I'm almost ready!" Abigail hollered back.

"She'll be down soon," Janette said to Abigail's friend Jack Lacombe, Grundy's local sheriff. He and Abigail's other friend Lacy were celebrating her 21st birthday that evening. Secretly, he'd always admired Abbi and had other intentions with her. He offered willingly to be the designated driver for the evening, not knowing what lay ahead.

"You look fabulous, Abbi," Jack said as he eyed her black mini skirt and the cheetah print halter crop top that Lacy made her borrow—though not normally her style—because she'd said it was a special occasion. Walking down the stairs, she smiled bashfully at Jack's comment.

"You always say that," Abbi said, reaching for his hand.

They walked outside and Abbi commented on the cool fall air and the beautiful sunset, trying her best to keep things friendly as she knew that Jack wanted to make this a formal date though she did not. They got in the sheriff's car and headed for the town bar to meet Lacy. Being a few months older than Abbi, Lacy had already landed a job as the bartender at Suds—the local favorite—and was eagerly anticipating Abbi's arrival. Lacy was smiling and waving as Abbi walked in with Jack.

"Abs! Happy Birthday! What time is it? It's only 6:30? You're 30 minutes early! That's okay. You can be my first customer. I just clocked in. Let's get you wasted!!" Lacy exclaimed as she tightened her short black ponytail before tying on her waitressing apron.

Abbi took her seat at the bar and Jack hopped onto a stool next to her, hoping to win her heart by the end of the night. However, Abbi saw him as no more a friend and nothing would ever change that.

"What'll it be first, Abs?"

"Abbi's always seemed to me as a mojito kind of girl," Jack chuckled.

After an awkward pause and no response from Abbi, Lacy piped up, "Okay. A mojito it is. Coming right up!"

"How are things going with your job at the mayor's office?" Jack asked.

"Oh, um … It's the same as always," Abbi answered, glancing over to Lacy.

"I feel like it's been forever since we've had the chance to talk," Jack said as Lacy handed Abbi the mojito.

"Enjoy! I'll check back on you two in a few minutes. I need to wait on my other customers." She nodded to the men who were seated a few stools down from Abbi and Jack.

"Thanks, Lace," Abbi said and waved.

"So, um, … we're still friends, aren't we?"

Abbi felt the cold drink in her hands before drinking down the mojito, trying to decide if it was her drink of choice.

"Of course, Jack. Why would you ask that?"

"It just seems as though things are different between us now."

"Now?" Abbi asked, looking up at Jack.

"You know what I mean."

"You mean since we left high school?" Abbi asked.

Jack nodded, his blue eyes pinning her to her bar stool. Lacy handed Jack a glass of Coke on her way back from taking drink orders from other customers. He took a drink as he said, "We used to be really close growing up, Abbi. Hell, we're neighbors! I remember you coming into my yard and hiding in my tree house when your dad left your mom."

Abbi sighed and turned to Jack, "We aren't kids anymore. Things are different now." She took a sip of her mojito, savoring the sweetness of the white rum against the menthol flavors of the mint as the club soda fizzed against her tongue. She tried again to decide if she liked or hated it.

"How's that drink, Abs?" Lacy hollered as she poured vodka for a man at the other end of the bar.

Abbi looked to the end of the bar and nodded, holding up her half-full glass, "I'm still good!"

"We need a pic of your 21st!" Lacy hollered towards them. "Jack, snap a selfie!"

Jack took out his cell and posed with Abbi in front of the bar, quickly taking a pic. He posted it to social media with the tag: "Abbi turned 21 today! Time to partay!"

While Jack was busy making posts and the notifications on Abbi's phone started buzzing, Abigail looked around the bar. Arlington was right when he told her this town was no good for her. Though she'd never knew why he'd cared so much since he'd left her, and she'd always wondered what he'd meant when he'd said that. Now, as she stared at the choices in dating as she looked around the bar, she was beginning to understand.

Jack pocketed his phone, returning his attention to her, "Come on, Abbi. You know I've always been—"

Abbi cut off his words with the frustrated look in her eyes, "Just don't. Don't ruin what we have."

Abbi didn't want to admit that there was no one in her mind worthy of dating, not even Jack. She blamed the cause of this on Arlington. Her thoughts were distracted by the voice of a young girl and she looked down the bar to her left.

A young girl with black hair stood facing the wall, whispering in a man's ear. Dressed in Georgian period clothing, Abbi thought the child must've been celebrating Halloween early.

"Are there any Halloween parties in the town tonight?"

"None that I know of. Why?"

Jack reached his glass out to Lacy as she walked past and ignored what Abbi was trying to show him.

"Back to our previous conversation, I never see or hear of you going on dates, Abbi. This is a small town and people talk. Is there a reason for this?"

"You mean other than that my dad is a whack job?"

"You're an attractive woman. You mean to tell me that you don't intend on dating at all because of your father?"

Abbi quickly turned to face him and folded her arms, "What are you getting at?"

"I was sort of hoping, um, I …"

Jack trailed off, swirling the ice around in his glass. Abbi shook her head at him.

"You're my friend, Jack. You're my very good friend." Abbi hollered to Lacy, "Hey Lace! How about something else? Maybe stronger?"

Abbi glanced back towards the end of the room where the young girl had been standing, but she was no longer there. She was gone. Abbi felt a gentle tap on her shoulder. She turned around on her stool to see the mystery girl standing there.

"He is coming," the girl whispered before skipping out the front door of the bar.

Feeling completely confused, Abbi looked to Jack and said, "Did you just see that?"

He took another drink and scowled, "See what?"

"The girl. Did you not see the girl?"

He shrugged, "I didn't see any girl. I think you've had too much to drink already, Abbi."

✪✪✪

Hours passed as Lacy poured drink after drink for Abigail and continued to wait on other customers, while Abbi endured a now extremely frustrated Jack. It was about 9:00 p.m. when Lacy called it quits on a very wasted birthday girl.

"I think that's enough for you, lady! You are so drunk! I think you better take this girl home, Jack. Give her a hug for me," Lacy said.

"Nooo! I can handle mooore! The party's only beginnnnning! The moon just came out! Loooook, Lace! There's a full moon tonight! Lucky meee!"

She began laughing so hard that Abbi almost fell off her barstool. Jack reached over to pick her up.

"Come on. Let's get you home," he said.

But just as he touched her, she protested.

"No, Jack! I want to stay."

He was persistent and grabbed her up off her stool against her will. This only made Abbi only more upset.

"No, Jack! Let go of me!"

Abigail Taylor would never forget this moment. It was the beginning of her destiny.

Jack dropped to his knees unable to breathe, his heartbeat weakening. She saw his face turning blue as he began gasping for air. As soon as everyone in the nearby vicinity saw what was happening to Jack, cries for help began. Lacy came rushing out from behind the bar.

No one realized it was Abigail who was triggering Jack's current lifeless state as their hands continued their contact when Abbi reached out and touched him as he fell to his knees, gripping to Abbi's hand. But Abigail had been around her father long enough to know that weird things in her life were bound to show up eventually. Something inside her caused her to yank her hand away from Jack.

The instant she released her grip, she looked into his beautiful blue eyes and his body fell back, collapsing to the floor. The sky outside opened up, letting out a loud thunderous crack as lightning snapped across the sky and rain poured out from dark clouds. Abbi paused in her movement as she heard the thunder roar.

She looked around the bar and saw the reactions from the other customers, realizing that they'd all witnessed what had just happened. Some were whispering to one another while others were sending texts or taking pictures. She was concerned that someone was calling the police. Abigail would never forget Jack's words to her as he began to breathe again, "What's the matter with you?"

"It's storming madness out there," Lacy said as she looked to the window and saw the lightning flash through the sky and heard the thunder rumble.

"I'm calling Arlington to get you home."

How did this happen? she wondered. *What's happening to me? Will I never be able to touch anyone again for the rest of my life? What am I?*

Her thoughts continued as she sat back on the barstool and waited for her father to pick her up. Arlington arrived a short while later and reprimanded Abbi for being so drunk, but his suspicions about her were growing.

"I can't believe you're in this sloppy state that you're in," he scolded as she plopped on the couch of his two-story, Victorian brick house that was cluttered with spell books, jars of potions and leaves from exotic plants he'd collected in case of emergencies.

Several human skulls and animal bones were scattered around the house and near a large grandfather clock in the corner. A brick fireplace was nestled in the center of the wall across from the couch with a picture of Abigail as a young child hanging perfectly on the dark blue wall above it.

"Don't act like a dad right now, Arlington. Act like a … whatever it is you that are and figure out what is happening to me," she said before vomiting on his floor.

"Ugh … jeez, Abigail. Now, c'mon. You're cleaning that up."

She looked up at him with tears in her eyes, "Dad, I almost killed someone tonight. He's one of my best friends. I'm *really* scared. What's happening to me?!"

"That's what I'm trying to find out. Just go to sleep."

He walked away from her while she closed her eyes and wiped the tears from her face.

While Abigail slept, he stood and walked the length of the room in order to clear his head and ponder her situation. After reading several notes from a few spell books, he made certain she was still sleeping before he removed her drunkenness.

"Hancipaviaest!" he yelled out with his palm spread out over Abigail's sleeping face. Immediately, she awakened and inhaled. While keeping a close eye on her, he walked to the window and sat in a plush chair to make a call on his rotary dial telephone.

"Beatrice, I need you to come right now. Yes, I'll pay you double." Arlington hung up the phone and walked over to the bookshelf.

"What are you doing?" Abigail asked as she sat up on the couch.

"Well, I can't think with the stench of the puke in this house, and it doesn't look like you're going to clean it anytime soon so …"

"You're having that prostitute come and clean up the vomit?" she asked, scrunching her face.

Pulling out a book from the shelf, Arlington turned and looked back to her and grinned.

Disgusted with his response, Abigail groaned and flopped backward onto the couch.

"Are you ever *not* involved in anything questionable?"

Turning a page in a book, he smiled over at her and replied, "No."

She didn't reply. Her head was pounding; the room was spinning.

"Oh, Abigail! Can't you make it to the downstairs bathroom before you do that?" Arlington chastised as she vomited on the floor once again.

"Arlington?" Beatrice hollered as she walked inside his front door.

Walking over to her and grabbing Beatrice's arm, he gestured towards his daughter.

"Beatrice, you remember my daughter, Abigail," he said as he pulled her into the living room. Abigail skeptically looked at the prostitute she'd met a handful of times previously. Arlington had Beatrice around quite often. She was always dressed in something very skimpy—today it was a mini red halter dress with black stiletto pumps.

Abigail sighed, shaking her head at her father's lackadaisical attitude towards her mother. The pretty blonde woman's eyes widened at the pathetic state of Abigail before she said, "Yeah, Arlington. I remember. Did you call me here just to clean up this vomit? I'm not your housekeeper."

But Arlington brushed her long hair away from her ear and he whispered into it. Beatrice turned on her heels and walked toward the kitchen.

"Abigail, I want you to use your power on her."

"No!" she exclaimed. "I'm not killing your whore!"

"I don't want you to kill her, Abigail. I'm going to need her again … eventually. I just want to witness what you told me about. Show me what happened at Suds tonight."

She thought for a moment about what he was asking her to do, realizing how wrong it felt.

"Um … I'm not sure if I can. It's not like there's a switch."

Beatrice walked back into the room carrying a mop and bucket with some cleaning supplies. Arlington smiled. He decided to test a theory he'd had.

"Beatrice, put the bucket down."

Turning to face him, she scowled, "Well, do you want me to clean up the mess or not, Arlington?"

She placed the bucket on the hardwood floor in front of where she was standing. He reached back with all his might, slapping her across the face, tossing her down and into Abigail's lap. This started stirring Abigail's emotions, making her angry, igniting her powers. Immediately, Beatrice started gasping for air as Abbi's fingertips touched her skin.

"Arlington! What are you doing?!" Abbi screeched. Arlington reached out and touched Abbi's arm, wanting to feel the force himself.

"I need to feel it. You can't hurt me," he explained as his smile curled up and he looked to the window watching the surge of lightning shoot across the sky and heard the sound of booming thunder.

Abbi's brown eyes looked to Arlington as his face turned to satisfaction.

"No! This isn't right!" Abbi persisted. She quickly tossed Beatrice onto the floor, breaking the physical connection and allowing her to breathe. Arlington pulled Beatrice to her feet and looked severely into her eyes, "Deleatur memoria."

Beatrice blinked and stepped away from Arlington and stepped over to Abigail.

"It was nice to see you again."

She looked to Arlington and shook her head, "I'm not cleaning that up." She pointed to the vomit one last time and stomped out the front door. Abigail stood and walked over to the cleaning supplies and began cleaning up the mess as she spoke.

"What did you do to her, Arlington? How does she not remember what I just did to her? … Do you believe me now?"

He hadn't realized it before. He'd thought the Slayer powers showed up earlier in life and just weren't mature until age 21. But with Abigail, she'd showed no signs of Slayer abilities at all … until now.

"Yes," he answered. "I believe you. But I also believe that you are awakening a force stronger than what I'm able to handle. You are very powerful. I'm taking you home now, though. I have a lot of research to do."

"What do you mean?" she asked, stopping the cleaning to look over to where he stood.

"It'll all be revealed to you soon. Trust me, Abigail."

"Why would I trust you?"

He grabbed her arm, quickly walking out of the room. Without answering her question, Arlington drove her home. Arlington was not reserved in anything he did, even when it came to traveling. Arlington's car was a 1957 British classic. He drove a mint condition, standard, black Austin A55. Abigail always wondered where he found the money to pay for things like that when he didn't work a job.

When they pulled up to the driveway of her small white house, that wasn't nearly as large as Arlington's, Abigail moved to exit the car. Arlington stopped her, "I will pay a visit to your friends, Jack and Lacy. We need to be sure that neither of them recall what's happened tonight. Also, do not speak of this to your mother."

"Arlington?" she asked.

He raised his eyebrows, wanting her to continue.

"What about the people in the bar and their phones? They took pictures and were making phone calls."

He thought for a moment before saying, "I have ways on handling such situations."

"Like?"

"All you need to know is that everyone who was there tonight will not remember what happened."

"How? Tell me! You don't even know who was there!"

"In about 10 minutes I will see for myself."

"What does that even mean? What are you? How can you do all these things!?"

"We will speak on that another time."

"Fine," she groaned, knowing he wasn't going to reveal any secrets. He never did. But just before she closed the car door, she turned to him again and asked, "What am I?"

Arlington's lips curled into a smile, "One of a kind."

One

Looking around, Delius noticed that Hell was nothing as he imagined it would be. The people of the world often described it as a fiery pit, a flaming furnace of inescapable torture, but from what he was seeing, it was just pure evil encompassed in its entirety. There were no flames or fire, and no inescapable torture; it was simply evil—full of eternal beings now trapped down there for all of eternity—every vampire ever staked, every witch ever burned, and every warlock ever doused with holy water, along with every bad or wicked person that didn't live up to whatever standard made the cut for Heaven.

Some of them were fighting with each other, some of them engaging in sexual behavior, and some of them eating and drinking and throwing a wild party in the darkness, where the only light was the radiating glow of the rod of Satan. There was enough to light up an entire world of its own—no one dared touch it for fear of incineration. Everyone wandered about as though they had been there their entire lives, as though they thought nothing wrong with being in the depths of Hell. Their desires and personalities intact, memories of previous lives still remained, but as with life on Earth, no moral code of conduct existed for them.

There were no walls confining them; it wasn't a house or a cage, but rather, it was just a pit of darkness that could only be entered and exited one way: down the stairway and through the gatekeepers—or the portal when it was opened. If someone wandered too far in one direction, they ended up right where they started again. There was no beginning or end to the massive room, only darkness.

The sight was a lot for Delius to take in. He had pictured a much different image of Hell inside his head than what was in front of his eyes, though the sight wasn't at all displeasing. Even Satan himself was not what people imagined him to be. He didn't have red devil's horns or red skin, but rather he walked amongst everyone else, blending in normally until he needed to show everyone who's boss. Then he was as sly as a serpent, literally. His sleek and handsome, blond-haired, masculine form transformed into the longest, sleekest, smoothest black serpent with a pointed, silver tail in order to unleash the Beast, his staff transformed with him in order to give him a sheen glow through the tough serpent's skin.

No one had ever seen the Beast released in their lifetime, that is, except one—Patrick Barclay. He knew the ways of the Beast. Its weaknesses, its purposes, and how to bring it down. Patrick was the oldest of all eternal beings and was considered to be the strongest and most powerful. He was also revered as the ruler of all, even of the Beast—though Satan would not obey him. Patrick and Satan were considered enemies. But no one knew how to find the key to unlock Patrick, no one except Arlington Domitius or Katherine Barclay.

Delius thought for a moment on what to do as he looked around at the scene before him. It was a smaller version of a wild, club party seen on Earth but being hosted by the most malevolent beings that had ever existed. It appealed to him and he started to wander around, noticing people he knew. Scarlett being one of them and Henry being another.

"Henry!" Delius hollered, "Knock that off and help me." He yanked Henry away from where he sat with Scarlett on his lap, kissing her, and pulled him to stand.

"Delius! What the bloody hell do you want from me?" Henry asked as he looked around, taken completely by surprise.

"You know why I'm here. I want that." He pointed to the Beast. "You need to help me. When you do, I'll help get you out of here. You as well, Scarlett."

"Sounds like a good deal. But how are you going to get it out? Those two never leave their post," Henry explained, gesturing towards two guards posted on each side of the Beast.

Delius contemplated his plan while he thought about the demon guards, who were quite a bit larger than he, the demon guards were nothing to go up against empty-handed. Their looks were intimidating with the contorted faces of humans. However, unlike humans, the guards had a raised, prominent, hairless brow with the smashed snout of a pig. Atop their heads were horns of rams and the huge wingspan of a bat and their hands were the sharp claws of werewolves. Each of the guard's demeanor was serious and focused, loyal and dependable.

Looking back at Henry and Scarlett, tightening his little brown ponytail, Delius replied, "I'm going to erase their memories. Our powers still work down here. Scarlett, use your infrared to keep watch. Henry, use your senses to listen in on nearby conversations. I need to be sure that Satan is not in the nearby vicinity. In fact, try and create a diversion while I gain control over this creature."

"How did you open the portal?" Henry asked.

"I didn't. Someone else must've. Katherine, I'm assuming. Tom must be around here somewhere. I used it to gain entrance down here. We need to hurry."

Delius glanced around while Henry and Scarlett reluctantly followed.

"How long does the portal stay open?" Henry asked, pointing toward the winding, howling funnel near the entry to Hell's gates.

"Katherine is holding it open for Tom, I assume. I'm uncertain how long it will stay open. I don't have time to mess around locating him. Let's just get started," Delius responded.

The portal was right outside the gates but could not be easily accessed by just anyone. When a vampire was staked, they're transported to the stairs right in front of the gates, the humans call it limbo. Limbo was where Patrick Barclay remained locked with a spell from his wife Katherine. But even his two sons, Henry and Tom, were unaware of his presence there as it remained a secret to all. Though everyone knew he remained locked in Hell, only two knew of his actual location. There's an allotted amount of time allowed there before a creature must enter the gates. Except for Delius. Delius's time in Hell was always temporary unless he's staked by a Slayer.

For all other beings, they briefly wait in limbo before moving to Hell permanently, kind of like a waiting room but without the cozy chairs and attractive secretary. When the waiting time is up, the gatekeeper calls the name and they must enter. After that, the chances of that vampire being able to be resurrected is far less likely; the vampire enters and the eternity is decided.

A vampire's process of resurrection (or any other eternal being for that matter) was far easier than a human's. Most sorcerers didn't like resurrecting humans because of the risk of not locating their soul. Human souls were kept outside of the gates of Hell and if a sorcerer resurrected the body but not the soul, there would be serious repercussions.

The time on Henry's and Scarlett's gates had not yet closed, so they could still make it back out to the portal. The gatekeeper demons keep a log of each vampire's blood. A blood droplet was required upon entrance and each drop is unique in its own way.

Delius was uncertain how to tame the Beast but knew he had to do it in order to gain control of the one creature that was able to compete against the Slayer with any kind of fighting chance. Much like many other eternal beings, the Beast was sensitive to pure silver and its cage was made of it in order to keep it under control. It had a high intelligence but an agitated temperament because of its wild bull personality and had a tendency to get vicious. The Beast was being held in a giant cage approximately 20 feet high by 15 feet long and 10 feet wide. The lock could only be opened only by the pointed tail of Satan, the Beast's controller.

The Beast itself resembled a large bison in body but had the head of a bull and the tail of a scorpion that shot out a lethal venom to anyone who agitated it. It could be killed, but not easily because of its ability to regenerate and heal itself.

Delius could see that the portal was still open, its spinning and turning of the time loop entry and the static and electricity being created between the two worlds. He looked over to the guards standing outside the cage of the Beast. He approached the guards alone, ready to continue with his plan to use his memory control on them.

"You don't belong here," one guard said, "Return with the other condemned."

Delius outstretched his arm, palm to the guard's forehead, "That which you once knew, will no longer be known. From this day forward, you will always remember as the day you belonged to me."

The guards were now wandering around aimlessly in the darkness without a purpose. Delius used his memory control and went for the Beast, erasing its memories and confusing it into thinking he was its master. Once that was completed, the Beast was tamed long enough for Delius to figure out how to get the silver lock unlatched, which was more difficult than he thought it would be.

"Damn that silver lock!" Delius yelled, looking down at his scorched hands.

He looked around, hoping to see how he could make this work. Luckily, he had plenty of time because Henry created quite the diversion with Scarlett when they started arguing over who was better looking than the other and most in the surrounding vicinity turned to watch.

"You dumb hag!" Henry yelled at her, as they climbed on top of a table.

"I am the more attractive one and I'll prove it!" He tore off his shirt and began flashing his muscles. All the females started yelling and hollering in agreement. With his bad boy attitude that made the ladies want to make him their prize, Henry was attractive at a towering six feet five inches with a lean yet muscular stature and dark hair that had just enough wave in it to drive girls crazy.

Scarlett just scoffed at him and yelled back, "Ha! You're just a laughing joke like your brother! I'm the hottie and we all know it! Okay, gents, who wouldn't want a piece of this?!" She slowly started unbuttoning her white blouse to reveal her black bra. The men started banging and clanging chairs and beer bottles and she gave them a thrill by tossing her black hair around and batting her eyelashes over her dark eyes.

"What about you, down there?" She pointed to a vampire with tattoos and long black hair. He agreed readily and stood making his way to Scarlett before Henry started again.

"Alright, but there are plenty of females in here who would jump at the chance for an opportunity with me! When I was alive, I came from a line of nobility!"

Scarlett's eyes quickly scanned the room while she made a shushing motion with her finger to her mouth to Henry. She jumped down off the table and walked toward the back end of the vast array of people. Henry assumed her infrared had picked up on someone she knew and wanted to make a mockery of, so he waited for her to finish. The people, however, continued hollering for their banter to continue, dissatisfied that they'd stopped. Seconds later, Henry found out why she'd wandered back there.

"Scarlett, get away from me! This is your only warning!"

Tom yelled as he stood up from a table to pace. Running his hands through his thick dark hair he tried his best to ignore Scarlett.

"Oh, but Tom, the people want to see that studly Henry has a sexy, identical twin!"

She turned to face the crowd, "Doesn't everyone want to see this hunk? Look, ladies! They're identical twins! You have not one, but … two!"

She hollered, clapping her hands, enticing the crowd. Scarlett could see that she was frustrating Tom, immensely. She continued by leaning down and whispering in his ear, "You may be identical twins, but we all know you're the true stud." She ran her finger along his strong jaw and turned to engage the crowd once again.

But while she was antagonizing Tom, Henry realized that Delius would be able to use Tom's mind power. He hurried off to let Delius know that Tom was nearby.

"Delius, Tom's here."

"Perfect! That's just what I need. Keep him occupied for me. I'll be right there. I'm going to need his psychokinesis," Delius responded as he moved away from the cage.

Henry walked away from Delius and back over to Tom. Tom, who was extremely irritated—Scarlett was unremitting with her taunting—and was trying his hardest not to lose his control on everyone in sight. Henry walked up next to Tom.

"Good of you to join us here, brother! It's a wild party down here, isn't it?! I'm rather enjoying myself. Too bad we aren't staying."

"That's right," Delius said as he approached Tom on the other side of Henry. "We aren't staying."

"I'll let you two get settled," Henry said, slapping Tom on the shoulder and walking away.

"Tom, your eternity depends on how readily you cooperate with me," Delius said.

"I'm not going to play games with you, Delius," Tom responded.

"Listen, Barclay …"

In a flash, Delius held his hand up to Tom's forehead, replacing his memories of Tom's previous life with only what Delius wanted him to remember.

Once Tom's memories were erased Delius said, "I'm your creator, your controller. You answer to me. Tell the gatekeepers to abandon their posts and not to return. Do it now, Barclay. Control their minds."

Following Delius's order, feeling very confused and only remembering that Delius was his creator and controller, he did as told and approached the gatekeepers.

"Abandon your posts. Leave now. Do not return," Tom mentally said to them and they walked away into the darkness as Delius watched from a few yards away. Tom immediately walked over to the cage of the Beast. Using his mind to crush the lock on the Beast's silver cage, Tom set the Beast free.

As soon as he was finished, Tom began to approach Delius once again, but was released from Hell and was taken up the portal in a tornado-like vacuum.

"Where did he go?!" Scarlett exclaimed.

"I have no idea," Delius said. "It was probably Katherine's doing, which means she's going to close the portal soon. We need to hurry!"

"You have a lot of nerve erasing Tom's memories like that," Henry said.

"What if he remembers eventually? He'll destroy you," Scarlett said.

"Enough of this! I've got to get the Beast."

Delius commanded the Beast like a pet owner gaining authority over a dog. Delius, Scarlett, and Henry along with the Beast exited up the funnel-like portal. Delius had forgotten a very vital piece of evidence though—he couldn't close the portal once he was out of Hell. Delius only assumed Katherine was the one to open it. If she didn't, there would be no one to close it and it would stay open.

Now, with no one to guard it because the gatekeepers were mind-controlled and with the Beast being controlled in the above world by Delius, the underworld creatures were realizing that they could escape. One by one the creatures of Hell went up and out the portal and back into the world. Every evil, malicious, and wicked creature that had ever lived was returning back to life to wreak havoc again. The gates were left wide open allowing creatures to fly up the portal and into the above world to whatever moment the portal was currently opened into. Hell's creatures, unfortunately, landed in 2018, the Generation of the Slayer.

✪✪✪

"Arlington!" Tom yelled out when he saw that he had been summoned by that warlock, Arlington Domitius.

"Hello, Barclay," Arlington responded with a sinister smile.

"What the hell do you want with me?! And what on earth am I doing here?"

Tom stood and looked around, understanding he was at his family's old estate and inside his old bedroom chambers but not yet realizing he had returned to 1787.

"I need you to fix a slight problem that has been detected that will soon be worsening," Arlington said as he exited Tom's chambers into the massive mansion's hallways. He stopped and looked back before closing the door, "You'll want to change into more appropriate clothing. You won't blend well looking the way that you are."

Arlington motioned his finger to Tom in an upwards and downwards gesture, referring to Tom's clothing from 2018. He continued, "You can't be seen in 1787 looking like you're a visitor from a far-off land. Do hurry though. We have to catch up for lost time and discuss the problem."

"Problem? What kind of problem? What are you talking about?"

Tom tried urging him to continue in order to get more information. Arlington was the kind of man never to do anything for anyone else's benefit.

"Just hurry. It will all be explained by the time you're turned again. Oh yes, by the way, you're a human again." Arlington exited, leaving Tom stunned and wondering what in the world was going on.

After tossing on tan breeches and his favorite deep blue waistcoat with a thin white shirt underneath, Tom stepped out of the chambers and into the hallway to speak with Arlington again … or so he thought. However, Arlington was nowhere to be found.

Two

As Delius had planned, Tom's memories of his time in Hell were erased. Tom began to adjust to life as normal, remembering only small bits and pieces of his previous time as a vampire—the parts Delius chose for him to remember.

Only a few nights had passed since Arlington sent Tom back to 1787 and to Greenvalley, Tom's wealthy family estate in 18th century England, but re-establishing himself to the customs of society was easier than Tom thought it would be. Immediately, he recognized the moment in time to which he had returned and he familiarized himself with his family and the household staff once again.

Having come from a long line of wealth and nobility, Greenvalley was a massive mansion with people and servants always bustling about. Servants were constantly busy with something or another. Greenvalley and its many subdivided business properties had a never-ending stream of visitors. Tom's father, Patrick, was an Earl, and Tom, being the eldest was to take up the title in his father's place eventually. That moment would never happen because there was soon to be an event that would change his life forever.

That morning, all the chatter was about the previous evening, as expected. For the several oldest members of the family had attended the highly anticipated masquerade ball, Tom and Henry included. Henry walked into the dining room dressed in what was considered only half-socially acceptable clothing, dark navy breeches and an untucked linen shirt, and joined his family for breakfast. He was tired and hadn't slept; nevertheless, he listened in on the conversation from nine of his ten siblings.

"I danced every dance!" Giana, the oldest sister, exclaimed.

"As did I!" Brielle, the second eldest girl, joined in with her, giggling together.

"How much longer do we have to hear about this dreadful ball?" 12-year-old James asked, annoyed with all of it.

"Until one of them dies, I'm afraid. I could arrange for that, if you wish," Edwin joked with his brother in his usual mocking style. James laughed, finding humor in his brother's joke.

"That's not funny!" Giana yelled back to him. "Father! Tell them to let us have our fun!"

Their father laughed too, however, amused at the scene. Henry laughed and agreed that his sisters could be a bit ridiculous. Their mother only smiled but looked Henry's way.

"Where's Thomas?" she asked. Henry only shrugged in reply.

"Was he awake this morning?"

"I don't know, Mother. I don't make it a habit to keep track of the regular habits of my brother. We may be twins, but we are *not* the same person," he said, irritated.

"I know where he is," three-year-old Charlotte spoke up from the far end of the long dining room table with a conniving grin.

Everyone looked over to her. Henry took a bite of his breakfast trying to hide his smirk, thoroughly amused by the quick turn of events. "Well?"

Their mother looked at her sternly, wanting Charlotte's explanation.

"He left out his window last night and didn't come back," she said nonchalantly and bit into her biscuit.

"Do you know where he went, Charlotte?" Lord Patrick asked.

"Well, I would think he went with the woman who was waiting below his window," she answered.

Edwin laughed, "Lottie, for a three-year-old, you seem to have the most knowledge of anyone in this family! How is that?"

"I'm the smartest!" she replied, sticking out her tongue.

"No, she's not. Her room is just situated in the best location! Right next to the biggest troublemaker!" 18-year-old, Ami, retorted. Giana and Brielle giggled, knowing full well that their middle sister, Ami—or Amelia—was correct. Tom was always getting himself into trouble, especially when it came to the ladies.

"I want *that* room," eight-year-old Marie pouted, "I want to know everything that is happening! It's not fair that she gets the best room in all the house! I don't want to be next to Ami! She's boring!"

"Of course, Marie," Edwin said and rolled his eyes, "You're the family gossip."

"I am not!" she whined, "I just like to know what is happening. Ami is so dull! At least put me next to Henry or someone else!"

"What do you think a gossip is?"

"It is not," she fussed.

"Of course it is," Edwin continued.

"Is not!" she argued back.

"Enough of this!" their father yelled at both of them. Henry looked across the table to Leonard, the next brother in line, and gave him a sly smile. They loved seeing the chaos that their older brother's schemes were causing.

"What are you going to do about him, Father?" smirked Giana as she took a sip of tea.

"It'll be sorted out," he said to Giana. He looked over to his wife with a concerned look.

"What about dear Lady Harriet? She won't want to marry him now!" Brielle relished in the idea that Tom's arranged marriage to Lady Harriet Loudgraves would be ruined over his scandalous ways.

"Why not?" Charlotte asked, "Why would she not want to marry him? I would marry him any day."

"You can't marry him, you stupid head. He's your brother," James said to her as he stuck out his tongue.

"Enough of this! All of you!"

Patrick yelled as he slammed his fists onto the table. Henry continued to find amusement and satisfaction in the entire situation, leaning back in his chair, arms crossed over his chest. His thoughts drifted to what Tom could've possibly been out doing and with what woman.

"Tom ... you never cease to amaze me. You keep the Barclay family full of interesting moments. I can't wait to see the look of horror on our father's face when you can't marry Lady Harriet Loudgraves. Ruining your engagement over a tradesman's daughter. We all know she's your secret lover. The secret lover you stole from me."

As Henry got lost in his thoughts, their mother, Katherine, gasped and grabbed her forehead. Everyone quieted themselves as Patrick rushed to her side and escorted her out of the room.

"Henry, go listen in!" Brielle urged.

Katherine claimed she was getting another one of her "headaches". Even though their mother claimed that they were headaches, everyone knew that she had some sort of higher power to see the future. The headaches were bringing her visions and she was able to see things to come and things that had not yet happened.

She was gaining powerful capabilities the older she grew. Although Katherine had not shared it with any of the children, one of them always listened in on the conversations about her headaches between their parents. This time, Henry was the chosen. He hurried out to listen outside the door of Patrick's study, where he and Katherine were quietly talking.

"What is it, Kate? I know you had another vision."

"It's Tom. I saw him with a woman in the distant future. I didn't see her face or any details. But I heard her say his name."

"The distant future?" he asked.

"Yes. She called him Hercules ... her Hercules. I fear that his future is about to change in a very drastic way."

"But you saw no details of her?"

Henry heard no response from his mother and assumed that she'd shook her head. His interest about this was growing enormously with every second. Henry was curious to know if Tom had returned yet, so he hurried down the hall and up the main staircase to the family's living quarters.

His chambers were situated on one side of Tom's with a connecting dressing room in-between. On the other side of Tom's chambers was Charlotte's. Continuing down the length of the hall opposite Charlotte's chambers was each of the other girls' chambers and their shared dressing rooms. Across the hall were the other boys' chambers along with their parents' chambers at the very end of the hallway. Any guests that stayed overnight slept in a different wing of the Barclay mansion.

Henry entered his chambers and then walked into the dressing room to listen for any signs that Tom might be in his chambers. But he was interrupted.

"Hello, Henry," said an enticing voice from behind him. Henry startled and quickly turned around to look at her.

"Claire! What are you doing here? This isn't our usual day to meet up."

"I saw your window open when I made my stop by the kitchen this morning."

She reached for his hand, leading him out of the dressing room and into his chambers. After planting a kiss on his lips she said, "Come with me, Henry."

He willingly followed Claire as she tugged him along, up and out the window, and down the trellis.

Out the window and down the trellis he went, following his heart's desires. Henry was madly in love with Claire and would do anything for her. Her playful demeanor and her childish freckles, green eyes, and long, strawberry blonde hair that curled up ever-so-slightly on the ends had a way of enticing him. Had she met Lord Patrick's list of approved women his father allowed Henry to marry, Henry would've been married to her already. But she didn't; she was only a milkmaid.

✪✪✪

It would only be months later that the Barclays would be soon trying to forget Henry ever existed. That very day that Henry left with the milkmaid was the last day the Barclays would ever see him alive and well.

"Wellington, can you be certain that Lord Thomas is awake this morning? I need him to be about at a reasonable hour today. We are expecting visitors and his father wants him to be present."

"Certainly, Countess, I will see to him immediately," Wellington responded.

As soon as Tom heard the conversation in the hallway cease, his chambers doors opened. He knew it was his valet, Wellington. Calling it a death felt wrong to Tom. No one really knew what happened to him. Henry's chambers were closed and the Barclays pretended it never happened. No one talked about it in the presence of Lord Barclay or Katherine, that is.

But the siblings whispered to one another daily and missed him terribly. Henry's brothers often went out to the fields late at night searching for anything they could find to bring him home. There was one specific instance that Leonard and Tom had gone out with James and Edwin. Even Amelia and Giana insisted on tagging along to help.

As the group of siblings trekked across the big field on the back side of the Barclay mansion, Edwin muttered to Giana and Amelia, "If you two are going to be joining, could you leave the whining about the bugs and mud to yourselves. Possibly at least keep it to a low whisper?"

"You men don't know what it's like for women to have to be in these bulky dresses all the time!"

"Complain, complain, complain. Just pull up the hem of that dress and let's go, Ami," Tom said.

They were headed to the wooded area on the opposite side of the vast fields. Tom and Leonard knew that Henry and Claire often hid away in the woods to be alone. Henry would go there with her; Tom was sure of it. The woods had a creek that ran through it. Henry would return through his window with muddy boots and wet breeches. Claire would be late for her deliveries to the kitchen with the hem of her dress, at least a foot deep, covered in mud.

"Who will be first?" Giana said as the group approached the edge of the woods.

Tom and Leonard looked to each other and Tom nodded, taking a step forward. The others followed.

"How much farther?" Ami asked.

"I'm not quite sure it was a good idea for you to come," Leonard said, glancing back to the girls.

"I told you, Ami," James said, "Girls should just sit in the library and read. This is a man's work."

"Then you definitely shouldn't be here, James," Edwin retorted.

"Will you all just pipe down!" Leonard snapped.

When they got to the creek, Tom looked to Leonard.

"We should spread out. Edwin and Gi, you come with me. Leo, you go with James and Ami and search towards the west end of the creek.

"What is this?" Giana said as they approached a makeshift shelter near the creek.

Tom moved the willow branches that had been laid over the top as a roof covering and looked inside.

"Tom?" Edwin said.

Giana gasped and covered her mouth at the sight of some of what was definitely Henry's clothes alongside a servant woman's dress.

"Come with me, Edwin," Giana said and pulled him out of the sight of possibly Henry's last whereabouts. "Why don't you go over to the creek for a moment while I talk to Tom."

Edwin ran the few yards away to the creek and Giana turned to face Tom.

"We know what he was doing here and we know who with, Tom."

Tom ran his hand over his face and didn't respond.

"Do you think …"

"I don't think Claire Davenwell killed Henry, but I don't think she's innocent. Let's go find the others."

Tom now knew he was going to have to speak to Claire.

$$\bigstar\bigstar\bigstar$$

The next evening, Tom rode his horse Moxie into town.

"Claire!" Tom hollered into her window where she lived on the poor side in the rowhomes. He banged several times on the frame of the window where the pale blue paint was chipping before she finally appeared and opened it for him.

"What do you want? If someone sees you …" she said as he stepped inside.

"Since when have you cared about your reputation? I'm here about Henry," Tom answered.

"I haven't seen Henry in weeks."

"You're hiding something; I know you are," Tom said, moving closer and pointing his finger in her face.

"What would I have to hide? I loved Henry, Tom. I miss him as much as anyone. You know that." She turned to walk away.

"Claire Davenwell!"

"What else could you possibly want, Tom?"

"Just tell me what you know."

"What makes you believe that I know anything about where he is?" she asked, wiping her tears.

Tom didn't say anything for a moment as he watched her quietly cry. After he contemplated that she might not actually know anything about Henry's disappearance, he remembered that she was the last one to be seen with him by the servants and in town. He also wanted to mention the servant woman's dress they found in the woods, but he knew she would only deny it was hers.

"Claire, the servants at the Barclay Mansion say you were at his chambers that morning. I've also heard from numerous sources that he was seen here in town with you that very day. You've also refused to deliver to our family since. What else would I believe?"

"It is true that I was with him that day. But I have not seen him!" She wiped her tears and Tom exited through the window. Tom believed Claire was hiding something and left unconvinced of her innocence but had no way to prove anyone of anything.

✪✪✪

"Lord Thomas, your mother requests your immediate presence," Wellington addressed Tom as he continued lying in bed. Not being particularly fond of waking early. Tom groaned and ignored Wellington. His father and mother had certain expectations of him, and Tom knew they had visitors he was likely to entertain. But it was not his concern to entertain any of their visitors, ever.

Wellington persisted, "Sir, Lord Barclay requests …"

"Who is it this time? Another eligible female?" Tom asked, peeking out from underneath the pillow.

Wellington smirked at him knowing that there would be no matchmaking taking place and answered, "I believe, sir, that Lord Loudgraves has brought his daughter for you to see … again. Shall I assist you?"

"No," Tom insisted and rolled back over onto his stomach, covering his head with his pillow once again.

"Of course, sir. What shall I say in regards to your mother?" he asked, understanding that she would want an explanation on his absence.

"Oh, right," Tom sighed, desperately not wanting to deal with her. He looked up to Wellington and continued, "Send word to her that I am ill. Spare me of this misery, please Wellington. Harriet Loudgraves is a detestable sight. I cannot be matched with that woman, Lady or not."

"Yes, sir. I will inform her. Let me just say, sir, that in all my years as a servant, I have never come across one as set against his role in life as you."

Wellington smiled and exited Tom's chambers.

Tom rolled his eyes and draped his legs over the side of the bed. He began to pace the room. Stressed and wondering what to do about, his father and all this matchmaking.

"What to do … I undoubtedly cannot marry this Lady Harriet. There's no way I am getting out of it because I need to marry a noble woman because 'That's the way it is!' says my father."

After hearing more steps in the hallway, Tom hurried to throw on his tan breeches and a clean white linen shirt, knowing it was his mother coming to demand to know why he wasn't presenting himself to Lady Harriet. He quickly did his usual escape down the trellis beneath the window. Tom had used it plenty of times before to have others climb in or to climb out. Tom felt not at all guilty for his life of leisure with the ladies, especially the servant girls.

"If I'm going to be fixed to a long life of marital unhappiness, then I might as well have my way with all the women I want while I still can."

He headed for the stables and grabbed his favorite black Belgian named Moxie. After a long ride through the countryside trying to avoid the woman his father was set upon his betrothal, Tom stopped at the end of the dirt drive where a big field rested the family cemetery. Though they never found Henry's body, the family felt it necessary with such a long absence to make it final and put up a tombstone, so the family could make their farewells.

Henry William Barclay
9 April 1760-23 July 1787

Staring at the tombstone brought back all the memories of their terrible relationship. Tom couldn't even recall why he and Henry hated each other. He couldn't even recall when it began. Perhaps it began when their father favored Tom because he was the heir. The relationship between the brothers worsened when Scarlett, the tradesman's daughter, began to prefer Tom as well.

Though Henry loved Claire, he had once sought after Scarlett and Tom knew it. Henry was angry because Tom couldn't marry Scarlett but still encouraged her affections. But when Tom found out about Henry's love affair with Claire, he made his own game of it and sought after Claire too, just to piss off Henry. However, Henry could've counted it a fortunate event because that's also when he discovered Claire's love was real; she hadn't shifted her affection to Tom only for the sake of immature games. Her affection stayed fixed on Henry and his love for her deepened.

Tom sat on the hillside and thought on Henry for many minutes as he stared at Henry's name etched in the tombstone, never thinking he'd be so young a man when he saw his own brother's name stamped on one.

Realizing that the sun was dipping down behind the trees, Tom stood and looked down to the tombstone one more time and said, "Henry, I know we had our differences, but I hope you are well, wherever you are. May I see you again someday."

When he turned to leave, he was startled by movement in the shrubbery.

"Goodness, brother! I didn't know you felt so strongly for me!" a familiar voice said.

"Henry?!"

"Yes, it's me. Surprised?" Henry asked as he stepped into view.

Tom's memory was stirred at the sight of Henry as a vampire and he recognized the red rings encircling the eyes that flushed the eyelids with a touch of red, the fangs, and the darkness in the eyes.

"No! Henry, back away! I've been down this path once. I won't do it again!"

Henry snickered. Walking out from behind the shrubs, Henry attacked. He began beating Tom around so brutally that Tom's memory began to stir even more, remembering Delius and his first life as a vampire. Teetering on the point of death, Tom began to cough up blood. Henry walked over, grabbed Tom by his shaggy, dark hair, pulling his head to the side to expose his neck.

"Had enough?"

Biting into Tom's neck, Henry forcefully drank his brother's blood. With barely any coherency, Tom felt Henry pull back and watched him bite into his own finger allowing blood to drip. Tom hesitated at first, not wanting to take it, knowing this would turn him into a vampire again. Henry forced Tom to taste the smallest dribble.

After just a drop, overcome by its sweet taste and healing effects, Tom drank Henry's blood willingly, unable to resist.

After a few moments, Tom pulled away.

"What happened to you, Henry?"

Henry didn't reply. He just grabbed Tom's head in one hand holding his body firmly in the other and snapped his neck, transforming his eternity.

✪✪✪

Tom woke later that evening amidst the shrubs where Henry had left him dying.

"Nice to see you've made a full recovery," Arlington said to him as Tom stood to take a look around. Tom felt his vampire urges and impulses returning, realizing he was a vampire once again. He had the sudden and intense craving for blood.

"What's this all about?!" Tom yelled as his eyes encircled with crimson and his fangs shot out. Arlington backed up, cautiously.

"Settle down. You'll get your blood. I needed you to be a vampire again, but I couldn't have you under Delius's control. I needed to break that bond. He couldn't be your creator, not this time. You needed a new creator. Who better than your own flesh and blood? Welcome back, Thomas."

"I feel so confused," Tom said as he began to scratch his forehead. Standing, he paced the grassy area near Henry's tombstone.

"Well, Delius has created quite a mess of things, and being who you are, *you* need to fix it. The Master of Sorcery has summoned you," Arlington said with a devilish grin.

"Being who I am? What do you mean? What has he done?" Tom asked and stopped his pacing and turned to face Arlington.

"He's released the Beast. Now he's mistakenly left open the gates to Hell, allowing all the creatures down there to walk freely. I need your power. And, yes, I do have a plan."

"My power? A plan?"

Tom's curiosity was growing. He'd heard of the Beast before but was unaware of what the consequences of Delius's actions were. Delius—being the oldest vampire in existence—felt he answered to no other vampire or being of similar likeness and frequently showed his believed authority because no one could kill him and Satan could not keep him locked in Hell without the order of Patrick Barclay or without the Slayer. Tom's power was unlike anyone else's and many eternal creatures often turned to him when looking for help.

Arlington's eyes grew sinister and his lips curled.

"First, we must pay a visit to 2018. Come. We must hurry. The creatures from Hell are wreaking havoc all over the earth. I know of only one who can stop this now, but she is … well, you'll see."

Three

The past year had been filled with more mayhem than any 21-year-old would ever care to admit. But now that Abigail was 22, her life was beginning to calm down. That was until one unique event changed everything for her … again.

✪✪✪

"I had a situation today," Abbi anxiously told Arlington, when she called him one October evening.

"What happened?"

"My boss was getting a little too handsy and my emotions were running high."

"Want me to kill him?" Arlington asked.

"Dad!" she hollered before realizing her mom was standing just outside her bedroom. Abbi peeked her head out to be sure her mom wasn't listening to her talk to Arlington.

"I'm guessing that's a no?" he asked as Abbi closed her bedroom door and leaned her back against it.

"Can you just be a regular dad, please?" she asked much quieter so Janette wouldn't hear.

"Continue."

"Well, he grabbed me and …"

"Do I need to hide a body?"

"Um …" she hesitated.

"Where is he?" he asked.

"Mayor Fulton is in my car's trunk," she whispered and looked out her bedroom door once more to be sure her mother had gone downstairs.

"You killed the mayor?!"

"I was working as his assistant, remember?!"

"Oh, yes, that's right. Bring the body to my house. I'll deal with it. By the way, hiding bodies for you isn't what regular dads do."

"Wait!" she yelled just before he hung up.

"What is it?" he asked.

"When I killed him …" she hesitated and started pacing her bedroom, feeling very nervous about having just killed Lacy's father.

"Go on," Arlington pushed. "I am a man of importance, Abigail. I don't have all day."

"Where do you have to be?"

"I have to meet a man about a girl."

"Oh? What girl?"

"You."

"That's creepy. Why are you discussing me?" she asked and looked out the window to watch Janette leave for her evening shift at the town diner.

"What were you going to say?" he urged, distracting her and going back to her previous statement.

"Oh, uh … immediately, like I mean the second he died and I pulled away from him, there was a lightning bolt that hit right outside my building. But it wasn't even storming before then. It's very odd because that keeps happening every time. The first couple times I thought it was coincidence but not now."

"I know this. It's why I have to meet a man. Bring me the body. I'll see you soon."

"Wait!" she yelled into her phone just as he was hanging up.

"What?"

"What's happening, Arlington? I'm really scared and I deserve answers!" she said and grabbed her jacket and purse and headed for the door.

"Remember last year when I told you that you were awakening forces that were out of my influence?"

"Yes …"

"That time has come."

He hung up without another word. Abbi frowned, staring at her phone. She was getting really tired of not having answers.

✪✪✪

"You know, Arlington," Abbi said when she showed up at his house later that evening, pointing him to the body still in the trunk of her car. "I told you weeks ago that Mayor Fulton was getting too friendly with me and you wouldn't listen."

Arlington made no reply as he lifted Mayor Fulton's body out of Abigail's car and put it into his car. Closing the trunk lid down, Arlington finally spoke, "I will arrange for you to have a new job within the week. In the meantime, don't touch anyone else, especially if you want me to be a regular dad."

He walked toward the driver's side of his car, pulling out his keys.

"Arlington! Wait!"

Arlington got in his car and started it. He waited as she walked over, "I would really like to take care of this mess before word gets around."

"I just wanted to say thanks."

He nodded and turned to back out. Abbi leaned against the car door and said, "What About Lacy? That's her father."

Impatient, Arlington tapped his fingers on the steering wheel, staring out towards the road. "Abigail, you will not be connected to the death. Lacy will believe it to be an accident, which it was."

Abigail nodded and smiled. She watched his car drive away, disappearing into the darkness. For a brief moment, she was grateful for her obscure father.

✪✪✪

Killing the mayor is what brought Abbi to where she was right now.

Arlington kept to his word and had gotten her a job where she could hide out as the evening manager at a boutique run by the local witch, Susan.

"Call me if you need anything," Susan said as she left for the evening.

"Okay, will do. Thanks, Susan."

"Abbi?" Susan glanced her head back inside the door before exiting, "Be careful. There are some weirdos out there at night."

"I will. Thank you for being so kind to me."

That Wednesday night as she clocked out, there was a startling noise coming from the back alley that led to the parking area where she always parked her blue Ford Focus. Used to strange noises coming from that alley, she thought nothing of it, blaming the bar two doors down, which was known for its drunken brawls.

Upon opening the boutique's back door and poking her head out, she quickly realized there was something different about what was going on. She changed her mind, pulling the door shut. This fight was unlike any fighting that she had previously heard from that bar. There was no yelling, no swearing, just banging—loud and brutal as the bodies banged into the brick walls and metal dumpster.

Though she heard the fight continuing and felt a bit intimidated, she had to exit out the back. After taking a deep breath, she had a burst of courage and opened the back door once more. Stepping out and into the alley, the scene before her was overwhelming.

Bodies were banging off the dumpster, walls, and doors, bouncing back and forth faster than she could follow. One of the two men let out a loud snarl, causing her to startle. Her heart sped up and she was so overcome with fear that she turned to go back inside. But she was stopped.

The boutique's back door slammed shut. The man who'd snarled said in a low, fierce growl, "Don't be afraid. Leave quickly." In a flash, he was gone faster than was humanly possible. Abbi's fear was replaced by keen interest.

She walked towards her car feeling dumbfounded. But just as she walked past the dumpster, she heard something stirring behind it. Unable to see what it was from the dimly lit alley, she slowly moved closer, peering into the dark. Her eyes widened, recognizing the other of the two men. Noticing the state of his brutally beaten body, Abbi realized that he would probably not survive until an ambulance arrived. Still, her heart wanted to help. She began the search into her behemoth of a bag for her cell phone. That's when he reached up and grabbed hold of her leg.

"Oh no … it's a vampire. You better run!" he laughed.

Taken aback by his words, she looked down and saw two marks on the side of his neck. It appeared as though he'd been bitten by a snake or a very large spider. Certain that those marks on his neck were not a good sign, she struggled to maneuver her leg out of his unusually strong grasp tightening around her leg. Before she could finish her call to get an ambulance, he let out an inhuman growl causing her to look down to him. That's when she saw the fangs.

She saw his eyes encircling in deep crimson as the fangs extended into razor-sharp, dog-like canines and they were very intimidating. Abigail's fear was increasing beyond what she could handle. Unable to conceal the terror, she screeched, crying out for help. But there was no one around.

She frantically tried pulling her leg from his tight grip, but it only aggravated him. "Don't be afraid. I'm just playing with you. Just let me mess around with you for a few minutes. It's not every day a vampire gets ahold of someone like you."

She had no escape against his grasp. She screeched again, "HELP! SOMEONE, PLEASE!"

A quick, figure flew past, knocking her to the ground, releasing her from the hold of the vampire. While her rescuer hovered over top of her, he scolded, "I told you to leave quickly!"

In a blink, he was off of her and over on top of her assailant, calling out for her.

"Hurry!"

She obeyed. Approaching him she noticed his strikingly handsome face. His face was almost too handsome, she couldn't remember a time in her life when she had seen someone so good-looking, He took her breath away. She stopped in her tracks as he looked over to her from where he was straddling the other man's waist with his legs, holding his throat with a sturdy grip of his strong hand.

"Quickly!" he demanded again in an unusually sensual voice. To appease his command, she snapped herself from her daze and hurried, noticing that he had the vampire unconscious.

"Yes?"

He looked up at her and pulled a long, wooden stake—about 12 inches in length—with a sharp, pointed end out of his belt. As he handed her the stake, she noticed his eyes were also encircled in a deep crimson color that flushed his eyelids and the outer skin with a brush of redness. However, the irises of his eyes were blacker than coal, seemingly unnatural, while the luminescent whiteness which surrounded that darkness kept her captivated.

"Take this and stab his heart with all your force," he said as he grabbed her arm and pulled her down in front of him, mimicking his straddle position. As she did, he inhaled deeply—reveling in her scent. He placed his hands on her waist and pulling her closer to him, igniting his passions.

He realized that Arlington's daughter was possibly the most beautiful woman he had ever seen. He moved in even closer, inhaling again, closing his eyes and enjoying the intimacy of their current position. Nervously, Abigail held the stake up above the unconscious vampire.

She shakily but forcefully thrust it down into the vampire's heart. It was like she had no control of her actions; something or someone else was compelling her to move. The vampire's heart burst, releasing blood forth like the water bursting from a geyser.

Blood spewed all over her. Horrified, she jumped back, knocking into her rescuer. He caught her, wrapping his arms around her and pulling her up. The staked vampire was now shriveling into a dusty corpse and fading away into nothing. As Abbi and the man touched, he realized there was something unique about her.

It was unlike anything he'd ever experienced in his vampire existence—humanity—she was causing him to feel. He wanted more and he stared into her eyes for a moment and was instantly under her spell.

"Oh my god!" she screamed, "What was that?!"

"Abigail," he said and tried to calm her, but she continued to stare towards where the vampire had been lying.

"What the hell was that?!" she repeated.

"That was a vampire out of the depths of Hell. You just sent him back. I'm Tom by the way. Your father sent me."

Her thoughts went in multiple directions at once. "My father? Hell? Why are you here? Why did I just do that? What is going on?!?"

"You will find out eventually. Look, I'm just doing my job." He held up his hands innocently.

"Your job? What's your job?" she asked, narrowing her eyes.

"To be sure you don't die," he replied, pointing at her. Tom turned and sped away, out of the alley and disappearing from sight. Leaving her mind in a whirlwind, Abbi looked down at the fresh blood soaking her clothes.

Dazed, she made her way towards her car, her mind remained fixed on how the events that had just happened could even be real. But as she drove through town replaying the bloody images over and over in her mind, her thoughts kept coming back to the man named Tom.

<u>Four</u>

Dashing out of the alley, Tom headed towards Arlington's brick house.

"Arlington! What's with your daughter!?" Tom said as he walked into Arlington's messy abode. Tom found Arlington in his kitchen, making a cup of tea.

"Ah, you find her beautiful," he chuckled, "I had a feeling you might. You always liked Claire and this one is far better looking than my other daughter, don't you think? Abigail has more of a natural beauty."

Seeping his tea bag, he continued, "But hands off. She's not yours to play with. Remember, we have a job to do. Would you like some tea?"

Tom growled at Arlington, annoyed.

"I'm not just talking about her beauty, Arlington. Her touch … I've never felt more human than when I *was* human! What the hell was that?!"

Tom began to pace the length of the kitchen, running his fingers through his hair. He felt Arlington was up to something more than he was letting on.

"Oh yes. I forgot to mention that *tiny* detail. She has a touch almost as powerful as your mind power."

Tom contemplated those words for a moment and then continued, "Explain."

"Gladly," he said and then he walked into his living room and sat on the worn and tattered green sofa. Tom started pacing the length of the room again. This time he was scratching his forehead, thinking and Arlington continued his explanation, "My daughter was born a Slayer, but her Slayer power is very unique. She encompasses a position as the Slayer. No one has seen or known of a Slayer for hundreds of years.

Someone with her power and uniqueness is valuable to the eternal kingdom. Slayers have the capability to bring down any and all vampires no matter the vampire's power, ability, or age. Each Slayer has a power exclusive to themselves—Abigail's being her superhuman touch and ability to cause vampires to feel their humanity."

"You're telling me she's the only Slayer to exist since before my time?"

Arlington nodded.

"Not only that, she causes vampires to feel human?" Tom asked.

Arlington nodded once more.

"From what I've seen firsthand and learned from literature, previous Slayers have been incredibly strong or fast; some have had unmatchable instinct or overwhelming senses; some have even had unique powers such as manipulating weather of a small area or a slight telekinesis similar to yours … things like that. Not one Slayer has had her unbelievable capabilities along with the power of her touch and the ability to bring out the humanity in a vampire. No one has ever come across any creature of her likeness in the history of the world. All the Slayers have been unique and they've all been powerful, bringing forth destruction to vampires whenever one came into existence. One touch from her and a vampire is completely under her control. The difference with Abigail is that she is dangerous to humans as well."

That particular statement caught Tom's attention. He stopped in his pacing and turned to face Arlington.

"How so? What do you mean?"

"She can't touch anyone. Her power works on humans *and* vampires. With humans, however, because they already have humanity, she takes their life. At the touch of a finger, if her adrenaline is up or her emotions are heightened, she steals everything there is of them. Every heartbeat, brainwave, and breath. Her finger steals it all the moment she makes skin-to-skin contact."

"Interesting … tell me more about why she's the only one that's existed for hundreds of years. I'm curious."

Tom sat in the chair next to the fireplace across the room. "Do you clean this house, Arlington? This place is a dump," Tom asked, looking around at the mess.

"I assure you, I know where everything is and I need all of it for my sorcery," gesturing to the piles of books, papers, and random items he had strewn about the room. Arlington continued, "In previous times, Slayers happened generationally. Abigail is the first to not immediately replace a previous."

"What do you mean? Like the world has been waiting for her?"

Arlington nodded. "This is what I was explaining to you about her line being wiped out."

"I see. We really have been waiting for her. There's a reason she showed up at this moment in time. But do we know why?"

"I have yet to figure that part out. I cannot figure out if she is the cause or if she's the effect."

"Does her coming have anything to do with Hell's gates?" Tom asked.

"Yes. I'm quite certain that it is because of her that the Hell portal has been opened, which you well know from our discussions. But what I haven't told you is that I don't know yet if the Hell portal was already being activated. "

"I understand. You mean because she was turning 21 … which came first? Did she interrupt it or vice versa?"

"Exactly."

Tom's curiosity was growing immensely. Even more so, though, he wanted to see Abigail again. Tom was drawn in by her unbelievable beauty and the humanity her touch brought out in him. Though he told Arlington he wasn't interested, he decided he would visit her the next night at the same place—the alley behind her work—even if there were no vampires to stake.

✪✪✪

For the time being, he ran to the far side of the county to occupy his mind and distract his thoughts from her. Tom entered the dark mine shaft that had been abandoned by humans for over a century. He sped through the long tunnels where the dirt walls were starting to cave in on the sides. The dirt pathway had many gaps and spaces that had already begun to collapse which made it inaccessible for human entrance and the whole tunnel smelled of rotting flesh as he moved the dead bodies of Antonius's kills along the way. If a human were to get trapped in the tunnel, Antonius made use of the body and ate it. He thought how Antonius might be able to shed some light on the current situation Tom had entangled himself in.

Tom sped through the hallways and kept heading deeper underground until he reached a concrete walkway. He slowed his pace to walk the few hundred feet to a steel-framed door. Tom hit the intercom to talk to Claudine.

"Hey, Claudine. It's Tom. Is Tony around?"

"Hi Tom," she responded.

"He's in the back. I'll let him know you're here. C'mon through."

She hit the door buzzer and unlocked it. Tom walked in taking notice that nothing around his place of residence ever changed. His was a place where many vampires often came to socialize, though not a formal bar, Antonius could always be counted on for vodka and women, and protection from the sun.

Antonius was really the only vampire Tom ever associated with. Created during the crusades of the 1200s, he'd been around a long time and had seen a lot of things. Tom wasn't nearly as old as Antonius but pretty much hated his existence as a vampire. Antonius was able to commiserate with Tom's bitterness about life in general, which gave him a pretty good appreciation for the bitterness of being a vampire.

Though Antonius didn't hate life as a vampire, he felt time tended to pass slowly and knew the frustration of being around for a very long time. When Tom was feeling tired of the unsatisfying experience of having no soul and the reality that the rest of all eternity would be this way, Tony was always right there to remind him that Hell was only a stake away.

Tom strolled into the main seating area of the lavish, two-story, underground apartment. The main seating area on the first level of his living space was fairly plush and elegant, with black marble floors and nine inch thick cement walls with a layer of steel on the very inside for safety and red leather sofas and chairs (for easy cleanup when needed). He also had several bedrooms. One for himself, which wasn't for sleeping but was for his own amusement, and one for Claudine.

Claudine had one that she used to retreat to when she when she needed alone time. Each of the human women Antonius kept had a bedroom, making a total of four bedrooms on the main floor. The sub level was a place Tom had only seen one time. Antonius's dungeon was only used when absolutely necessary.

Antonius kept a fully stocked bar and fridge because, unlike Tom, Antonius liked the taste of human women and needed to keep refreshments on hand. He kept a human plaything around to make sure those needs were always met.

"Well, well, well," Antonius said as Tom walked in, "It's been a long time. To what do I owe this great honor?"

Antonius spun around in his chair across the room and looked at Tom standing next to the sofa.

"Angelique! Get Tom a vodka and a glass of blood!" he hollered to his human plaything. "Have a seat, Tom. It's been so long since you were last here."

"I'm not here casually," Tom said looking over at Antonius's dark eyes, straight black hair, and dark olive complexion. "I'm doing dealings with Arlington and I need some advice." Tom looked over to the scantily clad woman behind the bar who was fumbling around for a glass.

"It's okay, Tom. My girls don't speak of the topics discussed here. I have them 'controlled'. You know what I mean."

"Do you manipulate all the women you bring around, Tony?"

"Yes, it's more convenient for me. I know they're on hand for me whenever I need something. But I also know they're like putty in my hands."

Antonius winked to Angelique, who blew him a kiss as she walked over with glasses of vodka and blood in her hands.

Tom smirked, shaking his head. "Arlington hired me to protect a girl—"

"A girl?" Antonius interrupted, taking his blood and vodka glasses from Angelique. Angelique handed Tom his two glasses, practically throwing it at him, splashing blood and vodka onto his shirt.

"Here, Tom," she said.

"Yes. It's his daughter," Tom took the drinks from her and quickly chugged the blood. Tom shamefully rested his face in one hand and wondered how he was going to get himself out of his current situation. Now that he'd met Abigail, he understood why Arlington thought her so valuable. But he also knew that he couldn't protect this girl. He was becoming too attached.

"That warlock has a daughter?!" Tony exclaimed with a slight laugh.

Tom nodded.

"Yes. He has two, actually. The other one is my brother's lover. She's … eh … nothing special. But this one …"

Tom shook his head and let out a sigh.

"Tom, buddy … are you in love with this girl?"

"What?! NO!" Tom reacted.

Antonius laughed, unconvinced. Claudine entered the room and walked over to where Tom and Tony were sitting.

"I'm not so convinced either, Tony," she said. As Antonius's created vampire, Claudine had the rare ability to detect what anyone was feeling at any given time.

"It isn't true, Claudine. Abigail is only a job," Tom persisted.

"That's not the vibe I'm getting," she said with a playful wink.

"Why does it bother you so much that he wants her protected?" Tony asked.

"By the time I found out what she is, I had already made my dealings with him. Then I felt her powers and she captivated me even more." Tom stood and started pacing the room, running his fingers through his hair.

"What is she?"

"She's … the only vampire Slayer in existence."

"Oh yeah," Claudine nodded. "He's definitely feeling something."

"Wait a minute. You're telling me she's the only vampire Slayer in existence and you are protecting her and *not* ripping out her jugular?!" Antonius yelled.

Tom looked to him and nodded once more.

"This is unacceptable. You are my good friend and we've been pals for nearly two centuries, but I'm going against you on this one. She is fated to kill us!"

"I KNOW!" Tom yelled back, shattering some glass in the room with his anger.

"You think I haven't realized this, Tony?! I have! Arlington gave me no choice! I thought she was just a job! I didn't realize the kind of power she has!" Tom started pacing again.

"What is the dealing he has given you?" Claudine asked.

"It involves Delius," Tom muttered.

"Leave it to Delius to be involved in something like this," she replied.

Antonius stood and walked to his supply of vodka as he thought about all that was happening while Claudine continued to question Tom.

"What do you mean 'her power'?" she asked.

"When she touches me, she can subdue me. Her touch brings out some kind of humanity in me. It's almost life-giving. I've never felt anything like it in all of my existence. I almost *like* it."

"Unreal," she said, astonished.

"No, Tom!" Antonius barked, "You need to break these dealings with that bastard warlock!"

"I can't!" Tom shot back, "I've been summoned by the Master of Sorcery. This is bigger than you can imagine. It isn't just about me or the money, Antonius."

"Since when does Adelemar have anything to do with vampires?" Claudine asked.

"Since Delius released the underworld and Abigail is the only one who can send them back!"

Antonius stared at Tom for a minute as he soaked in the realization of what Tom had just said. Shaking his head he responded, "It doesn't matter. You're a traitor."

Antonius pointed to the door.

Tom nodded and stood to leave. As he approached the door, he said, "Just remember, I can crush your beloved mine shaft with the blink of an eye."

He winked and motioned around the room as he turned to the door. Claudine gasped as she heard rumbles from the walls around them. Tom walked out but not before shattering every bottle of vodka with his mind.

Five

When Katherine learned that the portal to Hell was left open, she feared that somehow Patrick might have figured out a way to escape in spite of her spell on him. Not wanting to take any chances, she decided to take matters into her own hands before the underworld was faced with a crisis no one could contain—Patrick Barclay.

The opening to the portal was releasing demons out of Hell and directly into 2018, and the time of the new Slayer. Being the Witch Authority, Katherine called a meeting of every High Priestess in the eastern United States.

"Thank you for coming on such short notice, ladies. I've called this meeting of the High Priestess Council of the eastern United States because as you already know, the Hell portal is open and we need to close it. As the leaders of the witch covens in your regions, you are already aware that the underworld is in complete disarray—"

Katherine was interrupted by another witch, "How did the portal to Hell get activated? The portal has been locked for centuries!"

"We've heard of a Slayer. Is it true that the race of the Slayer has appeared again?" Susan—the High Priestess in Arlington's region—asked. Reluctant to give any details on that account, knowing Tom was currently protecting the Slayer. Concerned for Tom's safety around the witches who might go after the Slayer, Katherine only responded, "I've heard numerous reports of a woman who embodies the characteristics and traits of a Slayer, but I have not seen this woman and cannot confirm it truthfully."

The twelve witches in Charlotte's upscale New York apartment continued their chattering, but Katherine looked to her daughter knowing that they had a problem rising.

"We need to be ahead of Delius," Katherine continued.

"What's his plan?" another witch asked.

"He wants to use the Beast to gain authority over earth, but we don't know why. We also don't know how he got down there."

"He didn't open the portal?" Susan asked.

"He *used* the portal, but it is highly unlikely that he is the one who opened it," Katherine explained. "He doesn't have the kind of power to handle something of that magnitude."

"Could he be the reason for the interruption in the moon phases this time last year?" asked Ingrid,the New York region witch. She was the one always tasked with looking after Delius.

"What about Arlington? Could he have been the one to do it? Might he be involved in all of this? He's powerful enough," Susan pointed out.

"Arlington is a possibility. However, we don't believe Adelemar is involved in this and ultimately, Arlington answers to him," Katherine said as she stood.

"Follow me, ladies. We need to get started. Let us gather our supplies. Charlotte, you contact Tom. Delius already has the Beast, but we can close the portal before the rest of the underworld escapes. We need to keep Satan from escaping, or even worse, my husband."

"But Mother, isn't he locked down there with a spell?" Charlotte asked as she stood to follow Katherine.

"I'm not infallible. Let's get to work."

✪✪✪

The witches pulled together their powerful resources and began spellcasting in the far corner of the city inside an abandoned warehouse that very evening. Charlotte texted Tom and alerted him what they were doing, unaware that Delius had Tom's cell tapped and was screening every bit of activity conducted through his phone.

She waited a little while for his response while they collected the supplies.

"Half of you come with me while I go to the river and catch some rats, and find stones and driftwood," Katherine said.

"Half of you come with me to see Madame Fornisier, who will give us the candles, oil, and burning incense. Then we will stop at Tom's apartment to get an old shirt of his, which we will need for his sacrifice," Charlotte said. "Mum, we'll meet you at the abandoned warehouse for the spell."

"Who is Madame Fornisier?" Susan asked as she followed Charlotte to the parking garage.

Before she answered, she pointed between the BMW Tom had bought her and Susan's car, "Some of you ride with me and some ride with Susan."

As everyone got situated in the cars, she answered, "Madame Fornisier is a visionary. She's not a witch, but she supplies us with many of the materials we use. My mother has known her for a long time and it is rumored that she has connections with Adelemar."

That was all Charlotte had time to say before she got in her car and drove to the other side of the city to Madame Fornisier's Emporium, with Susan following behind.

Meanwhile, Katherine took several witches down to the riverfront underneath the Brooklyn Bridge.

"We just need to catch a few mice or rats, either will do. We'll also need some driftwood logs and a variety of sizes of stones and pebbles," she ordered as she took out her cell phone to call Tom.

"Thomas," she said.

"Yes, Mother."

"ETA?" she asked.

"I'm en route. Patience, please."

He hung up. Katherine quickly continued gathering her supplies.

✪✪✪

"I'll admit that I was expecting either you or your mother to show up eventually. I gathered your things," Madame Fornisier said to Charlotte as she walked inside the small, cluttered house-turned-shop, the other witches following behind.

"I'm assuming you already know of the current problem in the underworld?" Charlotte asked while she walked around looking at all of the oils, voodoo dolls, beaded necklaces, crosses and statues, bottles, potions, stars and moons, and all the other things on display for purchase for wannabe spellcasters. Madame kept her actual witchcraftery items in the back. The real spellcasters knew how to contact her.

"I have your things in the back," Madame nodded and walked through the swinging doors to the back of the shop, which was once a kitchen/dining room. A few minutes later, she returned with a large basket full of items.

"Tell Katherine this is everything she will need from me. I'll send the bill to Tom."

55

"Thank you," Charlotte said then turned to exit. The other witches stopped browsing the aisles of potions and voodoo dolls, spell books and oils to walk out the door behind Charlotte.

"Why do we need Tom?" one of the younger witches asked Charlotte as they walked to the car and she nosied through the items in the basket Charlotte was carrying.

Charlotte smiled knowing some of the younger witches found her brother attractive and looked forward to when she brought him around. She answered, "We need a sacrifice. Vampires are the easiest to resurrect."

"Oh, goodness! Poor Tom!"

"He'll be fine."

Charlotte rolled her eyes and put the basket in the trunk as everyone got in the car. They drove straight to the warehouse to meet Katherine.

✪✪✪

"Hurry ladies," Katherine ushered as everyone arrived at the warehouse. "We must work quickly. Everyone begin stacking the logs and stones for the altar and burn pile. Charlotte and I will prepare the oils."

Tom arrived just as Susan was placing the last stone on their altar, where Charlotte was dousing it with sacrificial oils.

"This better happen quickly, Charlotte," he demanded.

"Using my full name? Am I not 'Lottie' when you're in a rush?"

"I mean it!" he yelled.

"I just left Abigail in Grundy. There are vampires everywhere who are out for her destruction. And if she dies, Arlington will be sure I never make it out of eternity! Have I made myself clear?!"

"So, this Abigail woman … she's the new Slayer?" Ingrid asked Tom.

At her question, he flashed his fangs to her and his eyes encircled with crimson.

56

"As far as every witch here is concerned—besides Charlotte or my mother—Abigail doesn't exist. You are to stay away. I will see to the demise of anyone who does not heed to my instructions. Is everyone understanding this?! Are we under a concurrence?!"

At the force of his anger, the warehouse started to rumble around them. Katherine looked at him, troubled by his flaring temper. The other witches looked around at one another and nodded, wondering the truth about this Slayer and her abilities.

"Thomas, darling, do control yourself. Your anger has the tendency to flare and if we aren't careful …"

"Enough!" he barked, "Just get on with this!"

"Well, fine then …" Charlotte said as she motioned for him to remove his shirt.

Some of the younger witches stared at Tom as he unbuttoned his shirt, wide-eyed, hyper-aware of his handsomeness. Tom was used to that type of response from women and ignored it. Charlotte smirked, watching their reaction.

"This stuff smells terrible," he complained as Charlotte covered him with oil.

"Stop whining. Take it like a man." Charlotte teased. Tom growled at her as she finished covering him with oil. The other witches lit the candles that surrounded the circle, while Katherine began her spellcasting.

"Portal hoc quod est non sit et aperuit. Viribus meis invocabo maior corrigere quod male factum est. Pone tergum omnia quae fugit. Quid hic capere non pertinent. Haec mittite portas …"

But just as she was about to finish, she looked up to Tom. "It's already closed."

"What do you mean?" he asked, a little surprised, but also grateful that he wasn't getting stabbed in the chest. Charlotte seemed far too eager to stake her brother for the sake of the ritual.

"Someone else closed it. I fear that whoever it was, their reasons were not as honorable as ours."

"You mean?" Tom asked.

"Yes," she responded.

"I have to go!" Tom raced out of there and to the airport, urgently returning to Grundy but not to protect Abigail; his return was to gain information.

<u>Six</u>

Upon his arrival into Grundy later that night, Tom stepped into Arlington's house and demanded in a panic, "I need to know more about Abigail. It is imperative that you tell me everything you know about her history, the history of the Slayer … all of it. Why is the race of the Slayer gone or why was it?"

"First thing, improve your hygiene. I know those are witch oils. You've been to see your mother. Go shower and then we can talk."

"You're one to talk about hygiene. When was the last time you even looked in a mirror? You never brush your hair and your five o'clock shadow is becoming a full-grown beard. We don't have time for this."

"A vampire mentioning mirrors? The irony is too much for me to even speak upon. You only live across town; you'll be back within minutes." Arlington pointed to the doorway.

"The mirrors thing is only a myth."

"I will not speak to you about the reason for your visit until you no longer smell like a witch."

Tom growled at Arlington as he went to the door.

Several minutes later, after heading to his own house—and cursing Arlington the entire time while washing the witch oil residue off—Tom began speaking to Arlington again.

"I need to know about—"

Arlington cut him off. "I know about Satan's escape; I know about the portal closing; I know who did it; I also know that's why you're here."

"There's only one possible way he could've gotten out of Hell," Tom said. "Why would he want anything to do with Abigail?"

"Was that a serious question?"

"I only ask serious questions," Tom said as Arlington walked toward the door. "Where are you going?"

"I fear that the easiest way to explain it all would be to show you. I was there when it happened," Arlington said.

"When what happened?" Tom asked.

"In the Renaissance period, there were many witch burnings that took place, and Abigail's family line … Oh, just come on." Arlington grabbed Tom's arm and pulled him out the front door. As they stepped through, he said, "Tuncire," transforming the other side of the door into an entirely new time.

✪✪✪

Tom looked around and saw London streets that were full of people, carriages, horses, and work carts. Understanding they were no longer in Grundy and no longer in 2018, he asked, "Why are we here?"

"I told you it would be best to *show* you what happened to the Slayers. You are in the year 1587. This is when the witch hysteria began and the English government began seeking out anyone they believed to be practicing witchcraft. Come with me."

Arlington walked away, leading Tom down a back alley behind some rowhouses in a poor side of town that Tom felt he might've recognized, even though it was 200 years prior to the time Tom had spent in England.

"Where are we going?" he asked but quieted himself as they exited the alley and approached the town square where they heard shrieks and screams—a woman crying out in agony, begging and pleading for mercy. Tom saw the red glow of a fire as they neared, but he hesitated to move closer as he smelled the pungent stench of burning flesh.

"That woman …" Arlington pointed to the woman being burned, tied up to a pole in the center of the square on the top of the flaming brush.

"That woman is no witch, though they believe her to be."

"Who is she?" Tom asked as he watched the flames engulf her, hearing her shrieks and cries of pain cease as she disappeared into the fire.

"That is the last Slayer to exist before our girl. They believed her to be a witch because of her power."

"What was her power?" he asked, walking out of the square and back into the alley.

"Foresight. They thought she was mad because she was predicting events in the future and then they were coming true. They also believed her to be a murderer because people were disappearing and it was coinciding with her predictions, but she was merely staking vampires."

"I don't understand why there was never another Slayer after her until Abigail."

"Come with me."

Arlington led him into a small house at the far end of the dirty and dusty alley where they'd been previously, where a young boy sat crying in the corner. "This is the son of that woman. He grew and had a family but didn't have a daughter for centuries. The Slayer line could only come from his direct line. There were no daughters born from his direct family line until the late 1700s. It was like the universe was punishing the world for killing the only ones capable of ridding the world of demons."

"And now the underworld is being punished by having the most powerful Slayer in the history of the world," Tom added.

"Yes."

"Why was the next daughter born not a Slayer?" Tom questioned.

"Circumstances were … complicated," Arlington answered.

"How so? Did you always know of her abilities? I don't find it a coincidence that you—the most powerful warlock in existence—are the father of the *most powerful* Slayer to have lived," Tom mentioned as he walked out of the small and dirty house and back into the alley.

"No, I didn't know of her power, not right away. Abigail wasn't a mature Slayer until she was 21. I walked away from her until just last year, thinking that she was … that …" he paused for a minute stumbling over his words.

"Thinking what?"

"Come. There's something else I need to show you."

Arlington opened another door to a random house and once again saying, "Tuncire." On the other side, Tom recognized immediately where they were.

"We are still in England. But we're not in the 1500s anymore. I know this house."

"There's another woman you need to see," Arlington said.

"Why are we at Claire Davenwell's house?" Tom whispered as he looked around the inside of the house, stepping inside the entry hall.

"I know you know my other daughter in a *friendly* manner—as does your brother—but that's not why we are here. Although, I don't think Henry would approve of your relationship with her. If I do recall, isn't his attachment to her a bit more … affectionate?"

"Can we just focus and forget about Henry and me?"

"We are here about Claire's mother, Margaret Davenwell."

"What's she to do with anything?" Tom asked, glancing around the house, "She was only a maid. She wasn't anything spec—"

"Look." Arlington pointed into the next room in the direction of her as she appeared to be doing some sort of magic and was manipulating the furniture in the room, moving objects with her mind as Tom could.

"She's a witch?" Tom asked.

"No. Witches always have to use outside sources for their magic and she is not drawing from another source. It appeared to me at first that she could have been some type of sorcerer, but her magic never appeared to me as though she was casting a spell. Then I thought that it was possible she was a Slayer and I thought that another line had survived the burnings. But I searched continuously for evidence and found none. When I found out she was a prostitute, I knew that was my way to find out for sure, which is how Claire was born."

"But Claire isn't a Slayer," Tom looked away from Margaret and back to Arlington.

"Exactly," Arlington stated.

"You are making little sense, Arlington. Do be clearer."

"I was that little boy."

"Claire is the daughter born in the late 1700s?!" Tom exclaimed. "How did you figure out that she wouldn't become a Slayer?"

"Simple calculations. I knew that mine and my father's wizardry line would be more prominent in the child if Margaret was a sorceress. If she was a Slayer, then that line would win out. $1+1= \ldots$"

"I get it. Whatever traits were dominant would win and obviously, Margaret turned out to be a sorceress since Claire is. What happened to her?" Tom asked as he pointed at Margaret, who was using her mind to sweep the room.

"She died in childbirth, which was common back then, as you well know. How did you scavenge around from woman to woman and end up without bastards?" Arlington questioned.

"I was a man of high rank in society and of great wealth. I had no time for that nonsense. I did what needed to be done," Tom stated matter-of-factly.

"Well, lucky for your brother, Claire was one that I was willing to spare. I found her skills in sorcery to be useful to me. I took pity on her after the death of Margaret and sheltered her with a local family until her power became mature. You know the rest of the story with your brother and Delius."

"Yes. Why my family, Arlington?"

"Delius … he wanted you."

"No, I mean now, to protect Abigail," Tom clarified.

"I had no choice. Your mother envisioned you with her, did she not?"

"What?" Tom asked, surprised by Arlington's words.

"Ask Henry; he knows. Better yet, ask your mother," Arlington suggested. Stepping out the front door, he repeated the same phrase as before and returned to present day.

Seven

Abigail awakened the morning after meeting Tom to realize the only thing she'd thought or dreamed about all night was that fight in the alley. The vampires had her so intrigued. If what they had said and what she experienced was true, then she was certainly no longer the most abnormal creature that existed. It was a hard reality in life to be abnormal. Abbi very much wanted to talk to Tom again. She had so many questions for him about his relationship with her father and why he was there in the alley.

She desperately wanted to come across another vampire. She thought it was possible there might be one in the alley behind her work one night and that she could lure him in with blood. Her mind started wandering to all thoughts and possibilities of a vampire …

"What did he mean about being there to protect me?"

She continued to wonder *"Are all the myths I've read about vampires true? Do they feel as tortured and betrayed about life as I do? Do they also feel as though there's no hope for the future? How old are vampires? Is it true that they're immortal? Is he much like a human? Why were there bites on the vampire's neck? No!"*

Her inner-self screamed, snapping her out of her thoughts. After several minutes, she whispered to herself, "Vampires are killers! You need to stay *far* away!"

But something was drawing her to want to learn more and she found it hard to even make it to the shower and muster up the motivation for just regular, everyday activities. Trying to shake herself out of it, she went to the window. It was a beautiful sight. It was a bright sunny day and Abbi saw her mom out in the yard, working in the garden, as usual. Abigail and her mother have always been close in spite of the turmoil going on with her mother and Arlington.

Arlington left when Abbi was just five years old. He'd decided that a wife and a child were too much to handle and he left for better opportunities—his words. That's when she and her mother moved in with Janette's mother. Ever since, Arlington's had the tendency to show up for big birthdays or to annoy her by hanging around town. She always knew there was something peculiar about her father— as he's always been eccentric—but she never quite knew what it was.

Arlington's appearance showed his individuality at first glance, with his black, shoulder-length hair, which was beginning to gray, and his short beard stubble. He also wore the same thing every day—dark pants with a black, button-down shirt, covered by a long, flowing, dark, hooded cloak. Abigail was so used to his odd appearance that she hardly even noticed the cloak anymore. However, others did and frequently whispered about it when they were out together. His reaction to all the whispering was to curse them.

Arlington's eccentricity was always highlighted by events such as someone pissing him off and him responding with, "Curse you," or "You'll regret that," or "I will never let you forget that." Arlington's behavior scared and intimidated Abbi sometimes. The time he took her to The Grundy Shack to celebrate one of her birthdays and he threatened the cook who messed up his order indicated one of those examples.

Arlington said that there would be a curse for a thousand years on the cook's family. She never saw that cook in town again. Abigail didn't understand why he said those things or behaved that way and was embarrassed to go places with him. Could her father actually curse people? She wasn't sure. Did she actually want to know? Of that, she also wasn't sure. Yet, he was often a good father.

He made her feel safe and protected—his tall stature bringing her security—and when she needed help, he was there for her. He's also self-confident and provided for her financially and he often took her on nice vacations when she was younger. There were many aspects about him she admired. She took the good with the bad when it came to Arlington.

Now that she was out of school and getting older, moving out of her mom's house seemed appealing, but Abbi felt as though she'd be abandoning Janette, just like Arlington had. The thought of moving out had crossed Abbi's mind many times. A life of independence seemed ridiculously tempting. She'd thought about getting an apartment and living with Lacy. But Abbi didn't want to be the daughter who abandoned her pathetic mother.

Janette was never known in town for having her act together and she'd already been abandoned by her husband. After Arlington left, Janette struggled to pull herself together. She just never recovered from losing him. Arlington had left her shattered. She jumped from guy to guy, always on the search for love again, always calling and telling Abbi she was going out on a date.

After dressing and getting ready for the day, Abbi skipped breakfast and went straight for housework, trying to keep her mind occupied and off of vampires. After starting some laundry, she flipped through the stations on the TV without much success. Her mind kept wandering to the night in the alley, wondering why it kept getting stirred up in her mind. Abbi thought about the possibility of another vampire encounter was going to happen again. She desperately hoped it would. She found herself wishing for something exciting to happen in her life … something more exciting than Arlington.

Janette was headed to work by noon and Abbi's day passed like all the rest, except for the mounting anticipation and the arrival of Arlington at her front door.

"Abigail," he said as she opened the door.

"Arlington," she said at the sight of the father. He only came around in cases of distress, emergencies, or to lecture Janette about some business or another.

"May I come in?" he asked as he stepped inside and around her. She only shrugged, a little shocked that he was even there because he was always gone.

"What are you doing here?" she asked as he walked into the kitchen.

"I need to talk to you about a current situation involving you. I'm sure you are confused about a particular man who has recently entered your life—"

"Tom?"

"Yes. You've been introduced. Here's the deal, Abigail. I know you can touch him and that intrigues you. Don't let it. He's dangerous. Do not be persuaded. I've hired him for a job. That is all. When it's finished, he'll be gone and out of your life. End of story. Don't become attached. Understood?"

She nodded, agreeing. However, Abigail was never one to be persuaded easily.

"Arlington?"

He turned to face her as he strolled out of the house.

"What's the job? The job you hired him for?"

"Keeping you safe."

Arlington turned and shut the front door behind him.

She thought as she put her jacket on and headed out the door to work, *"Keeping me safe? What? Am I really in some kind of danger? I wouldn't be surprised. Arlington probably got me involved in some kind of terrible curse ..."*

For Abigail, work usually ran in the same dull manner. Being on the evening shift and outside of business hours, she worked alone. There were two other employees who worked the day shift, Jacquelyn and Cassie. The small shop was located in the next town over which was not much larger than Grundy, but leaving to go there each day helped to free her from the suffocating space of the confining mountains which enclosed her.

Upon her arrival that evening, Abbi was concerned to hear Jacquelyn and Cassie talking about some men who came into the boutique earlier. They had been acting strangely after spending time at the bar, causing a commotion, then rustled through items without making a purchase.

"We didn't want to tell you, but they asked for you," Cassie said.

Surprised, Abbi asked, "Well, what did they want?"

"They wanted *you*," Jacquelyn answered.

Startled at the thought, she wondered if she should call and alert Susan, the shop's owner.

"You better get going. I should get to work," Abbi said, trying to usher the girls out.

"Are you sure you're going to be okay?" Cassie asked as they exited out the back.

"If I need help, I'll call Sheriff Jack. Thanks. Goodnight."

She quickly locked the door just as normal and then got to work, closing and finishing up as an ordinary night. Midnight came and it was time to go, and again—like last night—something was different. Her fear was telling her that those men were waiting in the back and she thought for a fleeting moment about calling for help, but her gut instinct knew if these were regular, everyday, ordinary men, she could handle them on her own. It was exactly five minutes past midnight when she walked out the back door and into the alley. Her heart settled when she glanced around and saw no activity. No one was in sight.

Disappointment overtook her as she was hoping for some activity from a vampire and was sure one would come back. Then it occurred to her! The alley was especially quiet, no bar fights, nothing. She shrugged and turned to lock the door, when once again, it slammed shut.

Frightened, she spun around, but his arms extended up around either side of her, pinning her against the door before she could move further, with no escape. She kept her eyes closed—afraid to take a peek—but recognized that scent! It was intoxicating, overpowering, pushing her beyond her limits. He smelled woodsy, like he'd just spent the night sleeping outside. Yet, there was a mix of something more, almost spicy, like he had just eaten hot peppers.

It was Tom.

She opened her eyes to see him towering over her, holding the door closed with only inches between them. She was startled to see his face was ferocious, ravenous, evil, and almost hungry. But at the same time, he was glorious, and she was certain that he was the most beautiful thing she'd ever seen. The perfectly shiny whites of his eyes sparkled as they enclosed the very dark irises, which were captivating, and she'd never seen eyes so dark and so white at the same time and felt herself under a spell. Surrounding it all was a deep crimson color. Around the entire edge of his eyes, he had a ring of deep red that enclosed them and ran into his eyelids.

His wavy hair was like dark chocolate and he kept it combed back, with long sideburns. It was a retro style, very sleek like James Bond, and his features were strong and masculine, sharp and defined. They were eye-catching, intense, and powerful. Abbi found it difficult not to stare and felt—in spite of his moon-kissed complexion—that he looked like a model right out of *GQ*.

After having touched him for a brief second the night previous, curiosity overtook her and she let her sense of judgment become skewed. Abigail grabbed his arm. Although, as Arlington warned, she didn't hurt him; something else happened. He melted. Just like with everyone else, right into her grasp, like putty in her hands, he was hers.

His stance began to relax, his eyes became softer, and his arms dropped to his sides. The redness that encircled his eyes began to fade away and the beauty took over. His towering height no longer seemed so domineering. Abbi inched closer and tipped up on her toes to look him straight in the eyes. Those big, deep, dark and gentle but smoldering eyes stared right back at her. He began to back away, but she desperately gripped his arm.

"Tom, you don't want to hurt me."

"I know. I find you … captivating. What are you doing to me?"

"I think I should be asking you the same question. I find you just as captivating. Though, it seems as though I have you under my command, albeit not my original intention. But it appears to be working to my benefit."

"I don't understand your power. If this was not your original intention, Abigail, what was it?"

Smiling at the irony of the situation, she answered, "Normally when I touch someone, I drain the life out of them almost instantly."

Snapping her fingers to make the point, she added, "It only takes seconds. If I let go, the life or energy returns, maybe. The more I do it to one person, the faster it drains. But it didn't work with you …". She looked down at her hand—which was still firmly holding onto his arm—feeling somewhat bewildered, "… you're still standing."

"You're right. It didn't."

It was almost as if he found that part humorous because he had a slight chuckle to his voice when he answered. But his tone suddenly changed when he said, "But you intended to kill me when you reached out to touch me just now? Was that your plan? I saved your ass last night!"

"Hypocrite! Isn't that what you intended to do to me just now!? I was only getting business done first. Don't play innocent. I saw that redness surrounding your eyes," she scolded, holding his arm up again.

He looked down at her playfully, "Touché. But it appears we are at an impasse."

"Yes. It appears we are. What are we to do …" she replied incoherently, mesmerized by his smile, as though the rest of the world around her was disappearing. It was just the two of them existing in the entire world.

Thinking back, it was that moment in which he had entrapped her and she was lost within him forever. Of course, she hadn't known it at the time, but she was already falling for him in those first few moments. Her heart stopped for a few beats at a time and never before had she been so enraptured by something—or someone—in her entire life.

"Does he have this effect on everyone? Is it just me? Perhaps it's because he has the most angelic smile. His teeth sparkle like the stars and line his mouth perfectly."

Squinting her eyes, she looked closely to try and see his fangs again but couldn't.

"Curious about something?" he asked.

Tom knew Abigail was curious about him, but it was possible he was even more curious about her. The control she was gaining over him was infuriating but also incredible. The longer she touched him, the tamer he felt and more human he felt. It was unreal and he wanted more. He looked in the Slayer's eyes and wanted to toss her down on the alley floor and have his way with her. But more than that, he saw beauty in her eyes too. With each touch—as he was feeling his humanity—he was seeing a certain kind of beauty in her that he hadn't seen since he *was* human, or possibly ever. He desired more.

"If you want to see my fangs, I would be happy to show you," he said, smiling down at her again.

Her fear increased the slightest bit at his words, but his tone was still playful. As she heard a snapping noise come from his mouth, she raised her eyes saw them. Overwhelmed at the sight, her heart beat faster in her chest and her mind fogged over, and in all her staring, he'd backed her all the way to the door again. Trapping her against the door once more, he had both his hands extended to either side of her shoulders.

"Who is under whose spell now, little temptress?" he growled, snapping her out of the trance she was in.

Thinking in an instant—nervous that he was no longer playful—she threw herself at him, tossing one arm around his neck, clutching tightly to be sure she was touching his skin, one hand gripped firmly into his hair. She wrapped her legs around his waist, pressing their bodies close together. Her thoughts went into a panic.

"I had no idea a vampire's hair could be so soft! It is so thick and full! I want to bury my face in it! And oh, his voice! It is so sultry! Even growling at me he is so sexy! Now I'm in trouble … I have my arms around his head, with my chest in his face and my legs around his waist and all I can think about is how HOT this vampire is … Abbi, get a grip, girl!"

His fangs withdrew and the red around his eyes began to fade once more, allowing the beauty in the darkness to return. Then she put both of her hands on his face, looked deeply into his eyes, and said with as much sass as she could muster, "Actually, Tom, I'm pretty sure that you are under my spell."

"Yes, I do believe you are correct," he answered as his thoughts went obscene.

"What the hell is this Slayer chick doing to me?! She obviously has no type of experience with men because this position is ... damnit! NO! Arlington will kill me! Eh, life is overrated anyhow. She just jumped into my arms shoving her ... mmm!

NO, Tom! You are here to protect her! Stop messing around! Turn thoughts elsewhere ... She smells SO GOOD and this skirt she has on is very tempting. I could move my hands there and pretend like I'm holding her up ... that's a good plan. If she isn't careful, she'll wind up with more than a bite to the neck and get much more from Tom Barclay than she bargained for ..."

His hands were around her waist, but he began to move them to her legs to suit his mind's pleasures. She quickly realized that his hands were maneuvering for his own enjoyment as he began to relax his stance even further, stumbling backward. Their eyes met and his gaze became even softer. Yet, she was still very nervous as she felt at any moment, this very dangerous vampire could turn the tables and she could lose her life. Unknowing of how long her powers would work on him, she wasn't confident enough to test any theories and she let him be as comfortable as he needed. With her arms and legs still wrapped around him, he took one hand and braced her bottom, then took the other and touched her face.

"You're very pretty, you know? The prettiest human I've seen, and I'm very old."

"Well, then why would you want to kill me?" she tried to be flirtatious, trying to retain the upper hand.

"I didn't come here to kill you. You assumed that's what I was doing, Abigail. I was just fooling around with you. Life gets boring when someone's been around hundreds of years. I have to entertain myself somehow." He shrugged.

"Oh," she said, "I'm sorry. It was just the way you were acting."

She pointed toward the door, feeling sorry for her assumptions, and leaned in and hugged him. But as she did, he inhaled deeply. Realizing how stupid she was for hugging a vampire, Abbi quickly pulled away, bracing herself on his chest.

"Oh my! I'm so sorry. I don't know what's come over me. I … I don't know what to say. I've … never …"

"Met a vampire before?" he said and half-smiled.

"Yes," she nodded, nervous and unsure of his demeanor and mannerisms.

"Don't be afraid of me. I'm not going to hurt you. I'm supposed to be here to protect you. Though, Arlington didn't warn me that I would be so overtaken by you. You have a beautiful name, Abigail, and a beautiful smile." He reached up and touched one dimple with his index finger, then returned his hand to brace her bottom again.

"Thank you for the flattering compliments. I've never received compliments from a vampire before. I've also never been held like this by a vampire … or any man for that matter. You do realize that you and I are in a very intimate position. You really shouldn't be touching me the way that you are," she teased.

"*You* realize that you put us here when you jumped into my arms?" he said as he put her down. Tom sped over to the alley door and pulled out a stack of pallets. He pointed to them and sat down. Intrigued at what he was doing, she quickly joined him.

"Last night, when I needed your help, where were you hiding? How did you know I needed help?" she asked, taking a seat.

"I was sitting on top of the building. But I wouldn't have needed to be so close. I could've heard your scream from very far away."

He leaned back against his arms to look up at the rooftop.

"If you were so close, then why did you wait so long to come to my rescue?!" she scolded, lightly tapping his arm. He sat back up and crossed his arms and with annoyed expression, he replied, "I had told you to leave quickly and you did not listen. I felt that you needed to learn your lesson."

Her mouth gaped at his reply and she said, "I could've died!"

"Don't be ridiculous. I was watching."

She tapped his arm again as if to scold him and said, "You were watching?!"

"Of course I was watching. I couldn't very well let you die, now could I? Arlington would have my neck."

He winked at her and continued, "I was only letting you feel a little bit of fear so next time you would listen to me."

"Ha! Unlikely chance on that. How did you get up there?" she asked and looked around for a ladder.

"I jumped, obviously."

"What?!"

His face reacted ever-so-slightly at her response but he continued, "I jump very high and move very quickly, faster than your eyes can follow. I can also hear very well and can listen in on a conversation up to a mile away. My senses are very well defined. My inner senses, however, are more complex."

"What do you mean by that?" she asked.

Her curiosity about his mystery was causing him to feel comfortable around her—almost relaxed—even more so than he was already feeling from what her touch was bringing out in him. But no amount of comfort could keep him satisfied because he was fixed on being unhappy.

"Well, my outer senses are better than any other creature you've ever come in contact with. They are defined by things like my sense of smell, my hearing, my sight, or my touch. I am also never outdone in how fast I can run or how high I can jump. I'm stronger than anyone or anything you have ever met. See that dumpster right there? I could lift it with one arm and heave it across the alley with no effort and I could run from here to the other side of the country in one night. Things like that," he explained, arms crossed casually, as though being Hercules was no big deal.

"Wow. Very impressive. Could prove to be a fun toy. I wonder what else my new Hercules toy can do?"

"Show me," she said in a demanding yet innocent way.

"Excuse me?" he asked, pretending like he didn't know what she wanted him to do.

"I want to see you do it. I don't believe you," she said, walking to the dumpster, explaining exactly what she wanted him to do.

"I want to see you take this dumpster and heave it across the alley. C'mon, let's go." She motioned for him to go over.

"No. That's insane. I refuse." He shook his head.

"You *can't,*" she mocked, hoping to incite him, desperately wanting to see him toss the dumpster.

"I can. I assure you. But I won't. It's senseless to involve myself in human nonsense." He turned away. But she got his attention when she said, "But this isn't just human nonsense, Tom because I'm more than human. Do it … for me."

Something inside him awakened at her request and he said, "Sit over there," pointing to the pallets that he had piled up. She saw that he was annoyed as he took his time walking over to the dumpster. "Do not move. DO you understand?"

"Of course I do," she sassed, "I'm not an idiot. You may think that I'm a lesser being than you, Mr. Strong-dumpster heaving-blood drinking-human killing vampire man, but I can assure you that—"

"SIT down!" he yelled, pointing to the pallets.

She jumped at his temper, "Yikes!"

Crossing her arms over her chest, Abbi plopped onto the pallets, not liking being told what to do, while he rolled his eyes at her behavior. She could tell he was used to ordering others around and still had some human attitude in him. She was sure he would prove to be fun to have around, trying to hide her smirk.

Tom walked over to the dumpster, annoyed. Never had he ever been under the authority of a human before, and never did he think he would be, especially not some attractive, petite little vampire Slayer. Fury rose inside him, but something inside him couldn't be angry at her; he was pissed at Arlington because he felt Arlington knew this was going to happen.

He stood behind the dumpster with his back to her car, knelt down, and lifted the dumpster with one arm balancing it on his shoulder just like he said. It was effortless for him. He looked over to her, watching her amazement as her jaw dropped, unbelieving of what she saw. Tom heaved it across the alley.

Abbi was quickly taken by surprise when, as the dumpster was flying through the air, he sped over, locked her in his embrace, knocking her out of the way of any flying objects coming out of the dumpster as the top flew open. She was now on the alley floor, pinned underneath this bloodthirsty man that was able to lift and throw a dumpster with one arm and move faster than light! Her intimidation increased … just a little. When they heard the dumpster crash onto the alley floor and she flinched in surprise, he squeezed her tighter.

"Are you okay, Abigail?" he asked, wiping the hair back from her forehead.

Grinning excitedly, she answered, "Perfectly."

But Tom's reaction was much different as he laid there on top of her and red began enclosing his dark eyes; passion overtook him. When Abigail saw the red increase, she grabbed his face and said, "That was amazing! *You* are amazing! I've never seen anything like that in my whole life! Do something else."

He quickly stood up and extended his hand, being sure to keep hold of her hand to continue the skin-to-skin contact as they looked around at the mess of the dumpster. But Abigail's thoughts continued to Tom as she noticed that there was definitely something human in him. He was courteous enough to protect her from the dumpster debris, which she hadn't even considered herself and he reached down to help her up—like a real gentleman.

"C'mon, Hercules. Do something else!" She giggled excitedly.

"No," he said curtly, "I'm not your vampire plaything." He turned to look at her and started picking at her hair, pulling the garbage and dirt out of it.

"Very cute … my new Hercules toy! Who needs a bit of an attitude adjustment."

"Wow, you're so moody," she responded, brushing the dirt off herself and then turning to sit down on the pallets again.

"Yes," he agreed, sitting down next to her. "It's in my nature," he began to explain as he took her hand once more, wanting to be sure he didn't lose control of his vampire urges and kill Arlington's daughter and the only vampire Slayer in existence. Tom looked at his hand holding hers and continued, "You have now seen my strength and my speed, and I explained my other senses to you. I also have other powers that you have not fully witnessed."

He looked down at their hands, paused for a moment, then said, "My internal desires are less pronounced but a bit more complex."

"Are you telling me, that in addition to being Hercules, you have normal human desires?" she asked flirtatiously and moved her hand, placing it on his thigh. He looked up and smiled as she twirled her finger in a circular motion. His face quickly turned cautious.

"Almost," he warned and grasped her other hand. "Hercules did. Didn't he? But I don't remember it turning out too hot for Megara."

"Hey now, I saw that Disney movie and I'm pretty sure that Hercules saved the day and was able to live happily ever after with his beloved Meg after all the trouble and turmoil ..." she joked. Tom wasn't amused, clearly needing a good dose of Abbi's sense of humor, charm, and stunning wit.

"Abigail, of course I still have human instincts. My human instincts are what allow me to find you attractive. They're what allow me to feel overcome by you even when you aren't touching me, but are also what urge me to take your hand again," he held up their clasped hands.

"They're what make me wish you would jump at me and wrap yourself around me again, so I can be close to you and breathe in your scent. They're what make me desire you like a man desires a woman. My human instincts are what kept me from eating you that first night before you had ever touched me. They are also what made me protect you from the mess of the dumpster. But my human instincts have been overtaken by my vampire instincts for over 200 years. At this point, the vampire instincts are much stronger and more natural to me. But underneath my vampire layer, I am still a man with the desires of a man."

Letting go of one hand and turning away, he continued, "But ultimately, first, I am a vampire."

"I would've thought it was threats from my crazy father that kept you from eating me," she joked. But when he didn't see the humor, she leaned forward to look into his eyes—which were severe as though they were trying to warn her—and she sat back.

"You find me attractive?"

He thought over her question for a moment and then responded, "It is possible you are the most beautiful woman I have ever seen. And don't worry about your father. I've known him for a long time; he doesn't intimidate me."

Tilting her head, biting her lip bashfully, she waited for him to continue. He stood and walked away to leave.

"Don't go," she begged.

"This was a mistake. Goodbye, Abigail Taylor."

"Will I see you again?" she asked as she stood and took a few steps closer to him, sounding far more eager to see this vampire than she should've.

"Well, a deal is a deal," he said before vanishing.

"Tom?" She called out and walked down the alley, following his dust trail and suddenly having a bad feeling inside.

"Tom? Are you still there?" she hollered again.

Somehow, she felt safer in his presence. Sadness covered her heart as she looked down the empty alley and saw the overturned dumpster, wanting to replay the events. This was definitely more exciting than Arlington.

✪✪✪

As Abbi walked to the other end of the alley where her car was parked, two hands reached out from around the corner, forcefully grabbing her. Immediately, she let out a loud, piercing scream just as the gloved hand covered her mouth.

"Shhh, little human girl. We don't want your boyfriend to come back for you, now do we?" he whispered as he held her tightly in one arm and dragged her over to where the pallets were still stacked. Terrified, her heart was racing in her chest and she tried to yell for help but couldn't. He continued to speak, "I just want to play with you for a little while. I told your friends I would be coming for you. But first ..." He tossed her onto the pallets.

"Oh, Tom! Tom! That's it!" she thought.

Her mouth was uncovered now—as the man maneuvered himself on top of her, she knew it was so that he could take advantage of her. Abbi screamed louder than she'd ever screamed in her life.

"Help!"

The man reached for a bandana to tie up her mouth, but as he did, she managed to get out one more, "Tom!!" But in her screaming, she'd angered her attacker, and he reached back and slapped her across the face.

"Now settle down. Stop screaming for your boyfriend. He's long gone. Left you here, he did. Some boyfriend ..."

He slapped her again causing a tear to roll down her cheek, the salt from the tear burning her raw skin. She realized once her hands were tied together that this man, this hideous, disgusting man, intended to do something terrible to her.

"How did he know to wear gloves? He isn't a human because he called me a human. But is he a vampire? His eyes aren't red yet ... Ah ... there they go. Now I know I'm in trouble. Now they're encircled with a deep crimson."

His fangs emerged and he pinned her arms above her with one arm and reached his gloved hand down to grab at her skirt, but a quick figure flew past and knocked him to the ground with a loud thud.

Moving quickly to sit up, Abbi maneuvered herself out of the way and looked over, recognizing it was Tom! After gaining authority over her attacker, he looked over to see that she was tied up and used his mind to cause the bandanas to fall off. Abbi wondered how he'd done that.

"Hurry, Abigail!" he called to her from the same position he was in the night previously—man pinned beneath him on the alley floor, Tom straddling the other vampire's waist, and firmly holding his throat. Abbi rushed over and Tom yanked her down to join him once again, pulling her closer to him than was necessary for his pleasure. Tom handed her the stake but before she could plunge it into his heart, Tom hollered, "Wait!" and swiftly switched positions so that now he would receive the brunt of the blood spatter.

"Reach around me," he said with his back pressed against her chest.

She did as was told and thrust the stake into the vampire's heart from her position behind Tom, and the blood splashed up and all over him instead, leaving Tom a blood-soaked mess. The man shriveled up into a corpse, then disintegrated, and they bounced onto the alley floor. She tossed the stake aside, feeling once again, speechless.

He stood, picked up the stake, and took off his blood-saturated shirt. Then he tossed it next to the overturned dumpster. Abigail's eyes lit up at the muscular form of him as he tucked the stake into his belt and she found it hard not to stare.

"Are you okay?" he asked, reaching down to help her up. She nodded, blushing at the sight of him standing there shirtless.

He started pacing back and forth in the alley with a very serious look in his eyes and still covered in blood, before saying, "I don't think this is a good place for you to work, Abigail," he walked over and pointed to the back door.

"I had to leave my other job …"

"What was your other job?" he asked as he looked her over for injuries.

"He hit you. I'm sorry I left you here alone. Are you sure you're alright?" He reached up to touch her face.

Touching her cheek where the man had slapped her, she answered, "Yes … I feel overwhelmed. I thought that vampire was going to hurt …"

"He was," Tom interrupted harshly, "If I hadn't heard you scream …"

"Why did you turn back? Surely a vampire doesn't care about a human. Aren't we food to you?"

"That's true, but as you already pointed out, you are more than human. Plus, I've been hired to be your bodyguard. I knew that you needed my help … again." He rolled his eyes. "I could hear fear and terror in your voice. When I heard you scream, I felt both excitement and agony," he said as he started pacing, running his fingers through his hair.

"What?! I was in danger! Why would you feel excited?!"

He looked at her and answered, "I was excited because I had a feeling that I was going to have the opportunity to rip someone apart and because you were screaming for me. *Me*. No one ever wants me. Well, no one I want to want me. It was something to get excited about," he explained.

"Oh … well, sorry to disappoint. I apologize for the lack of people shredding, but I had a feeling you would be a great protector. I mean, you can heave a dumpster with one arm without even making a facial expression, Hercules." she flirted, winking. He didn't respond and dropped his head again instead.

"Why agony, Tom?" she asked.

He looked deeply into her eyes, repeating the same phrase. "Because I knew I was going to have the opportunity to rip someone apart."

Tom looked away from her knowing that he just shared his deepest most inner self which was unlike him, and he felt he needed to detach himself from his growing feelings for this woman before it was too late. He moved to stand, but before he could, she held her hand up to his face and began to wipe the dried blood off of his cheek with her jacket sleeve.

"What are you doing?" he asked.

"You thought enough to spare me of all the blood spatter. You deserve dignity too."

Abbi continued wiping his face, but he pulled away, disbelieving, not used to having someone care for his needs. He shook his head and looked away, running his fingers through his hair. "Abigail, you have made a great impression on me." She reached out to take his hand, sensing his frustration. Surprised at the gesture, Tom growled at her.

"Tom, I'm not going to hurt you," she teased playfully, but he wasn't amused at the irony.

"It's just that I'm not used to being handled gently," he replied.

"I'm a killer, Abbi. Gentleness is not in my nature. You need to go home before I do something regrettable," he moved away slightly, pointing to her car.

"I don't believe you. I see a different side of you that you don't want to show me. I feel a gentleness in you. What are you trying to hide?" she asked, moving closer, leaning up to kiss his cheek, allowing reality to take over. Even though he was a vampire, this was the first man in her real adult life she'd been able to touch without emotions getting in the way. Her father was right. She was forming an attachment.

He quickly moved away. Tom's eyes narrowed and he became very stern. "You seem like you are doing better."

"You didn't answer my question."

"Why don't you just go home?" He motioned to her car.

"Are you avoiding answering me?" she asked, eyes playful despite his sternness.

"Please, Abigail, I need you to leave." He motioned to her car again.

"Okay," she surrendered as he quickly ushered her over, helping her in.

"Goodnight, Abigail," he said, slamming the door shut and staring at her through the window.

Tom's thoughts were fixated on her as she drove away. But he knew he needed to get over it and fast. He couldn't be so drawn in by a human, let alone a Slayer. This needed to be dealt with quickly. Tom didn't realize that he wouldn't have time to deal with his growing obsession because another eternal being was just as enamored with her but in a completely different way.

Delius wanted her and badly. As with Arlington, Delius knew she was the only one who could take down the Beast and all the escaped creatures from Hell, and he needed to stop her before she stopped him. As Tom sped around the corner, he didn't realize that Delius had been watching them.

Too overcome with Abigail, Tom hadn't even recognized Delius's scent. Delius needed to find a way to get to her and immediately thought of Henry.

Eight

"Henry," Delius whispered into his cell phone as he paced the woods next to Tom's house in Grundy. He was watching Tom in the window, keeping track of Tom's every movement and decision over the Slayer. Abigail was at her own house, but Delius wanted to know every action Tom made.

"Delius?" Henry responded, "What do you want? Where are you? I'm busy."

"You're not busy. I know you're with Claire. Remember, I know everything you do."

"That's sick, Delius. Do you know that?" Henry replied, annoyed that he was being interrupted. But Delius was correct; Henry was with Claire.

"I need you to do me a favor. How soon can you get to Grundy?"

"I'm there now. Arlington has a house for Claire here. You claim to be aware of all my actions, yet you didn't know that? You're slipping." Henry chuckled.

"Just get your ass over here. I'm standing next to Tom's house. I need you to do something involving that Slayer. Hurry before your brother interrupts my plan."

Delius hung up and refocused himself on Tom, who was inside watching the news and keeping an eye on the vampire activity in the area.

"Get your thoughts off of her! Think of something else!" Tom thought.

But there was no use in trying. He was being enraptured by Abigail and was furious at Arlington for ensnaring him into the trap of this Slayer. Though unsure of what Arlington's plan was, Tom was certain Arlington wanted more than just to send all the creatures back to Hell. Now that he'd met the force of this Slayer, he knew that Arlington had chosen him for a reason. He sighed out of aggravation and kept flipping through the news stations, noticing there were reports of vampire attacks all over the area.

"Numerous cases of missing persons reported all throughout the tri-state area …"

Tom was certain that it was from the rise in vampire attacks because of the unleashed underworld and he now realized that even though Hell was closed once again, many creatures were still on the loose. Knowing only Abigail could send them back and concerned for her safety, Tom decided to head to her house and make certain she was safe.

He hurried to put on a clean shirt and jeans, since he was still bare-chested and his jeans had blood spatter on them from the scene in the alley. After picking a casual gray button down that he subconsciously thought Abigail might like, he opened the front door, but that's when he noticed an alarmingly familiar scent.

"Delius?! NO! Abigail! He will go after her!"

Tom sped out the door and darted to the far side of Grundy towards Abigail's.

But as soon as Henry arrived, Delius and Henry were rapidly following behind Tom to Abigail's.

"How will I get inside?" Henry asked Delius.

Delius responded, "I did some investigating and found out that the house is owned by Abigail's grandmother. Janette's mother was of witch bloodline and Abigail probably doesn't know about her grandmother. This means you won't need to be invited in."

✪✪✪

It was quiet when Tom arrived at Abigail's house. He observed that there was only one car in the driveway, not two, which he found peculiar since Arlington said his wife still lived there. Taking a deep whiff of the air, he tried to notice any scents similar to Abigail's. Relatives seemed to carry similar scents, so her mother's scent would be similar to hers, though still distinct. He smelled Abbi's, a few neighbors, the raunchy stench of the local sheriff ... but nothing similar to Abigail's.

He wanted to see her, so he jumped up on the porch roof and looked for her window. To his good fortune, it was the first one he looked inside. Tom saw her sprawled across her bed in just a t-shirt and some very revealing blue lace panties. Smiling in approval, liking those, he paused for a moment to have another peek and a good whiff of her inviting vanilla cake smell. He pulled her window open to get a better view. Abbi's old window creaked and startled her awake, causing her to sit up suddenly.

"Tom?" she asked as she looked over, surprised to see him at her window.

"What are you doing here?"

"I had suspicions you might be in danger tonight," he replied nonchalantly as though he wasn't seriously invading her privacy.

"Well, okay. But I have a front door ..." she shrugged and motioned to her bedroom door. Rolling her eyes, she motioned for him to climb inside.

"I can't come in," he answered. She stood and walked to the window, tilting her head. "I have to be invited," he continued.

"What?"

Just as she said that, Tom realized that he didn't need to be invited because half of his body was already inside.

"Abigail ... does your dad own this house?" he asked as he stepped in through the window, taking a look at her standing there in just the t-shirt and blue panties.

She shook her head, "No. It's in my gram's name. Why?"

He didn't respond, only started wandering around her room, looking at all her things, noticing her books and pictures. But he paused on a picture of her with the sheriff when they were younger and a fire stirred in him over that. He thought it was possible that he could be jealous, but he brushed it off.

"Tell me about her. I'm curious why I didn't need to be invited inside."

"She was my mother's mom. She died a few years ago. Again, why are you here?" she asked as she walked over to him, grabbing his hand—wanting the skin-to-skin contact and to feel in control. But just as Abbi did that, they heard someone else jump up and into her bedroom. Tom recognized the scent. He immediately tossed Abbi to the side, crashing her into the wall with much more force than he should've, and he lunged towards the intruder.

"What are you doing here, Henry?" Tom said as he pinned down Henry by the throat. Henry tossed Tom off forcefully. Henry quickly sped over to Abbi and grabbed ahold of her.

"Help me, Tom! Please, help me!" Abbi screamed as she struggled against Henry.

"I'm here for her," Henry said, flashing his fangs as he pulled her head to the side and exposed her neck.

"Go ahead, Henry. Have a taste. You could use a little humanity," Tom provoked.

Though unsure on what Tom meant and skeptical on why he was so easily giving up on his deal with Arlington, Henry bit into her neck anyway with a pleasing growl. Abbi let out a distressing scream, gripping onto Henry's shirt sleeves from the reaction to the pain. Her eyes looked over to Tom as he stood there passively watching, doing nothing to save her. The betrayal she felt pierced like a bite.

After a few seconds, Henry fell back and looked at his hands in shock from the effect of her powerful skin-to-skin contact. Wiping Abbi's blood from his mouth, Henry said, "What the hell?! What is wrong with her? What's wrong with me?! Her touch! I feel so … I'm out of here! You can deal with this, Tom. Let Delius and this Slayer be your problem. No way … forget Delius. He's on his own."

Leaving Abbi weak on the floor, Henry fled from the room and jumped out the window.

Tom rushed over to an unconscious Abbi in a panic.

"Abigail?" he said and tried to wake her.

"Abbi," he tried once more.

But Abigail didn't respond, she was nearly lifeless in his hands. Henry had taken more of her blood than Tom had realized.

"Damnit! What am I going to do?!"

There was only thing he could do. He laid her back down and stood to pace the room as he watched the life slip away from her.

"She isn't responding and there is definitely no way I am going to explain that Arlington's daughter is dead because I'm an egotistical asshole who just stood by and watched while I let my brother kill her … out of the question!"

He paced and stared at Abbi as her breathing slowed. He knew what he had to do. Tom rushed over to her and after rolling up his shirt sleeve, he tore open his wrist. With his blood spewing out and all over her, he took her wobbling head and turned it to purposely let some blood flow onto her lips, thinking the consequences of this action could be rectified later.

"Abigail, drink. It will heal you."

"No," she snapped, weakly. "Why should I trust you? You just stood by and let that other vampire try to eat me! I will never trust you. Go away or else I'll stake *you* …"

She let her head flop back to the side once more. Growling and frustrated, he steadied her once again .

"I hate this gig," he muttered, "You are the most infuriating … Ugh!"

He moved under her so that her head was situated in his lap. "You *will* drink because I am always in control."

He bit open his wrist again and forced her to take his blood. She tried once more to refuse, gagging as the blood poured into her mouth. But once Abbi had tasted its sweetness, she grabbed Tom's wrist and drank it willingly, feeling better almost immediately. She paused and looked deep into his eyes, feeling somehow connected to him. It was a strange but satisfying experience, unlike anything she'd ever had with anyone else.

After a moment, she sat up and wiped her mouth on her shirt, curious at how he made her feel better so quickly. But after sitting there for a few minutes in the mess, she stood and walked to her dresser to get a clean shirt. Tom's eyes were enjoying the view as she did, yet he was rebuking himself in his mind for his ogling.

"You have got to stop fantasizing about this Slayer. It doesn't matter how beautiful she is! Her intended purpose in life is to send you to Hell! Though, she is really gorgeous … wow … and you thought it was just her face that was beautiful. YEESH! NO! Think of something else … anything will do … my mother! Yes! No one wants to fantasize about their mother …"

As he started thinking about other things, Abbi turned to look at him.

"Either you turn around or leave the room because I need to change. I have blood all over me. It seems likely to become a trend when I'm around you."

She rolled her eyes and motioned for him to turn around.

"Right … okay."

He got up and sat on the bed, facing the opposite wall, removing his own blood-saturated shirt as he did. Tom realized he could still see her reflection in the free-standing mirror situated near the closet. Again, his thoughts reprimanded him and he began running his hands frustratedly over his face.

"You are behaving reprehensibly! You are the most powerful vampire there is and you have been hired to protect this girl so that the unleashed underworld world regains order once again. Pull yourself together!"

He took one more peek in the mirror and saw that she could see him watching her. He looked through his fingers at her as his hands rested on his face, resting his elbows on his knees. She pulled a tank top down over herself and walked back over, feeling shy that he had been making a show of her.

"You were supposed to be looking away," she scolded.

"This I know. But don't you realize how beautiful you are?" he asked.

She shook her head, sitting down next to him. Blushing and taking notice of his now shirtless chest. Abbi began feeling nervous around his very perfect, lean, muscular physique.

"I apologize. My behavior will improve," he half-smiled, running his fingers through his hair before leaning back on her bed.

"Thank you."

She intertwined her fingers in his. He looked down at her action for a brief second before maneuvering his hand to fully grasp hers. Her words struck a place of emotional confusion inside him that was causing him to wonder how he would retain control around her. He couldn't remember a time in his vampire life that he'd ever recalled someone thanking him for anything. Vampires didn't use common courtesies. But she was treating him as though he were human, as though he were her equal. He wanted to know why.

"Who was that other vampire? He looked exactly like you," she asked as she moved her body to stretch out next to him.

Tom sighed heavily knowing that everything which had just taken place couldn't be undone. "That was my brother, Henry."

"Your brother?!" she exclaimed.

"Yes, Abigail. There is a big world of vampires and other eternal creatures to which you have yet to be introduced. He is my twin. He's very powerful and very dangerous. He has senses which far exceed that of my own. His hearing capabilities are unlike any other vampire and his sense of smell is able to track anything or anyone. His touch is strong on contact and is able to remember someone's personality the moment he feels your soul. With vampires, he can sense our blood from the moment he touches us in addition to smelling us. His sight can detect even a tiny ladybug hundreds of yards away ..."

"Oh Tom!" she cried out frantically and wrapped her arms around him. Surprised at her actions, he laid next to her, stiff and unknowing of what to do.

"Hug me," she said, "That's what people do."

He enclosed his arms around her, pulling her body in close to his, wondering when the last time was that he had hugged someone. But even more than that, his senses were aroused by her scent and the feeling of her hair on his face. She tucked her face into the curve of his neck, he inhaled slightly. He smelled not her blood but the light fragrance of her strawberry shampoo, which reminded him of the strawberry fields near his house as a boy. He knew in that moment that she was causing something strong to happen inside him. He hadn't thought of his family's estate in over 200 years, not in happy memories at least.

She wrapped her arms tightly around him, and began running her fingers up and down the length of his spine, awakening other senses. As he laid there in her arms, his thoughts jumped back and forth from wanting to bite her and wanting to grab hold of that strawberry smelling hair and show her exactly how human she was making him feel. He moved her hair away from her face where it was covering her ear and started tracing her earlobe with his finger, thinking how he wanted to lean in and nibble on it.

"Tom?" she pulled back and looked up to him. "Thank you." Then she pulled his face in and kissed his cheek. She moved back to lay under the covers, motioning for him to join her. He hesitated, watching her move around in only that revealing tank top and those lacy panties was tempting him. He quickly recalled Arlington's words: *"Don't … Stay away … She's not for you to play with …"*

"I better just wait outside to watch for suspicious activity."

"Oh,"

"Goodnight, Abigail. Don't be afraid."

"I'm not afraid."

He walked over to the window and moved to climb out, but she interrupted his movements.

"Tom?"

He looked back to her, waiting for her to continue.

"What did you do to me? I feel … different."

He desperately didn't want to have *that* conversation right now.

"Uh … I healed you. My blood makes me heal very quickly and putting it inside you caused the same effect. Don't be concerned. You can't become a vampire just from a bite like Henry did to you, or from the blood as I did. There's a more complicated process."

He turned to leave once more, but she called out to him again.
"Tom?"
He let out a frustrated growl, facing her.
"Yeah?"
"Tell me."
"I'd have to kill you."
Her eyes widened. "You mean like drain all my blood?"
He sighed. "No. Now that my blood is in you, I'd have to literally kill you by my own hands. Henry created me. He gave me his blood, then he snapped my neck and killed me. Many hours later, I woke up in a field near our house and I needed to hunt … feed."

Unsure how to respond to that vivid explanation, Abbi said, "You wouldn't do that to me, would you?"

"No. But I couldn't even if I wanted. *You* can't become a vampire," he said and pointed to her as he walked over to the window once more, feeling uncomfortable with the conversation.

"Why not? What's wrong with me? Is it why these vampires want me?"

He groaned knowing he couldn't escape the question and felt annoyed that Arlington hadn't prepared her for this situation and her current circumstance.

Why the hell am I the babysitter? I'm just here to ensure the safety, not have the heart-to-heart conversations …"

Tom growled and slammed the window shut, then walked over to the bed, taking a seat next to her. She smiled happily, getting cozy, snuggling up next to him. But he looked at her and wondered why she was so happy to be sitting so intimately with him.

"Abigail, number one, there's nothing wrong with you for being unable to become what I am. I am the most horrific and hideous type of villain there is," he said as she wrapped her arms around his arm and snuggled in closer.

"Number two, your father hired me to protect you because of a situation that is going on in my world—the underworld. He feared your safety would be jeopardized once vampires started learning of your existence."

"Why does he believe that?" she asked, looking up to him, eyes curious and worried.

He contemplated his words as he looked down to her, noticing her beautiful brown eyes. He'd never considered himself a man to be especially fond of brown eyes—his previous interests having blue or green—but staring down at her right then, he was absolutely entranced by the depth of her eyes and found himself lost in them, unable to answer her.

"Tom? Why does he believe that?" she repeated.

"Because of what you are. They want you dead."

She gasped, sitting up suddenly. Tom, having given her his blood, felt her sudden fear and wanted to reassure her.

"But I'm not going to let that happen. Your father hired me, specifically, for a reason."

"What's that?"

"I'm the most powerful vampire there is," he reassured.

"How so?"

"Because I have psychokinesis," he said into her mind.

"What the … Quit that! Stay out of my head!"

Surprise crossed her face and she held her temples. He half-smiled.

"You wanted to know," he said inside her mind once again.

"It freaks me out! Don't do it anymore."

She shifted positions to rest her head on his shoulder, feeling relaxed. But he wasn't feeling at ease; he was very much on edge, unsure of why she was becoming so comfortable with him or seemed to want to be.

"So, you're more powerful than your brother Henry? Your twin?" she asked.

He nodded, "Yes. Henry is powerful, but his power is in no comparison to mine."

"Do all vampires have powers?"

"No."

"Oh? Why not?"

"Do all humans have freckles?" he replied, "It just happens to some of us and not to others, I suppose."

"Like genes."

"I guess so."

"Tell me about the whole being invited inside thing. I'm curious about these vamp myths," she said excitedly.

He moved away from her slightly, leaning back on his arms behind his head, and he explained, "Vampires cannot enter a human's home without being invited by the human who lives there."

"Hmm … interesting. So why could you come inside here?" she asked.

He shrugged, "It must have something to do with your father."

"But I told you my gram owns this house. Well, she did. It was in her name and we just haven't switched the deed yet. The taxes come to my mom."

"I'm not sure," he said, "I just know it means that if I can enter, any vamp can."

"That's not good. You need to stay here to protect me then," she winked, clutching his arm.

"What else?"

"What else … what?" he asked, confused at what she wanted to know. He was frustrated that she was right. He was going to have to stay with her.

"We could always go to my place …" he began, but Abbi quickly interjected.

"Nu-uh. Nope. Don't you dare think that you're going to just show up here and start bossing me around, telling me what to do, and all of that. I am still going to be my own boss and I will decide for myself what I do. Understood?"

He nodded but didn't say anything as he sighed and ran his fingers through his hair, leaning forward to rest his elbows on his knees.

"Mirrors?" she asked. He rolled his eyes and continued in her little game.

"Myth. Don't you recall just a little while ago I was watching you in the mirror?"

"Oh. Right. Garlic?" she continued.

"Doesn't bother us."

"Umm ... crosses?"

"False."

"Holy water?"

"No!" he snapped.

"Bats?"

"No ... Can we stop this now?"

Tom looked over to her grinning face. She giggled and replied, "No way! I'm having far too much fun driving you insane! Besides, there's got to be something that makes a vampire shake in his coffin at night," she winked.

"Silver?"

"Enough! No more!"

He sat up and moved away. His annoyance with her was peaking and he could feel himself seconds away from losing his cool. He needed to remain calm. He wasn't used to having this much energy. Vampires tended to remain calm and collected—without much outward expression of feelings—until they got angry. Then they were *very* good at showing feelings and expressing themselves. Abigail's effervescent temperament was bouncing him everywhere.

"Come on ... tell me more about these vamp myths! If we are going to be stuck with each other, I should at least know stuff about you! Like what about the sun? Does it burn you? Do you sleep in a coffin? Does silver hurt you? Are werewolves really your enemy? Can you eat food? Are you immortal? What about—"

Ignoring her relentless questions, he interrupted, "Do you have any vodka?"

He stood and paced the length of her bedroom, running his fingers through his hair, feeling overwhelmingly stressed.

"Arlington owes me BIG TIME for this ..."

"Umm hmmm ... my mom might have some in the kitchen. I'll go check."

She stood and walked out of the room. Once again, he enjoyed seeing her in just that tank top and those lacy, blue panties. He groaned at himself in irritation—and also with Arlington—as his passions ignited while he watched her walk.

Nevertheless, he continued pacing and thinking while she was downstairs and tried in an effortless fight against his own self to distract his mind. In the meantime, Abbi's mother had come home.

"Hi pumpkin, you're up late," her mom said.

"Oh … uh …" was all Abbi could spit out. Janette noticed the bottle of vodka in her hand.

"Vodka? Why do you have my Smirnoff? You never drink. Who's here? Abs?"

"Um … It's no one."

Abbi raced away and up the stairs. She hurried back into the bedroom, closing and locking the door behind her.

"I heard your mom," he said as she nervously handed the vodka to him. He took a few swigs as she walked to sit on the edge of her bed.

"Yeah, she just got home from work. She's a moonlight waitress at the Shack. But she works for the Mayor's office during the daytime hours. She holds two jobs so we can pay the bills. My dad doesn't help her. I help with what I can, but my job doesn't make much." Abbi shrugged.

"You drink vodka?"

He nodded as he took another big swig. *It helps calm me. You have no idea how much I need it right now,"* he said inside her mind.

"Oh? Why's that? Say something else. I'm intrigued now," she said as she sprawled out across her bed on her stomach.

"No. Besides, five minutes ago you *didn't* like it. You change your mind a lot; I can't handle you. Plus, you should get some sleep. Get back to bed."

He motioned for her to get covered back up. She scrunched her face in disagreement but did as she was told.

"You never told me earlier why you left your previous job," he said as he walked around her bedroom and chugged the vodka.

"I killed the mayor. I worked as his assistant."

At her words, he spewed vodka out of his mouth and across the room.

"What?!"

"Yes, Tom. I'm a killer too. But it wasn't my fault. He was being inappropriate. When my emotions get high and my adrenaline is up …"

"You are dangerous to humans. I know. Arlington told me."

"Is there anything in this life that I'm not a threat to?" she asked sadly.

"Me," he answered. "I don't fear you, though I should because one stake from you and I'm in Hell for all of eternity. But there's something about you that …" He groaned and started pacing the room again, taking another swig.

"What is it? You're upset. I can tell."

"Oh?" he responded, not looking at her. Maybe she did know he was frustrated, but she didn't know the reason why.

"How can you possibly know that?"

"I've noticed that you start pacing when you're upset. You're doing it right now."

She pointed her finger to mimic the back and forth pacing he was doing around the room in order to mock him but then reached to her bedside table to turn off the light. In doing that, she scratched her hand on the corner of the glass lamp where the metal was bent and warped out.

"Ouch!" she cried out as the blood started to drip onto the hardwood floors, a mistake for a very irritated and frustrated vampire who was sensitive to the scent of blood, especially hers.

As soon as Tom caught whiff of the blood, he was in vampire mode. In spite of the half of bottle of vodka and the growing amount of humanity inside himself, he could hold back no longer. He lunged at her, knocking her back on her bed, his eyes reddening, fangs emerging, blood-lust erupting from him like a volcano.

"Tom?!" she screeched as she saw the anger in his eyes, but quickly withdrew as he felt overwhelming fear flood her body. He looked at her eyes as she grabbed ahold of his arms and stared deeply into the depths of his, and collapsed onto the bed next to her. She leaned over him holding his face in her hands.

"Tom? Are you okay?"

He laid there, eyes closed, realizing that there was no way he could ever hurt this woman as he had originally planned. His idea of giving her his blood seemed perfect enough, and he thought once his job was finished, he would kill her in order to break his blood-bond with her. But now that he was feeling his presence inside her, he knew that it wasn't going to happen. He could never hurt her, not on purpose at least.

"Tom?" she asked once more.

"Yeah?" He opened his eyes to look at her delicate face.

"What was that?" she asked, her heartbeat quickening, fear increasing.

"Calm your heart. I can hear your fear. I'm not going to hurt you, not anymore. I'm sorry I attacked you. That happens to me sometimes. I told you, Abigail. I'm a vampire first, a man second. Is your hand okay?"

"Yes," she said and sniffled as she looked down to the cut which was now dripping onto her sheets.

The struggle between wanting to drink her and feeling his humanity was raging inside him. Tom reached for her hand and licked the dripping blood, savoring her sweetness. Abbi was the most pleasing blood he had ever tasted and it was hard for him to resist taking more. He felt her fear and looked at her beauty and stopped himself. Biting into his own finger to reveal a small droplet of his own blood, Tom wiped his blood over her cut. In just a few seconds, her cut was healed.

"That's so amazing," she said. "You're extraordinary." She situated herself under the covers and moved closer to him.

"I'm not the extraordinary one, Abigail. You are," Tom whispered as Abigail fell asleep.

She leaned her head against his shoulder while he stroked her hair. Eventually, one of her hands crept its way into the opening of where his shirt was buttoned and she clung tightly to his shirt until she fell asleep.

"I've never felt anything as good as tasting your blood, Abigail. I don't know how I'm going to retain control around you. What are you doing to me?"

He rehearsed over and over the many possible ways he could maneuver himself away from her side and bite into her neck to drain her of every drop of her blood without waking her, but he didn't. Instead, he kept watch over her, lying next to her the rest of the night.

✪✪✪

Across town, Delius and Henry were at Claire's house and Delius was reprimanding Henry for not following through on his plan.

"I'm your creator, Henry, and you answer to me!" Delius said as he sat in the armchair of Claire's living room while Henry laid sprawled out across the sofa. Henry never found Delius an intimidating man, though Henry was supposed to answer to him. Delius was just slightly shorter than Henry and had features that were accented by his high cheekbones and long nose. He had dark, wavy hair which he kept longer and pulled back in a short ponytail.

There was nothing overtly threatening about Delius—at least Henry didn't think so—as Henry's power far-surpassed that of Delius's memory control and Henry had proven that time-over. But some felt Delius was threatening, being that he was the oldest vampire and could only be permanently staked by one—the Slayer.

"You may be my creator, Delius, but you don't own me. I still make whatever decisions I want. I think I've proven that fact. Exhibit A? Scarlett."

"Yes. You made me quite angry with that one. But moving beyond that, it still benefits you to please me. You have explaining to do—"

"It wasn't my fault!" Henry exclaimed as he jumped up and off the sofa, defending himself.

"Number one, Tom was there. You know that even as strong as I am, Tom is more powerful. Number two, that Slayer's touch is a powerful force! I couldn't—"

"It's true," Claire interrupted as she entered the room handing Henry a bottle of vodka, sitting down on the sofa.

"I've heard my father speak of my half-sister's power. She has a pretty powerful touch."

"Tell me about her," Delius said, his curiosity roused.

"As soon as I touched her, I felt … tame. It was unreal. I've never experienced anything like it in my entire existence. But I continued on and I bit her. However, the longer I touched her and the more blood I drank, the more of my humanity I felt. I'm telling you, Delius. She's dangerous."

Delius's eyes sparkled with interest. Henry feared that Delius was coming up with another plan.

"What are your thoughts?" Henry asked.

"I'm wondering what your brother is thinking," Delius replied.

Henry looked to Claire and watched a slight smile appear on her face. Everyone was very interested to know what Tom thought of the humanity-giving vampire Slayer.

Nine

Tom sat in the rocker in Abigail's bedroom watching her sleep, wondering how he was going to get himself out of the current mess he was in, when he got an idea. *Charlotte!* He pulled out his cell phone and sent a quick text to his sister.

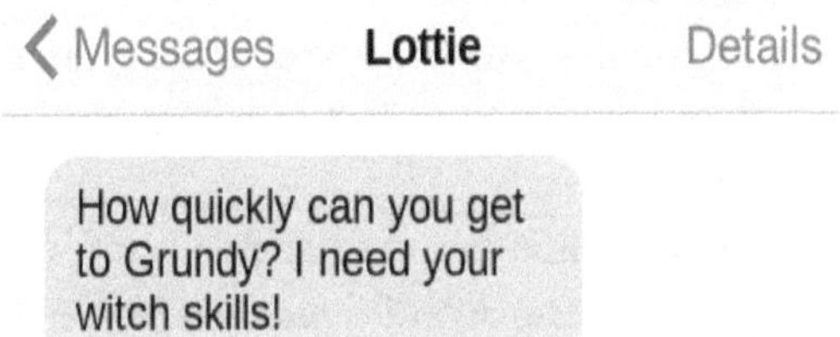

After waiting a few minutes for her response but receiving no speedy reply, he decided to occupy his time by watching the local news, watching for an increase in the vampire activity in the Grundy Hill area.

"Several reports of mysterious animal attacks are being looked into by the local Sheriff's Department ..."

"Shit!" Tom hollered as he turned up the volume and listened further.

"The attacks have all taken place in a similar manner: two bite marks on the neck, body completely drained of blood. Investigations believe it possible to be a rabid pack of wolves."

"They're not serious! Wolves?!" Tom yelled out. Angrily, he threw the remote at Abbi's TV, shattering the glass screen and causing Abigail to sit up suddenly.

"You're still here? What time is it? What was that noise?" she yawned and rubbed her tired eyes.

"Yes, obviously I'm still here, and I owe you a TV," he answered and pointed to her shattered TV.

"Oh! What did you do?!" she shouted. "I can't believe you! You're fired!"

"Heh, I'm not fired. And I believe that—" His words were interrupted as Arlington strided into the room.

"Take her from Grundy, Barclay," Arlington demanded.

"Dad! Don't you knock?!" Abigail admonished, covering herself with her blankets.

"No time for manners. I knew you'd be sleeping and I knew it would only be you and Barclay here. He needs to remove you from the area, immediately. Put some more clothes on, you're dressed inappropriately."

Abigail rolled her eyes at Arlington's orders and said, "I'm not going anywhere! And I'll wear whatever I want!"

Tom stood and started pacing again. This time he was scratching his forehead instead of running his fingers through his hair. Abigail noted the difference.

"Why the difference?"

Ignoring Arlington, Tom looked over to her, "What are you talking about?"

"Your pacing. You do it when you're upset. But when you're upset you run your fingers through your hair. This time, you were rubbing your forehead." She smiled at him, proudly. Abbi assumed he didn't like the fact that she was figuring out his mystery.

"False. You're wrong."

He continued in the pacing as Arlington spoke up.

"You know, Barclay, beware of this one. She just may have figured you out. Maybe she'll be the one to bring you down. On a more important note, I need to speak with you."

Arlington motioned for him to step into the hallway. Tom glanced to Abbi—noticing her wink as he walked past—he returned her gesture with a small smile, which was something he was not accustomed to doing.

"Listen here, vampire. I can sense that she's very attentive towards you. Put a stop to it. I know that parading around you in her skimpy clothing is enticing you, but I made myself very clear to you, didn't I? She isn't yours to play with. I'm being lenient with Henry and Claire because there isn't as much at stake there. But Abigail is the important daughter. Remember that."

Tom smirked at Arlington, knowing Abigail's growing interest in him was driving Arlington absolutely crazy.

"I'm not interested in her, even if she is interested in me. But something you should know, warlock, is you don't frighten me. There's a reason you came to me for help. Remember *that*."

Tom walked back into Abbi's bedroom and locked the door behind him. In his mind, he wanted to toss Abigail onto her bed and have his way with her just to piss off Arlington but also to suit his mind's fancy. Instead, he looked over to her and demanded that it was time to leave.

"It's time to go. You're in danger here. Henry will come back. If he doesn't, someone else of greater threat will. I cannot have that. I must remove you from this location."

"Ugh …" she groaned and sat up.

"You are dreadfully miserable. Has anyone ever told you that, Tom?"

He chuckled and responded, "Yes, quite often in fact. But I don't really care what others think of me. I do as I please and what needs to be done. So …" He walked over to her, picked her up, tossed her over his shoulder.

"Hey! What are you doing?!" she hollered out, protesting, kicking her legs, and pounding her fists on his back as he carried her to the bathroom.

"In you go. Time to get ready. I'll be back in ten minutes. Be ready when I come back," he said as he dropped her onto the bathroom floor. She let out a harrumph. Tom closed the door, locking it. Abbi turned on the water, her mind in a daze.

He jumped out her bedroom window and raced towards his house to grab one of his cars. He had to get Abbi away from Grundy and away from the destructive path of Delius and all of the vampires that were having a killing spree in the surrounding area. When Tom arrived at his house, he quickly grabbed the keys to his favorite car and a clean shirt, then sped back to Abigail's.

Upon his return, he jumped back in to her bedroom from her window, only to find she was still in the shower—much to his irritation. He let out an exasperated sigh at her absence and sat back down on the rocker to wait for her return.

"Abigail!" he called out as she nonchalantly walked across the room wrapped in only a towel, behaving like he wasn't sitting right there.

"Close your eyes. I need to get dressed," she scolded him.

"You were supposed to be ready! I told you ten minutes!" he fussed back, furious that she wasn't ready to leave but also enjoying the almost naked image that he was seeing.

"Well, we don't always get what we want in life, now do we?" she sassed. "Turn around or leave the room. I'm not your peep show."

She motioned her finger in a circle for him to do just that. He growled at her and stood to turn around. As with earlier, he positioned himself facing the mirror so he could still somewhat see her and remained watching, enjoying every glimpse of her now naked form as she dropped the towel to dress.

But she soon realized he was watching and she yelled out, "Hey! Stop that!" and she covered herself up with her blankets.

"I'm not even sorry," he admitted as he began to walk closer, running his fingers through his hair. "You're driving me crazy. You are bringing out instincts in me that I don't understand, impulses that I don't recognize. Plus … well … never mind." He looked away.

"What?" she asked and tightened the old, tattered, hand-made, floral quilt around her half-dressed body and moved closer.

"You're just so damn beautiful … your brown eyes and long hair … your stunning body …"

He looked back to her as she moved to finish dressing, assuming she wasn't certain what to do with his declaration. Abbi quickly took him surprise when she dropped the blanket, hurried over to him, reached up to his face, and planted her lips on his, giving him the most pleasurable kiss he'd ever received in his entire existence. Seconds later, he returned her enthusiasm—perhaps a bit more eagerly than she'd planned. Still kissing her, he picked her up in his arms for a brief moment before tossing her back onto her bed. He leaped on top of her ready to continue—eyes reddening and fangs emerging—but Abbi hesitated.

"Wait!"

"Ugh …" he groaned, dropping his head in defeat.

"You're my first," she said.

"First?" He raised his eyebrows, wondering if he was about to deflower Arlington's daughter. The thought pleased him far more than it should've.

"My first kiss. What did you think?"

Tom's eyes widened at the realization of how innocent she was and he sat back knowing he couldn't continue what he wanted. He moved away from her and sat on the edge of the bed, scratching his forehead.

"Tom?" she asked, scooting closer. But he didn't look at her, she was still in only a lacy bra and panties, it was far too tempting. She had no idea what she was doing to him.

"We have to go. You need to get dressed."

He stood, grabbed the vodka, and walked out of the room. His thoughts remained on Abigail and the complete understanding that if he was her first kiss then she certainly had never been with a man.

"Damn that Arlington! Why do I care about this girl so much?" he wondered as he paced the hallway, impatiently waiting for Abigail to finish dressing. *"She is only a job!"* He continued his internal reproaching.

Abbi stepped out just a short while later and Tom thought it no easier to resist his urges when he saw her dressed in a pale blue sweater and jeans. But then she opened her mouth and her complaints started running a mile a minute.

"You know, it's only like four a.m. I don't understand what's so urgent that we couldn't have waited until a reasonable hour to leave to wherever you are taking me. I'm not accustomed to being a morning person."

While her complaints continued, her mother heard them and stepped into the hallway wearing only her nightshirt. Tom, feeling uncomfortable at the sight, looked to Abbi, giving her a "Let's get going" expression.

"Abs? What are you doing? Who's your friend? Was your father just here?"

"Oh, uh, this is, uh, no one. Yes, Dad was here. You should call him later. Go back to bed."

But Tom, being the gentleman that was ingrained inside him, he spoke up.

"Hello, ma'am. I'm Tom. I'm a friend of Abigail's but also of Arlington's. Sorry to disturb you. Won't happen again. Pleasure to meet you."

"Oh, well aren't you a charmer! Abs, pumpkin, he's a keeper!" Janette responded, winking obviously at Abbi. Turning to go back into her room, she said, "Bye, pumpkin. Tell your dad I said hi and that he owes me money!"

As the bedroom door closed, Tom laughed slightly at Janette's remark and then looked to Abbi and grabbed her arm. "We need to go."

"I don't think you're a keeper. I can't decide if I like you or hate you," she snapped.

"You're no picnic either. Actually, I think you're probably the biggest pain in the ass I've ever encountered in my 231 years of existence. That's a hard feat, Slayer."

"You're really not so fabulous. I don't know why my father thought you such a great choice. And why did you just say that to me? What does that mean?" she asked as he firmly grasped her arm and pulled her along and down the stairs. Once he tossed her into the passenger side of his vintage Aston Martin, he walked around to his side and answered, "Your lot in life is to be a vampire Slayer. It's why I had you stake the vampires and didn't do it myself. All the vampires that have escaped from Hell have to be sent back by your hand. The only other that could do it is the original person who sent them but finding each and every one of them would be nearly impossible considering some existed centuries ago. You are the one—the chosen—hence, why they want you dead. You also have another job you need to do, but I'll tell you about that later. It's far too complicated to explain right now."

"Does this mean I have to stake *you*?"

"No."

He shot a glance in her direction as he started the car.

"There's a reason all the other vampires have been staked already. They were either out of control or were unable to live peaceably with humans. We have to keep things somewhat modest."

"Ha! That's absurd. Impossible. Vampires living peaceably with humans? That's an oxymoron."

He looked over to her as if to prove a point.

"True, but you've attacked me and I have an advantage," she pointed out.

"I concede. Even still, we can't allow vampires to go on killing sprees and wipe out entire towns. That's unacceptable behavior. They can't be turning children and babies … things like that."

"Turning children? That's just sick," she said, scrunching her face in disgust.

"It happens. There are children as vampires in Hell. You are going to have to stake children."

She gasped, horrified at the idea, tears filling her eyes. "I can't. I can't do it, Tom." Tears flowed faster than she could control them. He felt her upset but didn't know how to console her.

"Everyone has to face what they are, Abigail. I have to kill people every day in order to survive. I have to live with myself and the evil of what I am every day. I didn't choose this for myself either. I suppose you could say we are in this together. Both of our fates take the lives of others, just in different ways. You get to do it being a hero. I have to do it in order to not shrivel up into a corpse. No one chooses what they are, Abbi. We are born into it. Ultimately, fate decides us."

She contemplated his words as she watched the trees pass by her window as he sped through the back roads to get to the freeway. After some thought, she said, "I think that sounds like the most bitter statement I've ever heard. Because what I see for you is the opportunity for a hero as well, Thomas Barclay."

"What? You're mistaken. Vampires are monsters. And there's no need for name calling," he said, smiling ever-so-slightly, finding her use of his full name charming. The way it lightly rolled off her tongue and over her lips caused him to shift his eyes in that direction, noticing the beauty on her face once more as she spoke.

"Well, there is if you are being too hard on yourself. Because what I see is Hercules wrapped in a Batman suit. You're like the Dark Knight. A figure who lurks about in the streets at night, waiting for a kill. But you don't need to kill just anyone; you could wait for that perfect moment to snatch up the criminals and bad guys off the streets. You could capture all the ones that the police can't. You could catch all the real monsters … because I don't believe that's what you are."

He stayed silent, uncertain how to respond to her declaration of him being a hero. Finding her mind incredibly unique and fascinating, he turned his head to look at her eyes, searching for the beauty he had seen in them earlier. His views of himself were that he was a monster. Wretched, evil, and dead to the world. Then along came this Slayer, the one person in the world who should be loathing him, but she was energetic, beautiful, spirited, compassionate, and most of all, she was seeing good in him.

A few minutes of silence went by until she spoke up, "Arlington knew this about me? The Slayer thing? It's why I have the power I do, isn't it?"

He nodded. "The Master of Sorcery wants you protected. That's where I come in."

"The Master of Sorcery?" she asked.

"Adelemar. He is the peacekeeper amongst all spellcasters and knows your value. Adelemar is just about as powerful as I am because he can cast pretty much any spell he wants, whenever he wants, and I can do pretty much whatever I want as long as I can think it. The only advantage I have is that I can move faster than his spells and I can get inside his head but he can't get inside mine."

Abigail absorbed the magnitude of the powers in the people surrounding her.

"The Master of Sorcery? Why is Arlington involved with him?"

"Do you not know about your father and what he is?"

"What he is? You mean, other than creepy as hell?" she joked.

"Abigail, your father is the most powerful sorcerer there is next to the Master. He is a warlock and a very influential one."

Abigail just stared at him dazed, stunned, and speechless.

After a few minutes of soaking in the realization of the news about her father, Abbi spoke.

"I always knew Arlington was something weird and powerful, but I never imagined … so, this Master, will I meet him too? Is he scary?"

"Most likely not. I've been around for two centuries and have only seen him a handful of times. Adelemar likes to remain concealed in his castle. He isn't a threat to anyone but doesn't like to be bothered."

"How did he become the Master of Sorcery?" she asked and took his hand off the gear shift, grasping it in hers.

Looking down to her hand in his, he thought about how he *almost* enjoyed holding onto her delicate hand and how her skin touching his was rousing feelings that he almost wanted to say he appreciated. But he didn't. He snatched his hand away and said, "At one time, centuries ago, he was merely a warlock like your father, who earned his robe through his spells but inherited his wizardry through his bloodline. Through time and the evolvement of his magic, he became the most powerful and his position became supreme."

"Oh. Was there a master before him?"

"Yes. A master can serve for two-thousand years and then must be replaced by the next most powerful, which is chosen by the current master. I believe your father aims to become the next master. If he keeps up his current pace, he will achieve that goal."

"How old is Arlington?"

"Several centuries."

She sighed, thinking again that her father was untapping a level of weirdness she didn't want to experience.

"Where are you taking me?"

"Somewhere safe."

She wasn't satisfied with that answer. She was annoyed that she was being taken somewhere against her will but made herself comfortable against the car's window and glanced around at the interior. She noticed its immaculate tan, leather seats and dashboard, but also noticed that it was obviously vintage because of the lack of modern amenities, except for the newer aftermarket stereo.

"This is a really nice car. It must have cost you a fortune. What is it?" she asked as she leaned forward to look in the glove compartment and started nosing around, finding CDs, bloody towels, old cell phones, and also finding an old, leather-bound journal.

When he saw her reach for the journal, he growled, "Get out of there!"

She shut the compartment, leaning back, scrunching her face and crossing her arms to protest. He smiled slightly at her reaction, liking how she didn't want to comply to his every command but eventually did so.

"It's an Aston Martin. It's James Bond's car," he answered with a raise of his eyebrows and a sly smirk.

"What?!" she yelped. "You're telling me you are driving James Bond's car?! Like the actual car."

"Well, no. Don't be so gullible."

He looked out his window and revved the engine, speeding onto the freeway. "Buckle up. I didn't buy James Bond's car to drive slowly." He looked over at her, winked, shifted the gear, and continued, "It's an Aston Martin V8 Vantage, 1987. I own one of the few makes and models that James Bond drove."

She smiled, shaking her head in astonishment at the black beauty, dream of a car, wondering how in the world he managed to afford such an expensive toy! Looking at the perfect interior, she knew that he didn't make it a habit of taking passengers and could tell that he'd bought it in mint condition.

"Someone has an inferiority complex," she muttered.

"What?" He looked over to her.

"Oh, uh … nothing."

She smirked and asked, "Tom, how much does a car like this cost?"

"More than your house. I saw the statement on your desk in your bedroom while you were sleeping. Oh, and do buckle up. I'm an eternal being. You are not."

He motioned for her to get fastened. She fastened her seatbelt and looked his way, "Do you plan on crashing this beautiful toy?"

"Of course not."

"Then I won't be needing this." She pulled the seatbelt off in order to raise his aggravation, then she reclined her seat back, getting comfortable.

He growled at her, irritated that she wasn't listening to him. But as he looked at her there, he was starting to feel intrigued by the high-energy personality she carried, deciding he liked her spunky spirit and feisty temperament; it was keeping him entertained, and he wasn't used to entertainment, not like this at least. He reached behind the seat and handed her his leather jacket to cover her arms, and she wrapped herself up inside it, appreciating the gesture.

She glanced up to him from under her long lashes. Abbi smiled and blushed, Tom knew right then that he was developing some type of feelings for her that he was unfamiliar with. With his nerves on edge, he drove the Aston Martin at its top speed to his apartment near the Charleston, WV airport knowing that the sun would soon be up and he needed to be hidden.

As soon as they arrived to the city, Abbi recognized where they were. Arlington frequented Charleston and whenever she traveled with him, he made Yeager Airport a regular occurrence. For Abbi, the city of Charleston was a refreshing sight away from Grundy Hill. The sun was nearly cresting as they arrived, Tom had to move quickly. Tom pulled to the front of the apartment building, allowing the valet to park the car.

"Hurry Abbi, I need to get inside."

"Where are we?" she asked as she took in the scenery of the upscale apartment building which she was very surprised to see in Charleston.

"Good Morning Mr. Barclay." the doorman said as Tom approached the elevator with Abigail and she looked around at the lavish apartment complex. It was an older apartment building but still pleasantly nice. She glanced to her right and noticed a beautiful, winding, marble staircase with an intricately detailed iron hand railing running along the side.

Next to the staircase was a beautiful lounge area with blue patterned antique wingback chairs and a yellow antique sofa which were situated in front of a white marble fireplace. Hanging above was a very large and extravagant, crystal chandelier. Her gaze remained captivated by the scene before her until he pushed the down button and ushered her onto the elevator.

"Quit pushing me! Why are you in such a hurry?" she fussed as he forcefully shoved his finger into the button for the Lower Level. She crossed her arms in protest and moved away. But he smirked and looked over to her, noticing how pretty she looked with her still wet hair tucked into a low, messy bun. In spite of the frustrating experience she was for him, he found attraction in her, enormously. Tom realized she was unlike any woman he'd ever met before and knew she was bringing a life back to him that he *almost* appreciated.

"I have to get out of the rising sun. I need to check the forecast," he said as the elevator opened and he exited, pulling her along down the dimly lit hallway.

"Oh," she responded, "So it is true? Sunlight does burn you?" she asked as he stopped at the end of the hallway and typed a code into a door allowing them access into an apartment.

"Yes. I have to be out of the rising sun. Direct sunlight burns me."

They walked inside and he moved around the apartment going about his business, and she pondered his lack of décor, thinking he was very boring. The apartment seemed bland to her with its black tile floors and white walls, track lighting, and very traditional style artwork, but nothing exciting—no photos or painted portraits. She began wandering around as he walked into a another room, but he walked back out and yelled at her when he saw her touching one of the paintings.

"Don't touch that!"

"Oh, I'm sorry. I was just ..." she nervously responded.

"Do you have any idea how much I paid for that?!"

"Um ..." she looked at him, waiting for him to continue.

"Just sit down! There's a couch right there! It's a perfectly good and able couch! You can't just come inside and sit? You know, curiosity killed the damn cat! What is it with humans and always touching things?!" he yelled.

But at his anger, she felt very trapped inside this vampire cave with only four walls and no windows.

She dripped a few tears before saying, "I need to pee."

"Over there," he pointed to the door behind her. She walked away and into the bathroom. Needing a few moments to think and not actually needing to pee, Abbi closed the bathroom door. She was feeling very overwhelmed and still trying to absorb everything that was happening to her .

Deciding to be her usual nosy self, she poked around in his bathroom. It was elegant with a cherry cabinet and a white marble sink and a white marble tile floor.

She wondered as she looked around at the very white bathroom if it was easy to bleach. After reprimanding herself for her thought, she reasoned that she could've been correct in her assumptions. It *was* the cleanest bathroom she'd ever seen. There was a white towel hanging next to the sink.

"It's so white and clean and placed perfectly on the rack. Does he even use it? Maybe he has a maid … Nah … He would eat her."

Abbi splashed some water on her face and then dried off with the towel. She held the towel close to her nose.

"Mmmm, it smells like him. Yes. He definitely uses it. He smells so good! How does he do that?"

She pulled open a few drawers to waste some time but not seeing anything that she thought normal human men had in their bathroom drawers, like Playboys or condoms. Sitting down on the clean floor in front of the door, Abbi wondered about that.

"How does that work for him? His body no longer functions normally. But then again, he chugged nearly half my mom's bottle of vodka like a human. So, it's quite plausible that he's more human than I'm giving him credit."

Her mind continued spinning as she kept nosing around in the drawer next to where she was sitting. Even still, she didn't find any razors or shaving cream, no deodorant, or cologne. There wasn't even a shower in the room.

"Wonder if he sweats? Does his facial hair grow? Does his body work at all? Perhaps he has another bathroom."

There was a part of her that found attraction in him and thought him the most handsome man she'd ever seen. Yet, at the same time, she thought about her confused feelings for him and how infuriating he could be. She didn't like how he frightened her, yelled at her, bossed her around and treated her like a child, along with so many other things. Even still, she couldn't get past the overwhelming sense of attraction she was having for him, she was drawn to him. She had been since the moment she first saw him. Those feelings were overtaking her mind and body.

She listened to him outside the door as he moved about the apartment. She rested her back against the bathroom door, putting her ear against it so she could more freely listen in on what he was doing. As she listened, she wondered what he thought and felt about her. Allowing her tears to flow freely, a thousand different thoughts banged around in her head like a thousand train cars derailing all at once. Crashing one into another, dragging each other around, into the ground, explosions, derailing, complete and utter chaos. The thoughts took over her mind … she needed to gain composure.

Sensing her upset, Tom knocked on the door.

"Abigail, are you alright?"

"I'll be right out," she answered shakily, which most certainly gave her away. But he didn't seem too concerned because he responded with, "I'm running to Grundy to get the purse you left at your house. I can run faster than I can drive. It'll be quicker if you don't come with me. I've looked around for it and I know it's not here. It irritates me you don't have it. What if you need your ID? It's better for me to leave you here where I can lock you inside. I left some sweats in the bedroom for you. I'll return shortly."

Curious, she opened the door.

"Wait. Why do I need my ID and what about the sun?"

Tom didn't answer her question.

"I don't want to leave you without any way of contacting me. I figure we are at the point of exchanging numbers. After all, I already have yours."

"You do?"

"Arlington gave it to me."

She felt a buzz in her pocket.

"Check your messages and save my number to your phone. I'll be back soon."

He walked into the kitchen and Abbi heard him opening cabinet doors. Abbi pulled her cell from her pocket.

It's Tom. Does this take our relationship to another level?

Surprised by the text, she walked into the kitchen, where she saw him consuming vials of blood.

"Tom?"

Tom looked over to her.

"Why didn't you say anything about having my phone number?"

He shrugged. "Didn't think it was a big deal."

"So you were just going to be all creepy and stalker like?"

He growled at her and walked out the front door, leaving the mess of the vials of blood on the counter. Abbi walked out of the kitchen, frustrated he left her there and realizing she was still very tired. She sighed and surrendered to her growing sleepiness and searched for his bedroom.

Upon entering his bedroom, she saw that the room was plush and felt it was far too fancy for one vampire man. Abigail rolled her eyes at the sight figuring he probably used it for entertaining women. Quickly moving beyond the sight of the four-poster bed, she hurried to take the sweats and t-shirt and entered another bathroom—this one with a large glass shower. After changing, she climbed under the black blankets of his bed. However, just as she got comfortable, someone knocked at the front door.

"Tom! I know you're home! I saw your Aston!" a woman's voice yelled from the hallway. "Who are you with? Don't make me use my key! Tom, just open the door!"

Abbi hid under the covers, not quite sure what to do, afraid that it was another vampire. The front door opened and Abigail froze, holding her breath.

"Tom? It's me, Gina. Where are you? Why are you ignoring me?" The woman walked closer to the bedroom and inhaled deeply. Abbi stayed absolutely still.

"It is a vampire! I'm in for it! Is it a lover of Tom's? I don't know what to do! I need a stake! But surely, he doesn't have one around his own apartment. I'm certain a vampire's own apartment is in short supply of wooden stakes. I knew better than to trust him! He probably set this up himself! Why would he just leave me here?!"

"What do we have here? What's Tom been doin' with his time?" Gina pulled down the covers. Abbi peeked out and saw a very beautiful, vixen-sort of woman with shoulder-length hair dyed a flashy bright red.

"Who are you? Tom's latest plaything and a human. Aren't you cute! You're even in his clothes. No one gets to do that. You must be a favorite. Stand up, let's have a look at'cha."

She motioned for Abbi to stand. Nervous, Abbi did as commanded. Gina stared at Abbi for a moment before saying, "Well, I don't really know what he sees in you. You're kind of small and plain." Gina picked and fussed at Abbi's hair and face for several seconds.

"Tom is coming back," Abbi said as she pulled her face away from Gina.

Gina laughed. "You think I came to see him?"

Abbi moved a few feet away and grabbed her cell phone off the nightstand to try and text Tom.

"Who *are* you?" Abbi finally got the courage to ask as she looked down at her phone.

Gina laughed and answered, "Oh sweetie, I'm anotha one of Tom's luxuries. He'll come back to me when he's tired of you. He always does. He gets tired of all of them eventually. Then he comes back to me. Tell him Gina stopped ova! Bye, dahling."

She waved and left Tom's bedroom.

Abbi thought about the woman's thick and unusual accent and where she might be from. Abbi heard her walk out the front door and popped her head out of the bedroom. Thinking it was safe, she went to lay on the couch and not back in Tom's playboy bed. Once she was comfortable, she heard a ding come from the kitchen and realized Tom had forgotten his cell phone. Abbi walked into the kitchen to see who sent the message.

Abbi was troubled by the message. It felt more of a threat than a casual observation. A few minutes later, another knock was at the front door, but there was no introduction. Assuming it was that woman again, Abbi opened the door. But when she saw a man standing there instead, she was inundated by fear. Realizing it was a vampire, she was undoubtedly in big trouble.

"Hello, Abigail. It's nice to finally make your acquaintance. We're having a party in your honor," the vampire said as he grabbed ahold of her with his gloved hand and tossed her over his shoulder. He quickly ran to the stairway passing Gina on the way, who was standing in the doorway of a neighboring apartment.

"Goodbye, Abigail. No one wears Tom's clothes. No one except me, that is."

She sneered and waved tauntingly.

Abbi's thoughts panicked as he tossed her in the backseat of a very nice luxury car in the parking garage underneath the apartment building.

"Stay there!" the vampire with a long blond ponytail ordered as he sped around to the driver's seat. Abbi tried escaping and reached for the door handle.

"I said stay there!"

He reached for her hair and yanked her back with a strong grip against her bun from where he was sitting in the driver's seat. She let out a yelp as she dropped back onto the seat, he had the same quick reflexes as Tom. She sat on the opposite side of the car in the back seat. With her legs tucked up to her chest, he raced to wherever they were going. Looking out the window noticing the cloud-covered sky, she understood what Tom must've meant by "direct sunlight". Realizing that vampires could go about their business during the day as long as the sun wasn't shining.

Wondering where they were headed and what he wanted with her, she spoke up, "Where are you taking me?"

He let out a snide laugh.

"You're a prized possession. I'm selling you."

"To who"

"My business."

"How did you get to me so fast?"

"It only takes a few minutes or even seconds for vampires to get anywhere," he scoffed.

"Why do you want me?" she asked as he stared at her through the rearview mirror.

"You're the only one who can send us back. Now, shut up. Would you? We're here."

She thought about how she had staked the vampires in the alley with Tom and tried to come up with a plan, but she didn't have a stake.

"Why would Tom just leave me there?!"

She berated him in her mind as the vampire parked and pulled her out of the car, dragging her across the ground to an abandoned factory where there were many other vampires waiting for her. Another man got in the car that they'd arrived in and drove it away.

"There goes escape plan number one."

✪✪✪

Meanwhile, on his way back from Grundy, Tom's senses were awakened by Abigail's fear and hurt. He reached into his pocket to check for messages and realized he'd left his phone at the apartment. Tom rushed back to his apartment not realizing Abbi was gone.

"Abigail?" he called out as he walked in, but he was alarmed to find she was not there. Instead, an exasperating voice of his past greeted him.

"Hello, Tom, dahling. Abigail? Abigail who?" Regina said from his couch.

"Regina! NO! Where is she?!" he yelled as Regina stood and walked closer. He wanted nothing to do with her and needed to find Abbi. Tom pummeled Regina to the floor and yelled, "I'm not playing games with you. Tell me where she is!"

"Easy, big fella. I don't know where they—"

"They?!"

"Yes, I happened to be talking about your new lover to a group of vampires at a bar around the corner when …"

As soon as he heard that, he was up and out the door. He took a whiff of the air to track her scent, closing his eyes in concentration. As soon as he located Abbi, he took off at his top speed to the far side of town and towards an abandoned factory. "So, you're the Slayer that's got all the released underworld in such a fuss, eh?" one vampire said to her though Abbi didn't think he looked like a vampire because of his darker, olive-toned complexion. Abbi didn't respond as he walked closer. There were ten or so vampires surrounding her. They had her tied to a chair so she couldn't use her power on them and they all knew to wear gloves.

"You do realize that we aren't going to let you leave here alive, don't you? We know that you plan on staking every single one of us, eventually. It's nothing against you. Well, in the grand scheme of it all … yes … it is," said a very beautiful woman with long blonde hair, blue eyes, and bright red lipstick.

"It's you or us."

As she spoke those last few words, all the windows surrounding them shattered.

"He's here," Abbi said.

"She's right," another male vampire said as he walked over to her.

"That doesn't leave me much time."

He straddled her lap and sat on her, laughing, but she fought back at him. Tom felt her heartbeat quicken, knowing something was wrong. As the vampire grabbed her neck and moved in to bite, Tom started throwing shards of the shattered windows around the room with his mind to keep the vampires distracted. Then he spoke to Abbi mentally.

"I'm so sorry about this. I'm going to drop down in right next to you. Don't be afraid."

As he jumped down into the building, he knocked the other vampire back and off Abbi, holding him down. He used his mind to untie Abbi and quickly snapped a rod from the chair to make a stake. Abbi joined him, knowing what she needed to do. This time, she moved close to Tom on her own.

"Go to Hell!" she yelled out as she plunged the stake into the vampire's heart. Tom pulled her up and out of the way of most of the blood spatter and grabbed the stake, sliding it securely in his belt. Then Tom grabbed ahold of another vampire and they repeated the process. He looked around, seeing that the rest of the vampires had scattered … all except two.

When he saw who it was, he picked Abbi up, facing him, and pulled her against his chest. Abbi tucked her face in the curve of Tom's neck, wrapped one arm around his back and one around his neck, and her legs tightly around his waist. He appreciated the closeness of their position and liked that she seemed comforted by his presence. Holding her securely in his arms, he spoke as he approached the two remaining vampires.

"Antonius, Claudine. You have some explaining to do."

"Explaining? Me?" Antonius retorted. Abbi lifted her head off Tom's shoulder to take a glimpse of Antonius.

"You're the one with explaining to do, Tom. She is a Slayer! You're protecting a Slayer, my friend. Do you see nothing wrong with that? This is your kind. *Vampires* are your kind and you're helping this *Slayer* destroy us! These kinds of things aren't easily forgotten in our world, not even to good friends. We will deal with this later. I need to eat …"

Antonius winked at Abbi and turned to leave. Tom put Abbi down and hurried after him, tackling him to the ground, grabbing both of Antonius's hands tightly with one of his own, forcing Antonius's head down with his palm.

"Don't forget, friend, that one stake from her and you're locked in Hell for all of eternity. Watch yourself."

Tom stood and let him up. With Claudine following him, Antonius quickly scurried off. Tom picked Abigail back up, lifting her onto his back. She gripped tightly around his chest as they ran off, stopping at the top of a hill to look back at the empty factory. Setting her down on a large boulder, Tom turned to look back at the building.

"Are you okay?" he asked.

"Yes, thank you. My body is sore from being dragged across the ground and I'm a bit shaken up, but they didn't *really* hurt me. One guy tried to touch me, you know … like inappropriately …"

"Was it Antonius?!"

Tom's eyes burned with anger.

"No. It was the first man I staked."

He turned again to look at the building and collapsed it into rubble with his mind. She shrieked at the sight of the old factory falling in on itself.

"Goodness! Was that you?!" she exclaimed.

"Obviously, Abigail," he replied. "I'm sending a message to stay away from you. If any vampires are still around, they'll know I mean business. Here …" he walked over and bit his finger, lifted her up and shifted her to sit on his lap. He put out his bleeding finger for her to take. Abbi took his finger willingly. Her whole body ached and his blood not only helped her heal, but it also tasted so good. His blood made her feel connected to him and she liked that. Though, she wasn't sure why because she thought him the rudest and meanest person she'd ever met, even more so than Arlington.

"Tom?" she asked after a few minutes of sucking on his finger like a pacifier.

"Yeah?"

"Antonius … he's your friend?"

Tom nodded.

"Abigail, I live the life of a vampire outside of you. When your father hired me at the request of Adelemar, I thought I was only doing the underworld a favor. Now I see that it's becoming much more. The vampire world thinks me a traitor. Which essentially, I am."

"Then why do you do it?" she asked as she rested her head against his chest.

He enclosed his arms around her and answered, "Well, the first reason is that I'm being paid a rather large sum of money. The second is because I suppose it's the right thing."

Tom shrugged, giving her the short, quick, and easy answer. Tom had a much longer answer he could've given that might've explained why he enjoyed holding her in his arms so much.

"Who was that woman? The one at your apartment."

"Regina?" He sighed heavily and said, "I have a history. I apologize for her. She feels like she has a claim over me."

"It's okay, Tom. It's not like we're in a relationship," Abbi said. "But she frightened me. I'm scared about all these vampires."

Abbi maneuvered herself to face him—arms around his chest, legs wrapped around his waist, sitting on his lap. He didn't say anything for a moment as a fire was ignited inside him by the position they were in and froze, contemplating her words. In his mind, he kept repeating the words, unable to get beyond them for some reason.

"I need to get you back to the apartment. You can get cleaned up and I can make plans to get you to another place of hiding," he explained as he stood and tossed her onto his back again. "Hold on tight. I run very fast."

He took off running and she tucked her head into the curve of his neck out of fear, wrapping her arms tightly around him, clinging to his chest, moving her hand in through the pucker of his shirt where it was buttoned in order to feel his skin and began digging her fingernails into his skin. Tom sensed her fear and wanted to comfort her, but the only thing he could think to say was, "I've got you, Abigail. I won't let you go."

When he spoke those words, her legs tightened around his waist just a bit more and she kissed his neck where her face was hiding. The curious man inside him wondered what that meant, but he never asked. When they got back to his apartment, he plopped her down onto his bed and told her to go take a shower.

"I'll leave some fresh clothes out for you and wait in the other room."

He started to walk out when she said, "Please stay here. I feel safer when you're around. I find it ironic that I'm supposed to be killing exactly the one that I feel safest around. I don't know what it is about you, but I need you."

"I'll be … on the bed …" he groaned and walked over; her words hit him forcefully.

"She needs me? No one needs me. I'm only a vampire … dead to the world … a killer in the darkness."

With a smile, Abigail happily walked to the bathroom to take a shower. Tom laid down on the far side of the bed to wait for her, mind frazzled between deciding on making love to her and wanting to drain her of all her blood and leave her lifeless on the floor. He considered that there might be a remote possibility that he was in love with the Slayer, but then he reasoned there was no way a vampire was capable of love. *Never.*

✪✪✪

Delius, however, was in a fit. Tom was proving to be more of a match for him than he'd originally predicted. Arlington had chosen the right man after all, and no matter what Delius was throwing at him, Tom was overcoming it.

"Regina!" Delius said as she walked into the New York office. "What the hell happened? You have explaining to do!"

"Go to Hell, Delius. He isn't interested in me anymore! Besides, he wasn't even there! That Slayer's thoughts are hard to read anyway. Her mind is so erratic; I couldn't keep it all straight. I went to the men that you hired and they captured her, but I couldn't keep Tom away because he wasn't even at his apartment. When he got back, he didn't even look at me! It was like he wanted *her*! Like he was interested in *her*!"

Henry chuckled from the corner. "So, you're telling me that my brother is falling for this Slayer?!"

Regina nodded. "Yeah. That's what I'm sayin'. Now, give me my money, Delius. You promised me 250 thou'. Pay up."

"Fine," Delius said.

"Wait a second," Regina said and looked to Claire where she sat on Henry's lap. "This is interesting …"

"What is?" Henry asked.

"Isn't she Arlington's other offspring?" Regina asked, looking at Claire.

"What's your point?" Henry asked.

"Well, I just find it curious that the two sons of the underworld's most powerful creature are now involved with the two daughters of

126

the sorcery world's most powerful warlock. Do any of you believe in coincidence? Arlington has never been entirely innocent in his life."

"Your thoughts have been noted, Regina. Here is your money," Delius said.

Delius paid her and ordered her away because he had bigger problems than Regina.

"We need to break out the big guns now," Delius said.

"Why?" Henry complained. "I don't even know how to contact her."

"If Tom is vested into this Slayer more than through Arlington now, if he is developing feelings for her, then he is going to be very emotionally involved in this. What moves and turns the heart motivates the man," Delius growled. "We need her! Call her!!"

"I don't know where she is!" Henry snapped.

"You're her creator!"

"True," Henry responded. "But she's made her own vampire which broke her ties with me. I haven't seen Scarlett in 100 years."

"Would Tom even be interested in her anymore?" Claire asked.

Henry smirked. "My lovely, Claire. Scarlett is my twin brother's biggest life scandal. He can't resist her."

"We'll find her. For now, we will let him encourage this love affair with the Slayer. Then we will introduce Scarlett and break the little Slayer's heart. After that, we will make our move."

<u>Ten</u>

The more Tom thought on this situation, the more he realized Abigail was in huge danger. They couldn't sit around and wait for every single vampire to come looking for her. But he also didn't know how to go looking for *all* of them. However, this wasn't a task for him to take on alone. He also considered that he needed to find out more about her. Tom wasn't a naïve man and was curious about why Adelemar's interest in Abbi was so stirred. He needed to pay a visit to and have a discussion with the Master of Sorcery. Thinking England might be a good journey away from the area, Tom decided to call his mother.

"Katherine."

"Hello son, what is it you need? You only call when you need something," she answered.

"I'm coming to England to see Adelemar. But I'm bringing a human and I need to be able to walk in the sun. How can you help me?"

"That's a tall favor you're asking. Why should I do what you ask?"

"Because you know I have the only vampire Slayer in existence under my protection and if she dies the entire underworld will remain unleashed for all of eternity," he explained.

"She's going to do it, Tom. I know she will! She's just playing a hard game! You know how Mum is! Also, can I meet her? This Slayer girl? I've been watchin' the news about all these 'animal attacks' but I knew they're vamp attacks!" Charlotte hollered from the background.

"Hi, Lottie, and no. This isn't playtime. What are you doing in England? You better not have charged that to my credit card. Katherine, take me off speakerphone!"

"She's not in England, Tom. I'm still in New York. I haven't left yet. Come to New York and I'll work out an arrangement with you. I want to meet this Slayer."

Without another word, Katherine hung up the phone. Tom began pacing his living room, frustrated that now he was going to have to fly to New York. He figured he could also take care of some business while he was there. As soon as Abbi was finished getting ready for the day, he informed her it was time to leave.

"We're leaving. I'm taking you somewhere else. I need to meet up with someone."

"A lover?" she sassed.

He growled at her and responded, "No. My mother."

"What?!" she exclaimed. "You have a mother?!"

"Of course I do. Everyone has a mother," he replied with an annoyed expression.

"I know. But you're a vampire from hundreds of years ago. How is she even still alive?"

"Um … that's complicated," he responded, walking into his closet. She sat on his bed impatiently waiting. He stepped out in well-fitted black pants, a black button-down shirt, and a loosely fitted gray jacket. She smiled at the sight.

"You like black?"

"Well, it is fitting. I'm a walking funeral. Time to go. Are you ready?"

"I didn't know you were a funny guy."

"I can be whatever the occasion calls for me to be."

He winked, moving her along.

"Okay then. Why do you get to look so presentable and I have to look like a schlub?" she complained.

"You're fine. Those sweats are Armani."

He handed her jacket and purse to her as he ushered her out the door and down the hallway to the elevator.

"But they're too big!" she held the oversized white shirt out to the side and smiled at his baggy clothes on her petite frame.

"We'll get you some clothes when we arrive. We have not the time nor the resources right now."

"Fine."

She rolled her eyes and followed him out.

"Tell me about your mother. Believe it or not, I'm capable of understanding."

She crossed her arms and pouted as they stepped onto the elevator.

"Of this I am aware, but it would be easier for you to just meet her, and you will, shortly."

They went to the parking garage under the building where Tom's driver was waiting for them next to a luxury Bentley.

"To my plane," Tom said to him, stirring quite a reaction from Abbi.

"Your plane?! What?!" she exclaimed as she climbed into the backseat of the car.

"Please don't start. Yes, I have an airplane. No, I'm not going into the details on how. It doesn't matter. You'll be safe. It has a professional pilot."

"Did you steal it?" she joked.

He glared at her without answering.

"Jeez. What's eating you? I was only joking," she said as he messed on his phone for a few moments.

"This!"

He handed her his phone and showed her a news article from *The Manhattan Times*.

"A Mysterious Animal Attack …" she read the news headline out loud. "I don't understand," she said, handing his phone back.

"They're predicting my every move. I'm taking you to New York because I have another apartment there. But I have a feeling Delius is already there commanding these unleashed vampires to attack in that area. I fear you won't be safe there either. But I have no choice. I need to see Katherine and Lottie."

"Oh … Why? Wait, who's Lottie? And who's Katherine?"

Sensing her distress, he kissed the top of her forehead and continued, "My mother, Katherine and my sister, Charlotte—or Lottie, as I call her—are witches. That is why they haven't passed on. They are eternal beings. My mother is more powerful than Lottie, but Lottie has a very unique witch gift that she inherited from my father, who's also an eternal being. Although he is incapable of use in his current state … that situation is … *very complicated*."

"Tom. Your life is … it's so enchanting. It's like a storybook," she said as she gazed admiringly up at him. She scooted closer and wrapped her arms around his arm, sighing.

"Ha! More like a horror story. The Barclays are so messed up."

He hung his head in his hands, cradling his face.

"Tell me about your father. He can't be worse than Arlington, the hooded crusader. In fact, I would have to say that there probably aren't too many people who are."

She laughed slightly, as did he.

"You've got me there. I concede. My father is also very powerful, but he did not use his power as was to the benefit of all the eternal world and my mother had to … nothing. Never mind. I don't want to discuss this."

He shook his head, discontinuing the conversation.

"You can tell me anything, Tom. I make a good friend, even though I don't have many friends. The only friends I have are Lacy Fulton—the former Mayor's spoiled, selfish, self-centered daughter, who was only my friend because my father allowed it and set it into being—and Jack Lacombe, Grundy's sheriff. But he was only my friend because he wanted to get me into bed ever since high school. Be my friend, Tom. I need someone I can trust."

She snuggled closer and held his arm tighter, resting her head on his shoulder. He sighed and looked down at her, thinking that he didn't want to be her friend.

"Friends are overrated," he said stiffly in reply. He needed to keep up the charade, not wanting to let her know she was affecting him.

After a two-hour plane ride and a lot of vodka consumed by Tom, they arrived in New York. When they landed, Tom tried to quickly usher her through the concourse without being seen, but someone noticed their presence anyway as they exited. A reporter with her phone hollered, "Mr. Barclay! Who's the lady?" and snapped their picture. Tom tried to cover Abbi's face as she looked over, but he was unable to.

"I'm so sorry, Abigail," he apologized as they entered the elevator for the parking garage.

"Who was that?" she asked, feeling shy and confused.

"You'll find out soon enough. Unfortunately, not in a way you'll appreciate."

They walked through the parking garage and got in another very nice and expensive car. The driver was also there to escort them to meet Katherine and Charlotte at Tom's apartment.

✪✪✪

Abigail was impressed by the luxuriousness of his New York apartment. Essentially, it was pretty much the same as his other—simple with black tile floors, white walls, no pictures of loved ones or people—but a touch larger and a bit newer. It was very sleek and upscale and nothing she'd ever imagined herself being in.

"Hello, son," a tall, dark-haired woman said as Tom and Abbi walked in. She hugged him, but he didn't return the gesture. Abbi scolded him.

"Tom!" she quietly reprimanded, "You should hug your mom!"

He ignored her and said, "Let's just do what we need to do. Abigail, keep yourself out of trouble. Lottie, you do the same. Katherine, come with me."

They walked into the dining room. Charlotte looked to Abigail and reached for her hand. Abbi exclaimed, "No!" and quickly pulled her hand away from Charlotte's grasp.

"What is it?" Charlotte asked.

Abbi stood there for a moment, unsure of what to say. She noticed that Tom and Charlotte were strikingly similar in appearance—Charlotte also having dark, almost black, hair and angular, defined features with a tall stature—but Charlotte's eyes were blue. Abbi assumed that Tom's probably were at one time as well. Abbi also noted that Charlotte was dressed very nicely in a purple pencil skirt and white button-down top and black heels with her long hair flowing down over her shoulders. Abbi glanced at Tom's mom and saw her black dress slacks and gray cowl-neck sweater. Abbi suddenly felt very out of place in Tom's sweats.

"I'll hurt you. I have a special power," Abbi finally said when she was able to refocus her thoughts.

"Nah. I keep a spell of protection on me at all times. One never knows what one will come across. It's better to be safe than sorry. Look …" She reached out and touched Abbi's hand. "All's good."

Abbi breathed a sigh of relief and smiled. "Well it only happens when my emotions change, but if you're sure …"

"Trust me. It's fine," Charlotte assured.

They walked into the living room and sat down on the black leather sofa. Abbi looked around at the very plain decor but noticed his oversized TV and large, fully stocked bar and thought again how obscure he was, for a vampire.

"Now, tell me. Are you and my brother … you know?"

Abbi laughed. "No! It's not like that at all! He is hired to protect me from the vampires who are out to kill me. That's all."

"What?!" Charlotte looked Abbi up and down and gave her a questioning look.

"What is wrong with him?! He is usually the first to jump on any pretty woman that walks in his direction. But you … you are like THE most beautiful women even I have ever seen and he isn't jumping at an opportunity with you? Is he broken?!"

Charlotte stood and walked into the other room. Abbi stood up from the sofa and quickly followed Charlotte.

"Thomas Barclay!" she hollered at him as he stood in front of Katherine next to the dining room table who was holding her hand on his bare chest.

"I'm a little busy, Lottie!" he yelled back to her.

Charlotte leered at him and turned to leave, but Tom cried out in pain as Katherine said, "Sol non uret te ex die fiat. Omnes vires intendens ostendere pax erit vobis partum a praesidio atque inter mundos. Ista maledictio mortuorum erunt ultra. Gratias autem probationem. Ultimo comburantur!"

As she muttered the words, a beam of flashing light appeared on Tom's chest like a fire, knocking him back and onto Abigail, who was standing a few feet behind him in the wide door frame that lead to the dining room. Abbi felt awkward as he laid there on her, shirtless. His face looked pained and she didn't want to move him. Feeling sorry for him, Abbi did her best to carefully adjust him on her lap as she sat up and looked at his scorched chest.

"What just happened?" she asked, watching him grimace from the burn on his chest where his mother had created fire in the palms of her hands.

"My mother made a tattoo of the sun to protect me for all of eternity. Look."

He pointed to his upper left chest above his nipple over his heart where there was a black tattoo of a sun enclosed by a circle that was about three and a half inches in diameter.

"What's it for?" she asked as she traced the burned-on markings with her index finger, and gently held his head with her other hand, tracing his earlobe with her thumb.

"To protect me from the sunlight. She used the sun's rays to burn the tattoo onto me, protecting me from its light. Now, when I step out into the daylight, I won't get burned. I've been burned by the sun for the last time. That's what the tattoo represents."

"I see. She's a genius."

Abbi touched the tattoo again and then leaned down to kiss his cheek. Charlotte noticed Abbi's reaction and realized that even if

Tom hadn't shown interest in Abigail, she was definitely showing interest in him.

Tom's inner emotional turmoil was once again being ignited by his current position and the amount of care and concern Abbi showed over him. He shook himself off and stood back up, reaching his hand down to help Abigail to a stand, knowing that he had to do something about the reaction he was having.

"Thank you, Katherine. I don't need anything else. You can leave," he said, turning to look at her as she was gathering her things.

"Tom!" Abbi scolded. "Be nicer to your mother. She just did you a favor. At least hug her goodbye."

Abbi motioned for him to go and hug her. Charlotte giggled in amusement.

"Who's got the bull by the horns?" Charlotte asked with a smirk. Tom glared at her as he walked to hug Katherine, knowing entirely that Abbi was in complete control.

"You can call me sometime even if you don't need me," Katherine said as Tom leaned in to hug her and she tightly wrapped her arms around him.

He didn't reply.

Katherine reached her hand up to his face and touched his cheek. "You are still my son."

Tom glanced over to Abbi and noticed her smile. "I appreciate your help." He pulled away and approached Abbi as Katherine left his apartment.

"Tom," Charlotte started as he grabbed Abigail's hand to walk out of the room.

"What is it?" he replied, turning to look back.

"How could you bring this poor girl into the city dressed in your sweat pants? She needs a shopping trip."

"No. It isn't going to happen. I'm trying to keep her presence here a secret. Besides, I hate shopping and you're not a responsible protector," he told her.

"I never get to do anything I want!" Charlotte complained.

"It will continue to stay that way."

"I'm not three years old anymore. Stop treating me like a child!"

Tom pulled Abbi along and up the stairs to his bedroom.

"I'm sure that everything going on has you exhausted. You hardly slept last night. I can see the dark circles under your eyes."

He handed her a pair of sweats from his closet and a clean shirt.

"Put these on and I'll get rid of my sister. When you wake, we'll figure out everything else. Okay?" He squeezed her hand reassuringly and pointed to the bed.

Abbi sniffled but didn't respond. Tom sat down next to her on the bed.

"What's the matter? It's going to be alright. I'll pro—"

"I kinda like Charlotte. I want to go shopping, especially if it's on your dime. By the looks of this place you keep here and all your fancy cars, and the fact that you have your own plane …"

He held his finger up to shush her and said, "Okay. You can go shopping. I'll make arrangements for you to go later. But first, you need to rest. I can't have a grumpy Slayer on my hands. I'm not taking any chances with that," he joked, winking at her.

In that moment, she allowed herself to give into her heart's urging, and she flung her arms up and around his neck, pulling him in to kiss her. A surge of passion rushed through her. Abbi moved up to straddle his lap, cupping his face in her hands. His hands began exploring every glorious inch, moving underneath her shirt and eventually finding their way to where they most wanted. In a flash, he had her pinned underneath him on the bed, eyes encircled in crimson, fangs extended, the heat between them increasing.

"Abigail, I don't know what I can reasonably handle. It's been a while since I've hunted," he confessed as he kissed along her neckline, enjoying the pulsing flow of her deliciously smelling blood. "In spite of how human you make me feel, I still have this monster inside me that I can't tame. I need blood."

"Okay. Eat me," she urged and held her neck up to him, causing the blood vessels to become even more aware to him. Being overwhelmingly hungry, he couldn't resist. He shifted on top of her, towering over her, holding her by her hair and shoulder and he bit. She yelled out from the pain, digging her fingernails into his hair, trying to yank him away without success. After only a few moments, he pulled back, looked into her eyes and understood even more of the power she had over him. He pulled off his shirt, wiped his mouth with it and said, "The power you have over me is unreal. I've never felt anything like it my entire existence."

Then he moved to continue kissing her. Abbi was curious about what Tom meant and she pulled away.

"Explain."

Tom shifted his body and sat up.

"Now?" He ran his fingers through her hair and pulled her close again as he began kissing along her neckline.

Abbi persisted and moved away. "Yes. Now."

He sighed. "Every time you touch me I feel ... a little more human. But it isn't just that. I can feel the humanity lingering on me. It's like you're taming my vampire instincts just enough to make me ..."

"Tolerable," she said and grinned at him.

"I suppose. Just now when I drank your blood, it was like a surge of humanity rushing through me. It was unnerving because I've always been known as the vampire to go to for killing and jobs if another vampire needed something done. Tom Barclay doesn't have morals. Before I met you, I was quite hated by most vampires. If I wasn't hated, I was feared and for good reason."

Abbi moved closer and placed a soft kiss on his lips. "Well, I don't hate you. The feelings I have are far from hate. And as far as killings and jobs, morals, and whatever else you mean ... let's say you just forget all that and focus on the *only* job you have now?"

Abbi pulled his face to hers and moved over onto his lap.

Tom groaned and said, "This… this is the power you have over me. I've never made the company of humans, not even my mother or Charlotte. I have been alone for over 200 years."

Abbi kissed him again. "Not anymore."

Tom pinned her once again to the bed, but they were soon interrupted by a knock at the door.

"Abigail?" Charlotte asked as she walked in. Tom looked over—annoyed that she was coming into his room—and moved to sit up.

Abbi moved her hair to hide the bite marks and responded to Charlotte, "Is everything okay?"

"I thought I heard you scream and just wanted to check."

Charlotte shrugged and went to walk out but turned back to her just before exiting. "Oh, and you're a little liar, but that's okay. I figured as much."

She winked at Abbi and closed the door behind herself.

"My sister drives me crazy. What's she talking about?" he asked, moving to sit on the edge of the bed, regaining his composure and rubbing his forehead with his fingers.

Abbi blushed.

"She asked if we were … you know. I told her that we weren't, but she didn't believe me. She said that I was the prettiest girl you'd been with or something like that. Anyway, I guess she thinks this proves her theory."

"Oh. Well, Lottie likes to cause commotion. Don't pay any mind to her. I never do."

"Do you have a girlfriend, Tom?" Abbi asked as she stood to change. He didn't answer her right away as he watched her remove her shirt right in front of him, enjoying all the beautiful form that she was. Realizing what she'd just done, she quickly turned to face him and scolded him, "Tom! Why didn't you say something to me?! I can't believe you just sat there watching me!"

"You're yelling at me? You just stood there and stripped down to nearly nothing right in front of me and it's somehow my fault? Ha! There is not one man in the entire world who would look away from a beautiful woman who stands and undresses right in front of his face. Not one, Abigail! Especially not one who … never mind."

"Who … what?" she pushed him, wanting him to say more, but he moved beyond what he was going to say and answered her previous question. He walked into his closet to get a clean shirt.

"No, Abigail. I don't have a girlfriend, nor do I ever intend on having one."

✪✪✪

Across the city, Delius stared at the tabloid article with a snide smile, pleased with himself.

"I knew they'd be headed this way. When I learned of Katherine's presence here, I had a very good feeling Barclay wouldn't be able to keep away from her. He needs her witch resources."

Delius praised himself and he slapped the tabloid onto the conference room table in front of Scarlett, Henry, and Claire.

"What does this prove, Delius? It proves nothing. It's a tabloid article …"

Billionaire Bachelor seen in New York Airport with Mystery Woman!

"It doesn't say where they are or that they're in the city or that he's even with *her*," Scarlett ridiculed.

"It looks like her to me," Henry shrugged as he downed a shot of vodka.

"Me too," Claire agreed. "Though I've never met my sister in person, I've seen pictures, and after seeing this one, I'm now sure you've gotten the better end of this deal, Henry. Abigail looks like a tiny little mess in that picture."

She leaned back in her plush leather chair and propped her feet up on the table.

"Will you all just stop your messing and be serious?" Delius reproved. "It's her. Barclay doesn't make the company of humans and *that* woman is not a vampire."

"Henry, you saw her. Hell, you *ate* her. Is this Abigail?" Claire asked as she walked over to him and sat on his lap, wrapping her arms around his neck, kissing on his cheek and nibbling his ear.

"Could be. It's a bad image and Tom's hand is covering it some. But the hair color is right. Abigail has a caramelly brown hair that falls to her mid-back, and she's pretty petite. Scarlett, she has your build. So, the woman in the picture could be her because she looks so small standing next to Tom. Abigail is no more than five-foot three-inches tall and Tom and I are six-foot five-ish. She's good-looking and is definitely more attractive than you. I'd say you have your work cut out for you," Henry said.

Scarlett blew out a breath and said, "Hmmm … I don't see what you see. I see a pathetic mess. But she does have my figure. Maybe that's why my Tommy boy likes her so much. Maybe when he's getting it on with her, he's imagining me. He must miss me so …" She half-smiled, raising her eyebrows.

"She looks very much like Arlington. If Tom's engaged in a relationship with her, he's definitely not thinking about you," Henry observed.

"We are getting off track! Can we all focus, please?!" Delius reproved. "There is a reason you are here, Scarlett. I need Tom away from her. That is all there is to it. Use whatever powers of persuasion and whatever means necessary—"

"What about her mother?" Claire interrupted.

"Arlington's wife?" Delius asked. His mind stirred at the idea of involving Arlington's previous love interest.

"Yes. Perhaps there is a way to split them up involving the mother. Aren't they pretty close?" Claire replied.

"Claire, my sweet, you are going to reap serious benefits from this," Henry said as he kissed her neck.

She giggled. "Ooo, tell me more!"

"Enough of that!" Delius yelled at them. "We need to get our game plan together. But first, they'll be around the city today. The forecast is cloudy and I'll be able to have some no-names watching their moves. Scarlett, start following them. Be prepared to make a move. When I tell you to act, do it. You know what he likes. I need to do some dealings with Tom's company in the meantime. Henry and Claire, you two go to Grundy and locate the mother."

Each left Delius's corporate office and went their separate ways. Scarlett headed in the direction of Tom and Abbi in order to cause commotion between them. Henry and Claire moving toward Grundy to watch Janette and stir trouble there. Delius didn't tell anyone his full plans for a *very* specific reason.

<u>Eleven</u>

Abigail woke up in Tom's bed with her hair all disheveled, feeling completely rested. She yawned and looked around for him but unable to find him. She stood to leave the room, when she heard voices from the hallway. She recognized Tom's, but the other man's she wasn't quite sure.

"Here's the thing. I've decided to be on your side. That's as simple as it gets. There aren't too many people in the eternal world with a power that supersedes yours, if any. So, I feel that it benefits me to understand why you want to help this Slayer chick. I've decided to have an open mind. It's not like you to just rush into something, Tom. That's not your style. If you're into helping out that Slayer then I've got your back," Antonius said.

"What's he doing here?! Antonius wants to help Tom?! Why? Is it a trick? Don't believe him!" Abbi thought as she opened the bedroom door to see them standing there. Antonius widened his eyes at the sight of Abigail in only Tom's t-shirt and her panties.

"Hell-o," he said with a wide grin.

"Well, Tom. I see some of what has you so enamored. Hi, sweet thing." He winked to Abbi. "I'm Antonius."

"Enough of that!" Tom smacked him on the back of the head and walked into the bedroom, slamming the door closed behind.

"What's going on?" she asked and looked sternly at him.

"I don't know what you mean." Tom shrugged.

"That vampire helped kidnap me! Why is he here?!" she reprimanded.

Tom started pacing the room, running his fingers through his dark hair. He hated being the one stuck in the middle between his best vampire friend and … well, all she really was to him was a job. Even still, he wasn't treating her that way and he was having some type of growing affection for her. Instead of answering her question, he offered, "You've had some rest, are you ready to go out into the city for a little while?"

"No."

"No?"

Abbi turned her back to him and repeated herself. "That's right. I said no."

Tom growled at her. "Why are you being so stubborn?"

Abbi started tapping her foot while Tom patiently waited for her reply. Abbi spun around to face Tom.

"I'm not being stubborn. I'm sending *you* a message."

She walked away from him and sat on the bed.

"I don't know how to handle you behaving this way. Is this one of those female things? You know, like a mood swing?"

He stood and stared at her on the bed. Abbi glared at him.

"Got it. Not a mood swing."

"I don't know if I can trust you!"

"All because of Antonius?" he asked as he approached her.

She sniffled and covered her face with her hands, wiping her tears as she did.

"Abigail. Why do you believe you cannot trust me?" Tom asked and sat down next to her on the bed.

She wiped her eyes and glanced up at him. "Tell me why I should."

"Because I chose you over him. I've been friends with Antonius for 200 years. You come along and I have to betray my friendship. I do it not for my own benefit but because he's the only damn person in the entire underworld that I can actually stand to be around!"

"Then why did you?"

"To protect you," Tom said, pointing at her.

"That's the only reason?"

Tom thought about her question for a moment, not ready to admit his feelings for her.

"Yes."

"Oh …"

"Please just trust me."

Abbi nodded and grasped his hand. "Where is Antonius now?"

"Does it matter?"

"Right. I'm trusting you." She sighed.

"Now, would you like to go into the city?"

Abbi liked the thought of Tom's suggestion, but she looked down at what she was wearing and didn't like the idea of being seen in public with what she had on.

"What about my clothes?"

"Oh right. Let me see what I can do."

He turned to walk out and she sat on the bed to wait for him, but he turned to look at her just before he opened the door.

"Abigail?"

She looked up at him.

"I don't make a good friend."

She stood and walked over, took his hand and brought it to her lips, planting a tender kiss on it. Then she said, "I don't believe you. Because you already are." He reached out and brushed his hand across her cheek before walking out of the room.

A few minutes later, Charlotte returned with a few different items of clothing and some hair accessories. "Let's see what we can do to make you presentable," she said and laid some dresses and skirts out across the bed, but Abbi looked at them skeptically, thinking that they were all far too flashy and fancy for her. Also, she felt that Charlotte's body type was far different than hers as she was petite with an averagely medium build, but Charlotte was fairly tall and moderately slender.

"Okay, I've got a few dresses I think will work for your tiny frame …" Charlotte began, but Abbi interjected, "I might be a shorty, but …"

"Abigail, now isn't the time to be self-conscious. Here …" She handed Abbi a black halter dress. "This will accent your breasts nicely."

"Charlotte!" Abbi scolded. "Tom and I are NOT involved that way!"

"Yeah, which is why I see bite marks on your neck, blood stains on his bed, and a bloody shirt laying right there."

She pointed to his stained shirt next to the bed. "Let's just be real … Abigail, my brother is a hunk. You know it, and I know every female on this planet knows it. So, just be honest with yourself about the fact that if you're not doing the deed right now, you will be."

She tapped Abbi on the shoulder and handed her the dress. "Once you've changed, come back out and we'll fix your hair."

Abbi went into his bathroom and slipped into the dress. When she walked back out, Charlotte smiled.

"Yep. I knew that was the right dress for your figure! You're stunning! Now, let's do something with all this hair. Up or down? I say up. Then you can tease him with your sexy neckline."

Abbi only shrugged, unknowing of what to say. Charlotte was making such a fuss over her and she wasn't sure why. After pulling and tugging at her hair for several minutes, Charlotte managed to tuck it into a delicate, low-swept chignon with some strands of hair left subtly and strategically, hanging by her face.

Charlotte added a finishing touch with some mascara and some soft pink lipstick, then said, "Voila! You look gorgeous! You have beautiful skin so I didn't need to put on any foundation. But wow, girl, you look hot! Go look!"

She pointed to Tom's closet mirror and Abbi stepped over carefully because Charlotte's heels on Abbi's small feet were just a little too big.

As soon as Abbi stood in front of the mirror and looked at herself, Tom walked in.

"What the hell is taking so long, Lottie?" he griped.

"Oh, shut up and thank me," she replied, motioning to Abigail.

He looked over at Abigail.

"Abigail, … wow … you look … spectacular … breathtaking."

Charlotte whispered something into his ear and he shook his head at her. She gave him a stern look and then he nodded, conceding to whatever she had said to him.

"Are you ready?" he asked Abbi, holding out his arm, looking her up and down. She nodded and clutched his arm.

"Have fun you two!" Charlotte hollered as they left the apartment and headed for the parking garage.

"Café du Paradis, then Barney's," he said to the driver as they got in the car.

"Ooo …" she said as she moved closer to him as the driver exited the parking garage.

"What's that … café?"

"A restaurant, obviously," he replied.

"Is something wrong?" She let go of his arm.

"I'm just feeling … a bit on edge. I need to hunt," he admitted.

"Oh …"

He moved to the other side of the car and stayed quiet the rest of the drive. Abbi watched Tom help himself to the mini bar directly in front of them. He looked over to her several times, able to sense her discomfort, but he was unsure of what to say or how to bring her any happiness. Instead, he sat holding a shot glass of vodka in one hand, running his fingers through his hair with the other.

When they arrived to the Café du Paradis, Abigail was astonished at the courtesy Tom was receiving.

"We have your table ready, Mr. Barclay. Right this way," the maître d' said and pointed to the far back corner of the elegant dining room.

"Tom," Abigail whispered as he led her along to the back corner but he didn't answer. She was persistent, however, and continued in her questioning when they were seated.

"How did he know your name?" she asked as she sat in the booth across from him.

"I frequent here."

"You drink blood and vodka."

"Just look at the menu and stop giving me a hard time."

✪✪✪

Later that evening, Delius was headed in the same direction as Tom and Abbi, though not to the Café du Paradis or to Barney's. There was a bar just around the corner that Tom frequented. He often made dealings with the owner, Dominic. Delius walked in and made his business known.

"I'm here about your main man, Dominic. Has he been here?"

Dominic was in the center booth of the back room with a harem of skimpily dressed vampire women sitting on his lap and all around him. Dominic was a typical looking male vampire— attractive with masculine features. He had thick, sandy brown hair, and dark eyes with red rings. As Delius spoke, Dominic looked up and grinned.

"I'm sure I don't know what you mean. Barclay has been hanging around with a new crowd these days. I saw him in the tabloids just this morning. You know as well as I do that's the best place to find information about vampires, especially wealthy ones like our main squeeze."

Dominic laughed and kissed one of the women he was sitting with who handed him some vodka.

"He's right, you know," one of the females with him spoke up, "We saw him on the front page of the most popular vampire informational tabloid with a human woman. See for yourself," she said as she slapped the same article that Delius had been viewing just a few hours before down on the table in front of him. Delius picked it up, staring at it for a moment before looking back to Dominic.

"What are your thoughts?" Delius asked, knowing he was the one who sourced and printed the tabloid.

"My thoughts?" Dominic chided. "You are asking me my thoughts?!"

He slammed his fists down onto the table in a fury, eyes encircling in deep red. "I hired Barclay for a job over two months ago and it still isn't finished. He is known for doing things on his own time. He's always been the controller of his surroundings. That's who he is. But this … look at this picture very carefully."

He forcefully shoved his finger down onto the picture of Abigail and started tearing a hole into her partially covered face.

"What about it?" Delius asked.

"Whose face is covered?! Hers! Look at the way he tried to cover her face. She's only a human, and yet he was sure to protect her face from the nuisance of the tabloid reporters. He doesn't even do that for himself! He cares for this girl. Even more so, though, he felt he needed to hide her face. Now, Delius, my thoughts? Why … I want to know why!"

Delius hadn't given Dominic enough credit. He was smarter than Delius had predicted and understood that Tom was vested deeply in her.

"Look at this …" Ginger, Dominic's created vampire, said as she pointed to the picture.

"What?" Dominic responded, curious.

"Well, those can't be her clothes. She's so small and those clothes are so baggy," Ginger pointed out. Delius looked to Dominic.

"Damnit!" Delius yelled. "She's wearing his clothes!"

"I don't understand, Delius. Why are you so interested in this?" Dominic asked as he poured another shot of vodka.

"*That* woman?" He pointed to the tabloid. "She is a Slayer. In fact, she is the ONLY Slayer to still exist. That is Arlington Domitius's daughter."

"No way!" Ginger exclaimed out. "That warlock?!"

"Why does Barclay have her?" Dominic asked.

"Arlington …" Delius answered, "He wants her protected."

A woman to the right of Dominic asked, "Protected? From what?"

"All those killings that I've been printing in the tabloid. They're because dipshit Delius over here unleashed the underworld while he was down there capturing the Beast," Dominic responded.

"I was going to fix it! But Arlington screwed it all up!"

"And there's nothing in the bloody hell we can do about it …" Dominic said, nodding to Delius.

"Why not?" Ginger asked.

"Barclay is the most powerful vampire there is. None of us can compete with him," Dominic said to her.

The first woman asked as she maneuvered herself onto Dominic's lap, pouring herself some vodka, "What does he do? Is it why you're always hiring him for your jobs? Is he a good hitman?"

"He's the best hitman there is. He has psychokinesis," Delius said as he lit a cigar.

"Hahaha!" the women laughed in unison.

"Psycho … what?!" one of them mocked.

"Psychokinesis, you idiot. It means—"

"I'm psychokinetic," Tom said inside all of their minds at once as he walked into the back room. Abbi was walking closely behind Tom, intertwining her fingers from her left hand firmly in his, and tightly gripping ahold of the back of his shirt with her other hand.

"Barclay! Good of you to join us!" Delius hollered out as he watched Abbi hide herself further behind Tom.

"Glad to see you've brought us the prized possession. Let us have a look-see." He motioned for Abbi to move out from behind Tom.

"Stop pissing around, Delius. I didn't come here to see you. Dominic, explain yourself."

Tom slammed the tabloid with his and Abbi's picture printed on it down onto the table in front of them. Dominic laughed. "You've seen my latest edition. I had to let the people see Tom's new pussycat!"

The women in the room all started laughing.

Abbi whispered, "Can we just go?"

"In a minute," he told her mentally.

She tightened her grip around his waist. That's when she felt it—
the stake. Underneath his jacket, tucked into his belt, he had hidden a
stake. She reached under his jacket and maneuvered her hand to grab
ahold of it. Something in her was compelling her to take it, like
something beyond her control … something ingrained in her.

"*Don't do it, Abbi,*" he said inside her head. "*I know what you're
thinking. Don't take the stake.*"

Tom turned his focus back to Delius and Dominic. "Delius, while
I'm here …"

Tom began speaking to him about something Abbi was
uninterested in. She quickly scanned the room, noticing where
everyone was seated. She wanted to go for that man named Delius,
who she remembered Tom said—being the oldest vampire—could
only be permanently staked by her hand. She also remembered Tom
saying Delius was the reason for all of this chaos and Abbi felt a
sudden urgency to be certain of his demise.

In an instant, she grabbed the stake from Tom's belt, jumped out
from behind him and lunged at Delius, who was only a few feet to
her right. But she was knocked back suddenly. She heard, "No
Abigail!!" as she pounded into the wall next to them with great force.
Delius's lips curled up as he watched her tiny, fragile body bounce off
the wall and slam onto the floor. A frantic Tom realized he was the
one who'd just did it.

✪✪✪

"Why isn't she waking up?!" Tom yelled. Charlotte sat next to
Abbi on his bed with some potions and healing ointments, trying to
get Abbi to wake. Tom nervously paced the length of his bedroom.

"This is a pretty big bump on her head. Maybe you should take
her to a doctor, Tom. I'm only a witch. How long has she been
passed out?" Charlotte asked.

"Over an hour."

He sat and breathed in deeply, listening to her slowed heartbeat.
"She was heading for Delius, Lottie. I …"

He paused and looked to Abbi's unconscious, bruised and bloody face.

"I'm sorry. I was wrong. I was supposed to protect you," he said as he knelt down and touched the bruising on her cheek.

Charlotte looked at the angst written all over her brother's face and understood that in spite of his quick-acting vampire temper, he loved Abigail and was regretful for hurting her. Tom feared wouldn't earn her forgiveness.

"She'll forgive you. I can help. I know the ways of women and can teach you how to romance her. Perhaps all you've known until now is how to charm, but I will teach you how to give affection. I can tell you love this woman, Tom. I've known you a long time," Charlotte said as he held Abbi's hand in his and began wiping the dried blood from her face with a damp rag.

"You don't know what you are saying, Lottie."

He let go of Abbi's hand and stood. "Why aren't any of your witch things working?"

"I don't know! How hard did you throw her?"

He growled at himself. "With all my strength."

"Thomas Patrick Barclay! You probably killed her!" Charlotte reproved.

"She was going to stake Delius! What was I to do?!" he defended.

"Oh, uh … I don't know … LET HER! That bastard needs sent to Hell!"

"The consequences of that action are too great to be rectified, even for you."

"Well, something needs to be done, Tom. Delius is out of control."

"I know he is! But there is nothing you or I can do about it."

"Perhaps not, Tom. But *she* can," Charlotte said, pointing to Abbi.

Tom walked away from her and began pacing the length of the room as Charlotte continued working on Abbi.

"Nothing seems to be working, Tom. What about your blood? I know you've given it to her. I see that change in you."

Concerned for how much of his blood Abbi was consuming on a practically regular basis, he moved on from Charlotte's suggestion.

"Thanks for no help, Charlotte. What's our mother doing? I could really use her expertise right now!"

"She went to get food. You know, *we* are human; we eat food, but the only thing you keep in ready supply in this apartment is vodka and vials of blood."

He rolled his eyes. "I know, but I don't care. Right now, the only thing I care about is—"

"What?" Abbi asked as she sat up in his bed.

"Abigail?!"

He called out as he saw her put her hand to her forehead. Tom rushed over to her, grabbed her shoulders, and turned her to face him.

"How do you feel?"

She gave him a fierce look, then said, "Like I was just thrown at a wall by a very powerful vampire."

Charlotte smiled and said, "I gave you some healing oils for your cuts and bruises and a potion that soaked into your skin for that nasty bump on your head, but you'll still be sore. Goodnight, love."

Charlotte stood and quietly left Tom's bedroom.

"I'm so sorry, Abigail. I …"

"No. I have nothing to say to you. Get out," Abbi demanded, teary.

Tom bit his finger to give her a few drops to be sure she was fully healed. She refused.

He stood to exit, but before he closed the door, he said, "All of the new things we got you from your shopping trip are in my closet. I hope you enjoy them. I'm sorry I let you down. Goodnight, Abigail."

Carefully, Abbi stood and stretched her aching body. She went to the closet to get the clothes Tom had purchased for her earlier. She thought about the reason they'd stopped at that bar in the first place—the tabloid—and she was shocked to find out that he owned the Café du Paradis. Having lived her whole life in that tiny, little Podunk, backwoods town, she didn't know much about big business or life outside of Grundy. But Tom? Apparently, he was some kind of big deal.

After dressing in a nightshirt and brushing her teeth, she wrapped her hair up in a loose, messy bun and returned to the bedroom. But Tom was sitting there awaiting her return.

"I would like to speak with you," he said.

"You may speak, but I may choose not to listen." She walked around him and sat on the other side of the bed.

He growled at her and continued, "You can't stake Delius, Abigail. I'm sorry I reacted the way I did; I didn't mean to hurt you. I'm not used to my strength around humans and was immediately regretful. As soon as I felt the pain you were experiencing …"

"What? Explain what you mean."

She whipped her head around to face him and saw that he was turned in her direction. He moved to sit next to her and clasped her hand in his, holding it tightly.

"When I gave you my blood, not only did it heal you, but it also bonded you to me. It doesn't hurt you but it allows me to experience you on a whole other level."

Abbi started backing away, pulling her hand out of his grasp, but he held onto it firmly and continued. "No. Please, listen. It's a good thing."

"How so?" she asked, tilting her head.

"It's like when I create a vampire; I have to give that vampire my blood, and then we would be bonded together and that vampire becomes mine until that vampire breaks the bond and creates its own. But with you—because you're a human—it's for your lifetime. I feel everything about you. Your feelings, emotions, desires, wants, hurts, actions, location, even when you wake and sleep are all on display for me to see now. I know everything you do because my blood never leaves you. It's circulating inside you just as yours is, but mine stays separate. You're the only person I've ever done this for because it can potentially become an annoyance."

She put her hand up to cease him from speaking and stood to walk to the other side of the room covering her hands over her face as she began to cry.

"I don't care. I don't even want to hear it. I've heard enough."

She pondered over his words for a few minutes and said, "So this … my upset, you can feel this right now?"

Tom sat running his fingers through his hair with his elbows resting on his knees, frustrated and dismayed, concerned that she would never forgive him for his actions against her but also curious why in the hell he cared so much. He looked up to her and nodded.

"Yes. I feel everything about you. My blood pumps through your heart and moves through your brain. I'm a piece of you as you are to me."

"Can you read my thoughts?"

"No. But I can see your mind just the same as always. It's on my radar because of my power. That hasn't changed."

She turned away from him, angry that she had no privacy anymore. Abbi was curious about what he said about his power. She made a mental note to ask about that some other time.

"Tell me about your life. I feel like I'm stuck with a man that I don't even know. Like tonight … I found out about a whole other side of you," she sighed.

"You mean, my company?" he asked.

She nodded.

"When I was turned, my father knew that I wouldn't be able to work a traditional job because of the sun. So, he started putting away monies in stocks and investments for me. As time passed, I used that money to create a world for myself in the human side of life because, as ironic as it is, I don't particularly care for vampires all that much."

She laughed slightly.

"My company started small and I purchased a few hotel chains and restaurants, eventually expanding to airlines and car manufacturers. Now I'm ranked as one of the wealthiest men in the world."

Abbi gasped, "Oh my god … you're him. I know who you are. I recognize you now."

"Yeah. That's me." He nodded.

"You live … two completely different lives."

She shook her head in astonishment, looking away, unsure of how to feel having all of that dumped on her. Just as she looked away, Tom's phone buzzed in his pocket from a text. Abbi was curious if it was a woman or even Antonius. Part of her was still so very attracted to him and wanted him all to herself—though felt that could never happen—and was jealous of all of his women and was even still angry about Antonius. Abbi huffed out a breath, angry that she thought he might know how jealous she was.

"Who is *that?*" she asked.

He didn't respond, so she walked over, wiping her eyes as she sat next to him, trying to take a glance at the message before he pulled it out of view.

"Henry," he responded.

"Henry?!" she exclaimed. "What does he want?"

He sighed heavily and replied, "Well, he is my brother, Abigail. But in case you're wondering, I don't engage in life with him socially. He's playing games with me … look."

Tom handed her his phone. Abbi looked down at the text message.

> Riddle me this, dear brother. No need to invite me when one is just like the other. Daughter like mother or brother like brother. There's no erasing this bond, not even a trip to the past. Your time is almost up, so you better come fast. Tick tock, tick tock, goes the clock. Where it stops might be a shock.

"I don't understand," she said, looking to Tom who was now standing in front of her, pacing back and forth, scratching his forehead.

"They're … they're playing games with me!" he yelled at her.

She jumped back, startled, then asked, "Who?"

"Henry and Delius. This is a riddle. They're going to hurt someone. I have to figure it out before it's too late."

"Well, surely it can't be too hard to figure out. If it's about me, I only know like five people! We can just call Arlington's house and have him keep an eye on things there. He has a phone at his house, but he doesn't have a cell phone. Well, at least I don't think he does. Could you imagine him with Twitter? Ha! The whole world would be under a curse!"

She laughed at her statement, but Tom paused at her words and re-considered Henry's message for a moment.

"I have to make a call. We are leaving. Get dressed," he ordered.

"Ugh … It's always 'Abbi do this' or 'Abbi, we are leaving.' There's never a moment's rest when I'm with you!" She complained as she stomped off towards the closet to change again.

He looked back to her, and pausing where he stood, he said, "Your mother is in danger."

Twelve

Henry arrived to Abigail's house and knocked on the front door like a perfect gentleman.

"Hello, Ms. Taylor," he smiled as she opened the front door.

"Hello again! Abbi isn't here. I thought she was with you," Janette responded as she ushered him inside.

Janette walked into the kitchen while Henry perused the living room and looked over Abbi's family photos.

"Would you like anything to drink?" Janette hollered.

Henry didn't respond as he stared at a picture of Abbi at her high school graduation.

"How lovely."

He took the picture out of the frame and tore it in half then put it back in the frame. He saw one of Abbi with her mother and did the same before he texted Tom.

< **Messages**   **Tom**   Details

Your Slayer looked darling at her graduation. She really bears more of a resemblance to Arlington, I believe. So many family memories …

"Did you say you wanted something to drink?" Janette asked as she walked into the room.

"Now that you mention it, I *am* feeling a little parched."

He rubbed his throat and coughed as he slowly walked over to her. "I know just the remedy."

✪✪✪

"Mom! Are you here?" Abbi yelled as she opened the front door and hurried in a few hours later, searching the house frantically.

"I smell her blood," Tom said as he followed close behind.

"She's not here. My car is here; her car is here, but she is nowhere to be found." Abbi walked into the living room and walked the living room. She immediately noticed the pictures that were torn and yelled for Tom.

"Look at this." She handed him the frames with the torn pictures.

"Call your father. I'm going to keep looking around."

"Arlington," Abbi said.

"Did Barclay hurt you?" he answered.

"No! I'm back in Grundy and Mom isn't home. I'm concerned because I can't find her anywhere, but …"

"Eh, she's probably out with one of her boyfriends. I'm not surprised," Arlington dismissed.

"Arlington! Listen to me! Tom got a message from Henry saying that he was going to hurt someone. Someone has been here..."

Before she could finish speaking, she heard his phone click and there was a dial-tone. She stood to find Tom but it didn't take long. Tom was back to her side in an instant after his search of the house was finished.

He handed her a note.

"This will be the day that you will forever remember as the day your family belonged to me," the note read.

"How do you know it's him? It's not signed," she pointed out.

"That's very similar wording to what Delius said to him when he was turned," Tom responded.

"Oh. Were you there?"

"No. But I, uh … I heard of the events that took place."

"Don't you think it could be Delius instead of Henry?" she asked.

"No. This isn't his style. He would've stuck around, shown himself. That's more like who Delius is."

"And you?"

"Me?"

"Yeah, you. What's your killing style?" she probed.

"I'm not discussing this." He shook his head.

"I want to know, Tom. Tell me."

"You're not going to drop this, are you?" he responded.

"Nope. So, give in," she smirked.

"Fine. Generally speaking, I go after men in alleys. Women are too easy and I like a challenge. Men tend to fight back and I don't have to hear the shrieks and the 'help me' screams. I rarely show anyone my power."

"You showed me," she said.

"Yes, well, you are a special circumstance and I'm not trying to kill you."

"What do you do with them after?"

"I'm very uncomfortable with this conversation. But I will tell you I don't just leave them there. It's too risky for us."

"Because the authorities would find the bodies?"

"Yes, and let's change the subject," he said with a sigh.

"Alright. How are we going to find her? Do you think he killed her?" she asked as she wrapped her arm around his and laid her head on his shoulder.

"No. If he killed her, he would've left her here for you to find. I know how Henry works. He likes to show off his kills."

Just then, Arlington kicked down the front door with his foot, and walked over top of it to enter the living room.

"Barclay!! Explain yourself!"

Tom rolled his eyes and stood. Crossing his arms, he shook his head at Arlington's overreaction.

"First, warlock, I was hired to protect one Taylor, not two. And, second, I think you should be speaking to the other Barclay if you want answers about your wife. But perhaps, you should be keeping better tabs on your woman, Arlington. If I had a wife, I sure the hell would want to know who she was running around with, especially if it was a 27-year-old vampire who doesn't age and looks a hell of a lot better than you."

Abbi smirked and her eyes widened at Tom's comment. She bit her lip so she wouldn't laugh. Then she clutched ahold of Tom's arm and pulled him back down to sit next to her, whispering in his ear, "Behave yourself! Don't you know that Arlington is known for his flaring temper."

He half-smiled at her. "That may be so, but I've been known to be just as disagreeable," he whispered back and kissed her cheek. Tom looked back to Arlington, who was clearly unhappy with the closeness and familiarity that Abigail and Tom had developed.

"Whatever this is that's going on between the two of you can be explained later." Arlington motioned with his finger back and forth between them, insinuating his disapproval about their relationship.

"Barclay, I'm going to visit Delius and look into this situation. I know he has ties to Henry and Claire."

"Who's Claire?" Abbi asked.

Tom looked to Arlington, thoroughly anticipating the explanation he would give Abigail about her half-sister who was a sorceress from the 1700s and also Henry's lover.

"Abigail ... my dearest daughter, you have a sister ..."

"What?!" Abbi shouted. She looked to Tom, who only shrugged like an innocent bystander. Arlington continued, "Abigail, I've been around for many years..."

"Tom, did you know this?!" Abbi asked.

"How is this about me? Your father was a whore monger in the 1700s and somehow I'm getting scolded? Hell no! Tell her, Arlington! Tell her about how Claire's mother was nothing more than a servant who sold herself on the street and how Claire ended up as a milkmaid in my family's town and is my brother's lover."

"You knew her, Tom?" Abbi asked. Her curiosity about her sister was growing but her frustration with her father was deepening. Arlington casually smiled as he stood from the chair he had been seated in and crept towards the door.

"Yes, I know her. I told you; she's Henry's lover."

"But Arlington said he's going to see her now. Right Arlingto ... Hey! Where'd he go?!" she looked around and realized that as she'd been too occupied with reprimanding Tom and didn't notice Arlington had slipped out.

"Well, it looks like he left because he didn't want the same scolding that you were giving me," he growled.

"I'm sorry, Tom. It's just so shocking to find out I have a sister! But even more shocking to hear that you knew about this and she's your brother's lover!"

Distressed, Abbi rested her head onto his shoulder. He wrapped his arm around her, trying to comfort her.

"How heavily is she involved with Henry?" she asked, looking up to look in his dark eyes.

"He would've married her had he been able. But my family was of noble bloodline and Claire was only a milkmaid. My father didn't approve. Henry would climb out of his window at night to see her.

Sometimes I would hear her sneak into his room late at night. They had a long-standing affair … until …"

Tom discontinued speaking, shaking his head, dropping his face in his hands.

"Until?"

"Until Henry was turned. That's the moment that changed everything for my family."

"What happened when he was turned?"

Slowly, Abbi reached her hand out, pulling his face up to look her in the eyes.

"I don't want to discuss this. Now, you know that he loved her very much, but they couldn't marry because of the class system in that day. She's still alive because she is a sorceress, which is basically a female version of what your father is. Claire inherited your father's wizardry bloodline, while you inherited his other. They remain lovers now, but his regards as a vampire are only … sexual."

Abbi nodded, but the empathetic girl inside her could sense that there was a dark and serious secret he was hiding inside. She moved to his lap, held his face in her hands and said, "Tom, I don't know what secrets you keep and I fear that I may never unlock them all. But know this, nothing you could tell me would make me run away. Something inside me is drawing me to you and I have no idea why."

She straddled him, pushing him back against the couch and kissing him fervently. He let out a deep growl and swiftly pinned her beneath him on the couch in no time.

"What is it with you?" he asked as his eyes encircled in crimson.

"What's that?" she asked, tightening her grip on his hair, pulling him back to her lips for another kiss.

He pulled away again, saying, "I want to hate you. I want to do my job, protect you, have no care in the world about you, and move on. But …"

"But?" She pulled him in to kiss her again.

His kisses started moving downward. He paused on the juicy part of her neck where he inhaled a deep whiff of her delicious scent. But just as he did that, he put his finger to her lips to silence her, and she kissed on his finger for a moment while he mentally said to her, *"Don't speak. We have a situation. But I promise it will be okay. Take this …"*

He reached to his belt and handed her the stake. Then he planted one more kiss on her lips as he quickly pulled her to a stand and positioned her behind him.

She was expecting Delius, Antonius, or even Henry to come walking in the still busted-down door, but after seeing who walked through, she began to understand why her father wanted her protected.

✪✪✪

"Abigail!" Janette yelled out. "Abigail, it's your mother!"

"Janette," Tom responded, "I know you've been turned. I sense your blood has changed and know a vampire when I smell one. Where's Henry?"

Janette cackled and looked towards Abbi. "I'm here for her! You're a traitor, Barclay! Why are you protecting her? I'm here to do a job!"

"A job?" Abbi asked as she peeked out from behind Tom to look at her newly turned, vampire mother.

"Yes. My job is to make sure you … DIE!"

Janette screamed at Abbi. As she did, fire blew out of her mouth and across the room like an ignited torch, lighting up the sofa and most of the living room. The fire burned Abbi and scorched Tom. Tom quickly pulled Abbi out of the way, jumping through the front window, crashing the beautiful bay window to a million pieces. He realized that Janette's vampire power was fierce and she was going to need to be staked. They couldn't have a fire-breathing vampire on the loose.

Once outside and deep in the dark woods, he bit his finger to give Abbi some blood to heal her burns, noticing she was in tears. She reached her arms out for him and wrapped herself up in his embrace as she sucked on his finger and cried.

"Where did she go?" Abbi asked.

"Either the fire was too fierce for even her, you know we hate fire, or Henry must be near. I need to be on guard."

Tom looked around the area and breathed in trying to familiarize himself with the surrounding scents.

"Oh Tom …" she sobbed.

He looked at the reddened skin all down her arms from the burns, they were worse than he'd thought. He pulled his finger away and tore open his wrist. Abbi drank for a few minutes before pulling his arms around her. Tom flinched as his scorched arms hadn't quite healed.

"Are you hurting?" she asked, looking at his arms.

"I'm fine."

She stepped away and said, "I know you need to hunt. Why are you giving me your supply?"

"You're my priority right now."

"I'm healing."

She sucked in a shuddering breath, moving back closer to him and tucking her head into his chest. Abbi sniffled and wrapped her arms around him.

"Henry made her a vampire."

He nodded as he stroked her hair. "Abigail, you know what you need to do."

She pulled back to look him in the eyes. "I can't. I can't stake my own mother!"

"You can't look at her like she's your mother anymore. Look at this!"

He turned and gestured to her house just a few hundred feet behind them that was going up in smoke.

"She'll do that to others, Abbi. You said you don't want to stake children? Well, don't let her kill children either. Stop her while you can."

Abbi nodded. "I understand. But first, you need to hunt."

"Is the Slayer giving me permission to kill someone?" he asked flirtatiously.

She wiped her eyes and grinned, "Only if he does it Dark Knight style."

"Deal."

He kissed her forehead and went to toss her onto his back, but just as he was maneuvering her to take off running, another figure ran past, tackling both of them to the ground. Abbi was tossed several feet away from Tom.

"Tom!" she yelled in a panic as she fearfully looked around in the dark woods that was only being lit up by the flames of her burning house.

"Tom!" she yelled out once more, not seeing or hearing him.

But hearing her cries for him, Tom stood and immediately rushed over to Abbi's side.

Tom looked over to their attacker, who stood watching them nearby.

"Why are you here, Henry? Shouldn't you be keeping track of your new ties?"

"I'm perfectly aware of what my very powerful newbie is doing. I take it you've seen her skills? What do you think of your mumsies, Abs?" Henry taunted.

Abbi's anger exploded and she lunged at Henry, but he met her in the middle and pummeled her to the ground. On guard, Tom quickly interceded knocking Henry off of her and slamming him onto the ground. Tom pinned him down firmly against the ground with the strong grip of his hand to his brother's throat and his knee shoved forcefully into Henry's abdomen.

"Stay away. Understand? I can't erase what you've done to her mother, and now you've destroyed her home!"

Tom turned and pointed to the burning house several hundred feet behind them.

"But I WILL keep you away from Abigail."

"You love her, brother!" He chuckled and taunted. Abigail ran over, holding up the stake.

"Let me stake him!!"

Tom shook his head at Abbi, took the stake back and slipped it back into his belt. He reached for her hand, quickly pulling her up and onto his back.

"It's true, Tom. You're in love with the Slayer!" Henry teased.

Tom didn't respond but turned his head away, dismissing Henry and let Henry run off.

Tom and Abigail darted off in the opposite direction of Henry just as the firetrucks pulled up to take care of Abigail's burning house. His running slowed as he approached his Grundy house. Wordlessly, he sat her down as he walked onto the front porch.

"Tom," she said sternly, as he opened the double mahogany front door to his very old brick house. He turned to face her.

"I know you're upset about Henry, but I had a very good reason. Come inside and I will explain."

As he took her hand to lead her inside, Antonius was quickly approaching them with a young female vampire locked in his arms.

"Tom, your Slayer has to take care of this problem."

Antonius held out a young female vampire that was trying to kiss him.

"She was out of control, killing more people than I could even count, faster than I could watch … that's unacceptable! No one eats more people than me! I had to use my power on her to gain control of her, but now she won't stop trying to love on me. It's very frustrating!"

"What?" Abbi asked.

"I can't turn her off!"

Tom laughed and said, "You usually don't have a problem with women wanting to love on you, Antonius. What's the issue now?"

"She's a child, Tom."

Tom looked at her a little more closely and realized he was correct.

"Hmm … I suppose you're right. Would you say she's about—"

"Fourteen," Abbi interjected.

"Well that's why," Tom said. "She's just a teenager. She's like in puberty and all that nonsense. You shouldn't have tried to sex control someone of that age. Her sex drive is all out of whack."

"What are you talking about?" Abbi asked.

"Remember when you asked me about vampire powers?" Tom asked Abbi.

She nodded.

"Well, Antonius's power of sex control can cause anyone to become sexually attracted to him. He can use that power to sexually manipulate anyone he desires. However, once he uses it, he can't easily turn it off."

Antonius winked to Abbi, trying to stir a response from her before saying, "Turning it off usually depends more on the other person's drive. What about you, sugar? I see fang marks on your neck."

Abbi rolled her eyes. "No, thanks."

Antonius shrugged. "Well, alright but you're missing one hell of an opportunity." He blew a kiss at Abbi as she turned her back to him.

"Enough messing around," Tom said.

Antonius held the girl out to Abbi. "Stake her, Slayer!"

"I refuse."

"You have to do something," he snapped at her.

"You shouldn't have done it to her," Abbi said.

"I couldn't help it. It needed done. Here …"

He reached his arm out, handing the vampire girl over to Abigail as she longingly reached for Antonius.

"Do it. Stake her."

"I. Said. No!" she yelled, moving away.

But Antonius persisted, "You *will* stake this girl, or we'll see how quickly you have *two* sets of fang marks on that neck."

Tom lunged at Antonius, knocking the young girl onto the ground. Abbi caught her and held her firmly as she slowly set her onto the ground.

Abbi looked into the young girl's eyes and said, "No. I can't do it. I can't kill this girl!"

She looked back and forth between the three of them before she stood.

"Abbi, she's already dead," Tom said, holding the girl onto the ground with his mind. "You're only staking her, sending her to Hell where she belongs. You have to do it. I told you there are going to be things you have to do that you don't like. I can't erase that someone turned her. But this girl can't go on killing sprees."

Tom grabbed the stake out of his belt.

"No! Tom …" Abbi said as he yanked her down and forced Abbi onto the girl.

"This girl doesn't realize what she's doing! I remember being her age. Her impulses are that of a teenager!"

"Abigail!"

Tom knelt down next to her and grabbed her face in his hands. As soon as he touched her skin, he almost forgot what he was going to say. Their skin-to-skin contact began to soften his temperament and he looked in her eyes. Tom began to feel his humanity coming out faster by the second. He pulled his hands back and spoke with his mind.

"This is not a human anymore. She is a vampire! She has the impulses of a vampire and she will kill you the first opportunity she gets! Now stake this evil vampire!"

He handed her the stake and joined her on top of the girl's waist.

"Do it, Abigail."

His words were not a request but were a command and Abbi had no choice. He was forcing her, putting actions into her head and controlling her mind. As Tom held that girl still with his mind, Abbi reached up and she pierced that girl's heart with the stake. The girl cried out in pain as her heart spewed blood.

The blood came up and out faster than Tom could move Abbi out of the way. Abbi quickly removed her blood-soaked shirt, tossing it to the side. Not caring who was looking at her as she sat there shirtless, Abbi only cared about getting the girl's blood off herself. She began to sob as she watched the girl turn to dust.

Antonius stood by and ogled Abbi. Tom frowned, he didn't like sex-crazed Antonius staring at her that way. Tom removed his jacket and hurried to cover her with it.

"Abigail, I'm so sorry," he said as she sobbed. "Let me get you inside for a shower."

"That was a lot of wasted blood. Look, this has been lovely, but my hunting was interrupted and I left Claudine in the middle of an alley on the other side of Logan County. See you birds later."

Antonius ran off as Tom picked Abigail up to get her cleaned up. Tom carried her up to his bedroom and into the bathroom, turning on the water for her to get cleaned up. Abbi sat on the bathroom floor sobbing, unmotivated to do anything.

"I know you're angry with me, Abigail. But I told you that there was a reason all those vampires were sent to Hell in the first place. That girl couldn't control herself. She can't eat every human she sees. Do humans eat every piece of food they see? No. Vampires need to be reasonable as well. We have urges and impulses as well that we need to control—"

"I'm not angry at you, Tom. I'm not upset about that girl," she interrupted as she regained her composure and wiped her eyes.

"Oh?"

He walked over to her and sat down.

"My mother …" she began to cry again.

Understanding that Abbi was realizing she was going to have to do that to her mother, Tom walked over to the shower, turned off the water, then picked her up, and carried her to the bed. After stripping off her shoes and jeans, he covered her up with the blankets and kissed her cheek. He wet a rag from the sink and gently wiped the blood from her face and hands. As he did so, he thought about what Henry said and realized once more that it was very well possible that he might actually be in love with this Slayer.

"Goodnight, Abigail. No more worries for tonight. I'll be right over there. Get some rest."

"Tom?" she asked as he tossed the rag in the corner and took a seat in the antique wingback chair next to the old marble fireplace in the corner of the room.

"Yes?" he looked to her as she sat up.

"Why don't you ever sleep? Is it because you don't want to lay with me? Are you afraid I'll kill you? Because I won't."

"No. I rarely sleep. I only sleep to pass the time," he shrugged. He picked up a book that was on a table next to his chair.

"Oh. I thought—"

"My body is very resilient and strong. I *can* sleep, but I don't need it. When someone like me has been around for hundreds of years, time tends to pass slowly but sleeping helps it go faster. But mostly, I don't think to do it because I'm not tired. Get some rest. I fear that this isn't the worst of it."

He returned his attentions to the book he'd picked up off the table. But Abbi had other plans. She stood and walked over to him, removing the book from his hands and sitting on his lap. He very willingly allowed her to do so, especially since she was only in her lacy bra and panties.

"Abigail Taylor, what are your intentions with me?" he asked with a deep sigh and a half-grin.

"What do you mean?" she asked and twirled his hair in her fingers.

"I know that you are innocent in the ways of men, but you have to understand how hard it is for me to be sitting here with you like this."

He gestured to her sitting on his lap and then moved her hair away from her neck and started kissing at the vein he could see pulsating through her skin.

"Well, I'm desperately trying to get you to come and lie down with me."

She turned to face him, forcing him to kiss her lips. "Are you struggling to be here with me like this because you are a vampire? Or because you are a man?" She kissed his nose and began unbuttoning his shirt.

"Both," he answered as she finished unbuttoning his shirt and ran her hands across his chest while gently resting her head against his shoulder.

"Do you need to hunt?" she asked.

He inhaled deeply and stiffened his body from the way her hands were awakening his senses and replied, "You have no idea."

"Go ahead. Just be quick."

She kissed his lips, then stood and walked over to the bed, his gaze desirously following her as she moved.

"No. I'm not risking leaving you."

"Well, you can't starve. You need blood, Tom. What are you going to do? Take me with you?" She looked at him skeptically.

He pondered over that for a moment thinking it possibly held some merit. He could put her inside a nearby bar for a little while where he knew there would be other humans around and she would feel comfortable, and then he could wander into an alley for a kill.

"Yep. I'm taking you with me. Be right back …"

He walked into the next bedroom to get some of Lottie's clothes in the spare bedroom, grabbing the first dress he saw. He quickly returned to Abigail and handed her Lottie's dress.

"Here put this dress on."

"No! I'm not wearing your lover's dress! Where are my clothes from the city?" she protested.

"I left them there. We had to leave in such a hurry and I plan on returning, eventually. Do you always have to be so stubborn?! It's not a lover's dress; it's Lottie's." He handed the dress to her again.

Her demeanor changed when she heard it was Charlotte's. She reached out and took the red spandex dress.

"Oh, in that case, I'll wear it."

She walked to the bathroom to put it on, though she felt uncomfortable in the long-sleeved, mini-dress, which scooped low in the back, and hugged her every curve. She stepped back out to see Tom, whose eyes brightened at the sight of her wearing such a figure-hugging dress.

"I'm not so sure of this dress, Tom …"

"Well, it doesn't look like *that* on Lottie. It'll be fine, believe me. Now, you need to just wear whatever shoes you had on and we need to go before …"

He paused his statement and his mind turned once again to thoughts of wanting to make love to her. "Let's go, Abigail."

✪✪✪

Across town, Henry was pleased with himself at having turned Abigail's mother. He was positive that it would tear Tom and Abigail apart. Delius, on the other hand, was outraged.

"I told you to kill her, not turn her!" Delius yelled at him.

Henry sat in Claire's living room drinking vodka with Claire kissing on him as though he had not a care in the world.

Henry laughed and responded, "But don't you see? This gives me an edge. Now I can dangle the mother in front of them like a little pawn. Janette belongs to me. She's all mine."

"What you don't realize, though," Scarlett spoke up from the opposite side of the room, "Is that this is going to push them closer together."

"How so?" Claire asked as she moved off of Henry's lap and sat next to him.

"She's going to look for comfort. If he's already attracted to her, he'll give in to her. It's who he is. I know Tom. Vampire or not, he doesn't have it in himself to be an ass. Not that kind at least," Scarlett continued as she walked out of the room, feeling angered that she might have been defeated for Tom's affections once again.

"Do not worry, Scarlett. You will get him back!" Delius yelled to her. "This game is far from over!"

"Ha. Well, surely she won't be satisfied with him forever," Claire reasoned. "She's a human. Doesn't she want human things? Make her see what she'd be missing out on."

"You're a human, Claire," Henry retorted. "What the hell are you missing?"

She moved over onto his lap again, and grabbing his face in her hands again, she said, "Oh Henry, love. Don't be offended! I'm different. I don't desire other things. But Abigail? She's lived the life of a human. Eventually, she's going to tire of your dear brother."

"You make a valid point. She will want a normal life," Henry agreed.

"Who are her friends?" Claire asked.

"Why do you ask?" Delius responded.

"I have an idea …"

"Your idea will have to wait because once I learned of Henry's little scheme, I set forth a pawn into being that will set them way back," Delius responded.

"Oh? What did you do?" Claire asked.

"I made a deal with the devil."

Thirteen

Tom ran the length of the county—with Abigail clinging to his back—looking for a reasonable kill yet unable to find any until he was headed back towards Grundy and was in the next town over.

"And I said STAY out!!" the bar owner screamed as he threw the drunk man out into the alley.

"What about him?" Abbi whispered in Tom's ear, pointing to the man. She reached her other hand inside his shirt.

"Are you encouraging a kill, my beautiful little Slayer?" he asked.

She softly kissed his neck, pausing for a moment, allowing her lips to rest against his skin, and igniting the fire inside him.

"Dark Knight style," she replied. "I'm tired. You need to find one eventually. There's a reason he was thrown out of that bar. Do your business and take me home."

He thought about her words as he watched the man stand in the shadows where the light of the doorway only dimly lit up the alley. Did she feel so comfortable with him now that she felt his house was her home? He almost liked the thought of it.

Looking around for a safe place, he sat her down on an empty barrel. "Stay right there," he ordered. "I'll be right back."

Then he sped over to the drunken man who was staggering away. Not wanting Abbi to witness what he was about to do—not wanting her to think him a monster—he threw the man over his shoulder and hurried down the alley out of sight. Abbi felt nervous sitting there alone in the dark and stood to follow after him.

"Tom!" she called for him, repeating his name several times with no reply. But several other men came hobbling out of the back door of the bar at the sound of her voice.

"Ooo, gentleman! What do we have here? Look at this fine young thing!" one man said as he walked over to her. She started backing away but they surrounded her, mocking her, and she knew she needed to do something as she searched with her peripheral vision for anything she could use as a stake.

"I'm with a man and he will come back to help me …"

"Oh, I'm so afraid! Look at me shaking in my boots! She's with a man, guys! Maybe we should leave!" another man with shoulder length blond hair and especially masculine and attractive features said. He pushed her up against the brick wall directly behind her. Her heart sped up, her fear increased, knowing she didn't have a stake, and not even certain he was a vampire. She reached her arm out to grab his. But when her touch didn't hurt him, she knew right away that they weren't human.

"I knew it! He is far too attractive to be a human! I should've known better!"

He easily overpowered her and was too strong, even for her power. Her heart was pounding and her breath quickened as he moved her hair away from her neck and his yellow eyes encircled with black. His forked tongue shot out in a serpent-like slither, he whispered in her ear, "Now, you're mine."

As soon as he bit into her neck and Abbi cried out, Tom appeared behind the man, yanking him away.

"No one bites that neck except for me!"

Tom held the man against the wall and pressed a stake to the man's chest above his heart. He motioned for Abbi but she'd passed out on the alley floor.

"I'm not what you think I am!" he hissed as Tom looked back to his black encircled eyes. Startled at the sight of black—not red—Tom dropped the stake and quickly ran to help Abbi. When Tom looked back to the other man, he'd disappeared into a black cloud of smoke.

"Abigail!" he yelled, but she didn't respond. When he inspected her neck, he noticed an alarmingly peculiar bite and understood right away that man was not a vampire. He was unsure what else to do except dial Arlington.

✪✪✪

"What the hell did you do to her?!" Arlington yelled as he stared at Abigail's bruised and green oozing bite as she unconsciously laid on Tom's living room sofa.

"I didn't *do* anything. I was hunting because, I don't know, Arlington… maybe it's that I need blood in order to survive and if you want her protected then that's what I need to do to live!"

"Well, you've done a shitty job protecting her! She's practically dead!" Arlington exclaimed, walking over to her and examining the bite more closely. He turned and looked at Tom.

"This isn't a vampire bite, Barclay. I don't know what this is, but it's unlike anything I've ever seen. We should take her to Adelemar. Call up your resources. We are going to England."

"I'm sorry, Arlington. I know this is your daughter and you care for her."

"It isn't me who will be so distraught if she dies," Arlington said.

"Oh?" Tom tilted his head and looked curiously at Arlington.

As they walked quickly out the front door with Tom carefully carrying Abbi in his arms, Arlington answered, "It's you."

Tom looked down at Abigail's pale face—that was almost a blueish color—and considered the bite marks on her neck and blamed himself.

"He's right," Tom thought as he laid her down on the back seat of his vintage Aston Martin. *"I will never forgive myself if you die."*

After a lengthy flight, a lot of pacing and consumption of vodka and "red from the private cooler" for Tom, they arrived in Hertfordshire. During the flight Tom heard nothing but acerbic comments from Arlington about how Tom needed to end his very obvious affections for Abigail. Tom got a rental from the airport and drove them out the long drive to where Adelemar resided in his mansion built back in the 1000s. Gwarenmogt was where he kept many of his apprenticing spellcasters on site. Abigail remained unconscious and Tom's concern for her grew with each shallow breath she took.

"I know you're in love with her, Barclay. I'm no idiot," Arlington said. "But it isn't going to happen. I made myself clear. She isn't for you."

"I know not of what you speak," Tom replied as he drove through the dirt roads of country England.

"Pish posh. It's written all over your face. Your worry is undeniable. You love my daughter. I know love. I've been in love."

Tom rolled his eyes, scoffing at Arlington and made no reply.

"I'm telling you that you will get over this. End it now!" he yelled.

"What if you're right? What if I do have feelings for her? I can't make it just magically go away. You're the one who introduced her into my life knowing the powerful effect she would have on me. *You* did this, Arlington. You can't erase what is done," Tom combatted.

"Perhaps not on your end. But I can on hers, and I will intervene somehow."

"What is the big deal anyhow?" Tom asked.

"Because I know the future …"

"The future of what?" Tom interrupted.

"The future of what your relationship will bring to all the eternal world!" Arlington shouted at him as he pulled up to the main gate of Gwarenmogt.

Before pressing the buzzer to speak with Haledezzar—Adelemar's first in line sorcery adjunct— he thought about Arlington's words and what he might've meant. He also considered that it was Arlington—the biggest commotion maker in the history of the world—and figured it was no big deal. Tom looked back to Abigail and pressed the button.

"What's your business with Gwarenmogt?" Haledezzar answered.

"It's Tom Barclay and Arlington. We have urgent business with Adelemar."

"Come through. I'll let him know you have that Slayer," Haledezzar said as he pressed the button to unlock and open the gate. Tom's glance shot in Arlington's direction, surprised that Haledezzar knew of Abbi's presence.

"Haledezzar senses her humanity. His sorcery is not as strong as mine, nor Adelemar's, but he has a gift for sensing the location of others. Much like your lover, Scarlett."

Tom's ears perked up at the mention of his 1787 lover, Scarlett. She had a vampire power of infrared. She could sense the awareness of anyone within the vicinity of her and tell who it was before approaching them.

"Yes. I know so much more of your world than you think I do. Watch yourself, Barclay, or your secrets will be on display for all to see … and I mean ALL."

Arlington looked back to Abigail as he exited the car. Tom carefully picked Abbi up out of the backseat, holding her tightly against his chest and followed Arlington up the lengthy front-entry stairs.

"Wizards and sorceresses are like vampires in that we can be gifted with powers. Some of us have higher powers, like Haledezzar, yet some of us gain higher powers from achieving levels of magic, like me. Haledezzar was gifted with a higher power. Me? I gained my sorcery."

"Yeah, by selling your soul to Sat …" Tom paused and looked fiercely at Arlington. "I know what's wrong with her."

Arlington's interest was stirred. "Go on. You've got my attention. And I did not sell my soul to anyone. It doesn't work that way."

"That's a snake bite," Tom said as he moved Abigail's hair and showed the oozing bite to Arlington as they entered the giant castle doors.

When Arlington nodded and murmured his agreement, Tom's fury rose inside him faster than he could contain himself and he let out a violent growl that shook the castle walls. Tom knew that this was now far more serious than he had anticipated. The emotions he was feeling were new to him and now his concern for her over what he was certain was a serpent's bite was only going to complicate it all the more.

They continued to walk the long hallways and Tom looked around in order to distract his mind from Abigail. Its age was showing but was a beautiful sight nonetheless—with sandstone walls, candle wall sconces, and marble floors. Apparently, Adelemar liked to be simple. He made no updates like Katherine did to her mansion.

"Adelemar will see you now," Hadelezzar said as they approached him standing outside a large door that was the main sorcery lair.

Haledezzar was a normal-looking human with nothing odd or peculiar about his appearance other than his unkemptness. Much like Arlington and many of the other spellcasters, he had long, dark hair and his wizardry earned him a cloak, but in order to be hooded, he needed to gain the mastery of warlock. Haledezzar wore his long black hair in a messy ponytail that spread down over his black cloak and walked through the that castle, proudly considering himself the next closest wizard to Arlington.

All unmastered wizards remained unhooded. As their sorcery skill improved, the color of their cloaks changed beginning with maroon, navy, then gray, then ultimately, black. Arlington wore a hooded, black cloak, and the only others to have black cloaks were his apprentices. Each color had a mastered warlock that was hooded, but Arlington, being the most powerful, was the darkest hooded and no one had purple cloaks except the Master of Sorcery.

Adelemar's appearance, on the other hand, was quite startling at first impression—with his purple eyes and almost glowing skin. He wasn't frightening, but his appearance seemed abnormal at first introduction.

Tom cradled Abigail in his arms as they walked into the grand ballroom. Adelemar had transformed the ballroom into his own sorcery lair filled with candles, basins of water, and glass globes that radiated electricity and illuminated light; marble stones surrounded the doorway, forming a pathway directly to the pillar where Adelemar sat. He was sitting in the middle of the room perched on a large throne-like chair that was hoisted up on a tall, white marble pillar directly above mounds of dead rodents but living frogs and snakes. Next to him was his long wooden staff carved with the image of a swirling flame that rose to the top.

"Welcome," he said, jumping down off the pillar and uncovering his head from his purple cloak. He looked straight to Abigail draped across Tom's arms, knowing they were there because of her, and said, "Abigail Janette Taylor … daughter of my favorite warlock. It is so very nice to finally make your acquaintance," he grabbed her hand, kissing her knuckles. "I've heard extraordinary things about you."

"Quit pissing around, Adelemar," Tom scolded. "I won't play these games with you."

"Alright, Alright. I'll be on my best behavior, Barclay. Now, what seems to be the problem?"

Tom laid her down at Adelemar's feet and knelt down next to her, moving her hair away from her neck to reveal the still bruised and oozing bite marks.

Adelemar nodded and sighed. "Well, I don't know what you want me to do about this. It's out of my influence."

"What are you talking about?! You are the oldest and most powerful sorcerer!"

"Yes, well, this is above what my powers can fix."

Adelemar knelt down and held his hands over the two fang-like bite marks on her neck, closing his eyes, pausing for a moment before saying, "You need … You already know what you need and know him well. I suggest you call your mother."

Adelemar stood and turned to walk way. Tom saw that Abbi was waking and the bite marks were healing; the oozing was stopping and the bruising was fading.

"Abigail?!" he called out to her, then he looked to Adelemar. "I thought you said … Explain yourself," Tom demanded, standing.

Arlington merely stood, watching, observing, yet doing and saying nothing. It was almost as if he knew what was going to happen … like he knew the outcome.

"I didn't say I couldn't help her *at all*. I only said it was above what my powers can *fix*. She'll feel better for a little while, but that bite will come back to haunt her if you don't get that *nasty* snake venom out of her."

"What's it going to do to her?" Tom asked.

"It damns her to Hell for all of eternity as one of Satan's demons."

"What?!" Abbi screeched as she partially sat up and clutched ahold of Tom's leg from where she was lying on the floor. He knelt down again.

"Abigail, I don't know what you remember or of how much you're aware. But you were bitten in Grundy by something very powerful."

"I remember. He seemed like a vampire at first, but he had a forked tongue and yellow eyes. Then he said something to me."

"He did? What did he say?" Arlington asked, finally speaking up.

"That I belonged to him," she answered as Tom picked her up and they watched Adelemar return to his pillar throne. Abigail didn't answer right away as she was paying close attention to Adelemar as he moved. She discreetly pointed to Adelemar and whispered in Tom's ear, "Who's that weird looking man?"

But Adelemar, able to hear her, replied, "My dear Slayer, I'm Adelemar, The Master of Sorcery. It's a fine pleasure."

She turned her head around in his direction, taking a good look at his startling appearance, then she shifted her body on Tom to wrap her arms and legs around him, feeling frightened. Tom braced one hand securely on her bottom and pulled her in close with his other hand protectively on her back.

"Arlington!" Adelemar called out as he took notice of the intimacy of Tom and Abbi's position, "How are you feeling about this love affair that your beloved daughter is having with the reprobate sex-addict?"

Arlington looked over to Tom with a scowl, "It displeases me, very much so. But I—"

"What?! No! It's not like that," Abbi exclaimed and she looked to Arlington, afraid that her angry father might get the wrong impression. But Adelemar chuckled slightly and pointed to her arms clutching tightly around Tom's neck and her finger's gripped firmly into his hair.

"Slayer, you're not fooling anyone. Look at the way you're holding each other."

"He makes me feel safe," she defended. "The whole underworld is plotting for my destruction. Isn't that why I'm here?"

Adelemar made no reply to Abbi but turned to Arlington. "It's funny, Arlington. You convinced me to hire a vampire because her natural instinct tells her to hate them. How's that working out?"

"Time to go," Arlington scowled.

As they walked out, Adelemar hollered, "You need Patrick! Or you might contact Charlotte!"

When they got back to the car, Tom immediately dialed Katherine to inform her that he was heading her way. "Katherine, I'll be there in two hours. I need a favor …"

"You're going to have to manage on your own," Arlington said.

"I can get to my family's estate from here. Where will you be?"

Arlington glanced to Abbi in the passenger seat before he said, "I have a distressing situation I need to deal with."

"I understand," Tom looked between Abbi and Arlington and nodded.

Fourteen

Tom and Abbi arrived at Greenvalley and entered the Barclay mansion expecting to find only Katherine. However, much to his surprise, Charlotte came rushing into the Great Hall at the sound of their entrance.

"Where is she?!" Charlotte called out as she hurried down the main stairway.

"I'm right here," Abbi responded from Tom's side, lightly grasping at his fingers.

"Oh! Phew! I was so nervous! Let me see you!"

Charlotte pulled toward her to inspect the bite but quickly shot an angered look up to Tom.

"Thomas Patrick! There's nothing wrong with her! She's completely fine!"

"For now, she is. Adelemar closed and healed the wound. But Satan's venom is still there. He couldn't remove it. You know what we need."

"She's not going to do it, Tom." Charlotte shook her head.

"Lottie, I have to try. The future of the underworld depends on it."

"Oh really? I'm not convinced. Give it up. We both know what this is truly about."

Charlotte firmly took his arm and pulled him down the hall and into the old ballroom with Abbi quickly hurrying behind them.

As she followed, she noticed the workmanship of the beautiful old mansion and was entranced by the majesty of the once elegant house—which had lost its charm from the wear and aging over the years—but still had delicate and intricate detail crafted all over it. Abbi looked above where they walked and observed the hand-carved stone ceilings all throughout the walkways and realized that Tom's family was definitely *very* wealthy in their time.

When they entered the grand ballroom, her attention was immediately fixed upon the 30-foot, royal blue curtains that hung in the windows and were accented by the navy-blue runner that laid out-stretched across the entire length of the room.

Set on each far end of the room were two white-stone fireplaces—that had to be taller than she—and above all of it hung three sparkling crystal, candle chandeliers—one in the middle, and one at each end. Yet, her eyes could not be moved from the 10-foot-tall painting of the entire Barclay family, and she began walking in just that direction, entranced by it.

"Abigail," Tom called to her as she continued in her astonishment.

"Look at all of you," she said to him. "Which sibling is she?" she asked and pointed to a lighter-haired young woman with blue eyes, whom Abbi thought was especially beautiful.

"My oldest sister, Giana. She was about your age when …" he paused, shaking his head. "Never mind."

"It's okay, Tom. I don't need to know."

She reached up and kissed his cheek. "You know, you were just as handsome back then …" she reached up, pressing her lips to his.

Tom pulled away. "You can tell the difference between Henry and me?"

"Of course! You're my Hercules. Besides, you're far better-looking. That's you."

She stretched her arm up and pointed to Tom in the painting. He smiled, feeling happy that she knew the difference between the two brothers, when sometimes even their own mother did not.

He sighed deeply. "Come. We need to fix this."

They walked over to where Katherine was standing at the other end of the ballroom working on spells.

"I know what you want, son. I won't do it. Patrick deserves his fate. Everyone has a fate in life. Your Slayer will have to meet hers."

At her words, he grabbed his mother up by the throat and slammed her onto the ground, forcefully choking her. Abigail cried out frantically. "No Tom! Think of what you are doing."

He looked over to Abbi, seeing the fear on her face and loosened his grip on Katherine's throat, allowing her breathe. Abbi walked over, touched his arm, and placed her other hand on his face.

"This is your mother. You don't understand each other's ways anymore. But she loved you as a child, rocked you in her arms as a baby, and raised you to become a man. Think of your actions. They cannot be undone."

She grabbed his face in her hands and laid a gentle kiss on his lips and continued, "Love her. Love her for me."

Abbi stood and walked back over to where Charlotte was standing a few feet away and Charlotte whispered in her ear, "I've never seen anyone able to soften him the way you do. I *truly* believe he's in love with you."

Tom released his grip and allowed Katherine to stand. He started pacing, scratching his forehead with his fingers. Abbi knew that meant he was thinking about what she'd said.

Abbi whispered back to Charlotte, "No. Love and magic are two very different things. Remember, I have this strong force."

She held out her hand, palm up. Charlotte nodded to appease Abbi, but in her heart, Charlotte knew her brother was in love. Katherine knew it too, which was why she looked to Tom and said, "Have Charlotte take you back to 1787. Stop the events that took place. That's all I can do."

"I've heard people speak of a key? Is there no key?" he asked.

"Yes. You don't want to use that."

"Oh. Why's that?"

"She's the key."

Katherine pointed to Abigail.

"Is there no other way? You can't reverse the spell?"

"I'm sorry, son. Go to 1787. Stop his actions. That's what you need to do," Katherine replied.

Charlotte began preparations immediately to transport them back to 1787 in order for him to try and erase the moment that tragedy struck his family and locked Patrick Barclay in Hell for all of eternity. Tom needed to prevent certain events from occurring in order to reverse Patrick's fate, but in order to keep Abigail from the relentless path of Delius, he had to take her to the past with him. So, into 1787 she went.

"Tom, what happens if your past self sees your current self?" Abbi asked as Charlotte was preparing her spell to take them back.

"They won't," he responded, impatiently waiting for Charlotte.

"Why not?"

"It is impossible. They cease to exist. They are us," he tried to explain, but she wanted more.

"I don't understand. Tell me more!"

"Alright. Think of it like this … At any given time, there is only one version of you at one point in the world. You aren't duplicating yourself. You're only traveling through time. But you are taking yourself with you. Both the past self and the present self cannot exist simultaneously. Meaning, if the present self goes back, then your present self is now past self."

"That makes no sense…" She felt bewildered.

"Yes, it does. Lottie, are you almost finished?"

"Then how are they *all* there?" Abbi continued.

"Because they're all dead. They died in the past. Their past selves are their present selves," he explained some more.

"What about Henry and Katherine? Will they be there?"

"Their past selves."

"But what about their present?"

"Ugh … this is far too complicated to try to explain," he grumbled, agitated that Charlotte was taking so long.

"I think I get it. They're not traveling, so they don't cease to exist. Right?"

"Their past selves are only reliving a memory for us because they're not duplicating. If they were traveling through time, their past selves would cease to exist. Get it now?"

She nodded.

"Ready," Charlotte said as she held a puffy cloud of smoke in her hands, expanding it as she stretched it out in front of herself and spinning it like a funnel.

Tom and Abbi stepped right into Charlotte's bedroom through the pocket-of-time funnel. As soon as they all stepped through, Charlotte turned, sealed it up with her fingers, grabbed the cloud-of-time out of the air, and held it in her hands. Then she blew it out with a strong breath—locking them into 1787 until she opened the cloud again.

"Charlotte, take her into Giana and Brielle's dressing room and find her a dress. She needs to blend in with the time period. I'll be back in a moment after I change."

"Wait!" Abbi called out.

"What?" Charlotte asked.

"I need a spell of protection, Tom. I don't want to hurt your family."

Abbi raised her hands, wiggling her fingers.

"Oh, right. Charlotte, can you do that?" he asked.

"I'll see what I can do. Her power is pretty fierce."

"Do what you can."

Charlotte started on the spell as soon as Tom had left. She closed her eyes and opened her hands in front of herself in a cupping gesture until a little wave of electricity appeared in the palms of her hands. Abbi was in awe at Charlotte's amazing power and stared in disbelief.

"Fiat vis in quo mulier ad tenendum universum intra tempus conceditur. Quod roboris in medio eius, et prohibitus sum ad eam et extraxerunt ab ea praesidium!"

As soon as Charlotte said it, she jumped back. "Wow! Girl! I felt your force go through me! You are one strong woman to reckon with. Now, let's get ready before Tom comes back and flips out on us."

She nodded, as did Abbi, knowing Charlotte was right about Tom's temper.

In the meantime, Tom had rushed out of the room and to the next door, which led to his old chambers, to get himself into time appropriate clothing. After picking out his favorite deep blue jacket, tan breeches, and a thin white linen shirt, he returned thinking he'd given them some time to maneuver through all the layers women wore back then. Tom's sisters were fashionable and stayed up on the current trends in English society and opted for the growing trend of scooping necklines, higher waistlines, and less-restrictive corsets.

"Charlotte! Let me in!" he banged on the door.

A moment later, the door swung open and Abbi pulled him in quickly, slamming the door closed behind them. His dark eyes widened at the sight of her in only the chemise.

"What are you doing? My sisters could come back and see you! Even more, they could come back and see me in here with you! Come with me."

He pulled her out of the room and hurried down the hall into the next room before being seen.

"Where are we going?!" she exclaimed as he pulled her into his chambers. "Tom, I'm not even dressed!"

"Taking you somewhere I know my sisters won't see you."

"Where is that?" she asked, looking around at the lavish bedroom chambers.

"My room," he answered as he watched her curiously move about the room in only that chemise.

"You look cute, Mr. Son-of-an-Earl, fancypants," she flirted, glancing over his way, taking note of his untucked white shirt and tan breeches, as he tossed the deep blue waistcoat onto his bed. He half-smiled and looked down at the old-fashioned, 18th century clothes he was now wearing.

"Why didn't you get dressed?" he asked, staring at her as she turned and looked out the window, leaning out it.

"Careful!" he hollered as she began leaning far over. But in realizing he could just slightly see through the light muslin of the undergarment, which satisfied his senses, he allowed her to look out the window while he ogled, and he continued in his gazing as he reprimanded. "Abigail? Why didn't you get dressed?"

"Oh …" she looked up to him from the window, "Uh, your sisters are really skinny! The dress didn't fit. Charlotte went to get one of your mother's."

"Damnit. That won't work. She'll recognize it. Wait here."

He walked over to her, softly kissed her lips as he moved past, reached his hand around her head, and entangled his fingers in her hair before he lifted his leg to climb out the window.

"Where are you going?" she hollered down to him as he lowered himself down the trellis.

"I'll be right back. Just stay in my room." He blew her a kiss.

As he was out, she wandered the beautiful room taking notice of his luxurious lifestyle. Just as in his modern life, nothing in the room was shabby. The large, wooden framed bed was draped with a canopy to shield the morning light from the window. The bed was perfectly made up with white blankets that covered the white sheets, which was obvious to her that he didn't make it up every day himself. She looked to her feet and saw the beautiful wood floor and realized the house was far older than she could possibly imagine, and seeing the outer stone wall, she knew it was hundreds of years older than the century she was currently visiting.

"Here," Charlotte said breathlessly when she flung Tom's door open as she entered and tossed the exquisitely designed purple dress onto the bed.

"Tom doesn't want me to wear it. He says your mom will recognize it," Abbi explained with an exasperated sigh.

"Oh … That's probably true. Our father tailored all our dresses specifically for us." Charlotte shrugged.

"Were you very wealthy?" Abbi asked as she stood from the bed to look at the dress, holding it up in her hands and admiring the intricate details of it.

"Yes. Many women wanted Tom because of that, which was what made him so bitter about marriage, I suppose. I was his only real friend. I was his baby sister, but I was the only person in the whole world he talked to, that he felt safe with."

Abbi put the dress down and looked to her, "What do you mean?"

"I would come into his room at night when I was scared from a lightning storm, since my room was just next door, and he would tell me things that he didn't tell anyone else. I suppose he assumed—since I was only three—that I didn't understand, but I did. I knew that he was frustrated and lonely, and that he really only wanted one thing."

"What was it?" Abbi asked, wanting to give it to him.

"To be loved. He wanted someone to want him not for his position in society, or his name, or his wealth, but just for who he was—Tom."

Abbi sighed deeply, wishing that she could tell him how he'd stolen her heart but knowing she couldn't.

"I better take this back. I don't have a lot of time. I can't be here in the past." Charlotte picked up the dress and walked out, leaving Abbi to think about Charlotte's words.

After waiting what felt like an eternity, she got restless and decided to explore the connecting door to his room, which she thought might be a closet-like room similar to what was in Charlotte's room. But upon opening the door, she was greeted with the surprise of her life.

"Tom!" She cried out when she saw him in there with a woman.

"Henry," he corrected. "And you are?" he asked with an interested grin, eyeing her.

Remembering she was in only that chemise, she gasped and slammed the door closed.

"Tom is going to kill me!" she muttered to herself as she went to sit down on the edge of the bed. She dropped her face in her hands and began to cry.

"Why would I do that?" he asked, jumping back into the room from the window, holding a dress.

"I'm not going to tell you," she sniffled and wiped her eyes. "Because I know you're going to freak out on me."

"I'm not going to freak out."

He handed her the dress and corset. "Now tell me." He motioned for her to stand.

"I was curious about that door." She pointed to the dressing room, and he groaned knowing it connected to Henry's chambers. "I'm sorry. I didn't realize it was him at first glance. I mean, I did after …"

"It's okay, Abigail. I'm not upset. What happened?"

"Nothing. Nothing happened. He just saw me. That's all." She explained.

He was annoyed that she didn't keep herself hidden until he could introduce her properly, but he responded with, "At least it was only Henry."

"He was in there with a woman."

"Oh … What'd she look like?" he asked and began to help her with the corset, taking his time on the laces.

"A few inches taller than me … Long hair like mine, but a strawberry blondish color …"

"It was Claire," he said, spinning her around to look her in the eyes.

"My sister?" Abbi asked, wide-eyed as she held the loosely tied corset to herself.

"Yes. But I'm curious about why she's here. She doesn't usually meet him at this hour. They have a pretty routine schedule."

He walked over to the window, peering out, but not seeing anything. He looked over to Abbi who had taken a seat on his bed but was pulling and tugging at the uncomfortable corset.

"What do you mean?" she asked as he walked past her to look into the dressing room, again seeing nothing.

"No matter. What's done is done," he said as he sat down next to her, tying up her corset, and pulling it tighter than he should have out of frustration.

"I can't breathe," she gasped.

"Sorry," he loosened it then slowly helped her into the dress.

"Is Henry human again?"

"Yes. We returned to the point in time before Henry was turned."

"Then why aren't you a human?" she asked.

"That's more complicated in time travel since I'm only visiting this moment. But I think that once Henry transitions, if I stay here, he'll have to change me again, which is why we need to watch the time here very carefully."

"Oh, I see."

"Where'd you get the dress, Tom?" she asked, as he was leading her to the door.

"Uh, a friend," he said hesitantly.

"Wait," Abbi stopped where she was standing. "I don't understand how Charlotte is able to be here in the past ..."

"That's why we need to get her. She needs to leave this moment in time soon or else her three-year-old self will suffer consequences. Because 2018 Charlotte is here, 1787 Charlotte is not," he explained before leading her to the door again.

"Then how are you able to be here?"

"Because I died. I was frozen in time and removed from that moment. But Charlotte was not. If we put her back into that moment, she will replace herself."

"How is Henry here?"

"Because I went back to the moment in time before he was turned in order to figure out how it happened."

"So, that means you're not turned yet. You've come back and replaced your human self?"

He sighed and answered, "Technically, yes. But it doesn't mean much because I was being turned anyway and I know it. I just have to make sure everything stays the same. I'm just going to 'be human' while I'm here and make sure Henry still gets changed."

"Will he know it in his memories and will yours change because of this?"

"I don't know," he shrugged. "I'm not very experienced with time manipulation, especially for more than a few hours. Charlotte's powers are great and I don't use them often."

"But you've used them before?" she asked just as Charlotte walked in.

"Once or twice," he said and looked to Charlotte.

"I have to go! If I don't leave now, things for me will get very messy!" Charlotte exclaimed anxiously.

"Two days!" Tom said.

She nodded and closed her eyes. "Nos transferat in alterius regni declinare. Ibo. Ibo. testimonium hoc verum quia manere non ire. Vadam."

A small cloud of smoke appeared in her hands, and as she widened her hands, the cloud expanded and she spread it open, creating a funnel around herself, and stepped through. Once she was through, it quickly dissipated behind her.

"She's so powerful," Abbi said in amazement at Charlotte's disappearance.

"She's such an annoyance. I'll give you five thousand dollars if she's not back in two days," he responded.

Abbi laughed and said, "What do I have to give you? I mean, if she is?"

"Heh, nothing. Because she won't be. Now, hurry. We must find Giana. I need her to pretend you're a guest of hers."

"Giana?" Abbi questioned as he grabbed her arm and ushered her through the servant corridors and entry ways so as not to be seen before he found his sister.

"Yes. She's my oldest sister. Well, was … she's your age. I think you'll like her. That's the one you asked about in the painting. She can be a bit sassy but for the most part is enjoyable company."

"Oh. How do I behave around her? I mean, we're in 1787 and I'm from an entirely different millennium!" She laughed.

Tom looked back, smirking at her as they approached the library, and he said, "Just be yourself. Be cautious of what you say though. Don't give anything away. Keep conversation to a minimum because she might wonder about your 'accent' or lack thereof."

She sighed. "You're making me nervous."

"Don't be. It'll be fine." He smiled as they stepped into the library where they found her reading.

"Gi," he called to her. She looked up to him from where she was sitting in the corner and smiled, which caused Abigail to smile slightly when she saw their sibling interaction happening. She squeezed his hand tighter.

"I know what you want," Giana said looking to Abigail. "I'll do it. But … You have to pay me," she added, now looking at Tom and then to Abigail.

"She's the prettiest one yet."

Giana stood and walked away from them to sit in the opposite corner of the room. Tom looked down at Abbi. Abbi shrugged, unknowing of how to respond. He winked in response before pulling her along to where Giana was now sitting.

"Giana!" He hollered at her, frustrated.

Giana rolled her eyes and looked up at him from her book. "What else?"

"Have your maid fix her hair and have Mrs. Johnson give her a room but not in the guest wing. Put her in the empty room in the family wing."

Giana raised an eyebrow noticing her hair was unkempt and also because of his request for her to have the extra room in the family wing. It wasn't an odd or peculiar thing for Tom to ask Giana to participate in his charade so he could sneak women through the house, especially if they arrived unexpectedly or were from a neighboring town. But he'd never before asked for them to be put in the family wing. She'd wondered what the difference was and decided she would investigate when her maid was fixing the woman's hair.

"The family wing?" she asked.

"Yes. That's what I said. Go, Gi. Take Abigail to Brigette and please hurry. Be kind to her," he said sternly.

Giana stood and put her book down. Abbi whispered to Tom, "Your fake accent is pretty cute by the way."

Tom made no response and repeated, "Giana, please hurry. Treat her well." Before they'd walked away, he mentally said to Abbi, *"It's not fake. This was my life."*

Abigail looked back to Tom and noticed his eyes intensely fixed on her. Abbi walked away thinking that he might just possibly want to be moving his desires just a bit further.

✪✪✪

Giana and Abigail hurried to find the maid, Brigette, who was in the kitchen engaging in gossip with the cook. Giana interrupted them.

"Brigette, if you could come with me and do up my guest's hair for her? Her travels fussed it up a bit."

"Of course, Miss." She curtsied.

Before they walked out, the cook asked, "Miss Barclay, will your guest be here for supper?"

"She will," Giana replied.

They exited the kitchen, but not before Giana took two scones from the pile of treats the cook just pumped out.

"Here," she said as she handed one to Abbi and bit into her own. Abbi took a bite as they walked up the never-ending stairs with the quiet maid trailing behind. Noting how different the food tasted and how bland it seemed, Abbi now understood why the girls were so skinny.

"These are my favorite," Giana giggled. "I steal them whenever I can." Abbi gave a weak smile in response.

The women walked into Giana's room and once again Abbi noted their lavish lifestyle. There were two beds in the room—one at each end—but each were large and extravagant. Like Tom's, they had draperies to block out the morning sun. But unlike Tom's, the girls had beautiful, delicate colors on their beds, while Tom's was white. Giana's was covered in shades of blue, red, and flowers, and the other sister had lovely shades of pink, white, and lace. Also, unlike Tom's, they had paintings and artwork all around, decorations everywhere, where his was very plain and simple with only one long wall with a bookshelf.

Brigette started working on Abbi's hair and Giana began questioning as she sat on her bed.

"Abigail is it?" Giana asked.

"Yes. Abigail Taylor," she answered hesitantly, unsure of whether or not Tom would want her to converse with his sister.

"How did you meet my brother?" Giana continued.

"Uh, in town." It seemed like the most reasonable explanation and, in all reality, was the truth.

"Do you know about all the others?" She looked over to Abbi cleverly.

"Others?" Abbi tilted her head, and the maid scolded her for moving.

"You know he's in line for our father's title and has to marry a woman with a title. Our father has him engaged to Lady Harriet Loudgraves. However, Tom doesn't want to marry her because he thinks she looks like a horse. So, instead, he runs around with any woman he thinks is beautiful and plays with her while he has the opportunity. At the present moment, you just happen to be one of them. He has favorites and regulars. I read it in his journal when our youngest sister steals it from his room. He writes everything down in there.

His most favorite and regular is a woman named Scarlett. Tom can't marry her either, but she comes often. However, I do not keep her here overnight because our father knows her father, as he is a tradesman nearby and their family is not of high society and have no title. Our father knows of Thomas's games but does nothing because he knows Tom will have to stop eventually if he wants our father's money, which he will because it's a substantial amount. Obviously, he can't marry you either, unless you're titled. By the horrified look on your face, I'm assuming you are not."

Tears filled Abbi's eyes from the harshness of Giana's tone, words, and the reality of the information she was just given about Tom's promiscuity.

"Why would Giana be so cruel? Are all Tom's sisters so mean? Is this what wealth does to someone?" Abbi thought. She wanted to say something, but she bit her tongue, not wanting to show her upset.

"All ready," the maid said as she pointed to Abigail's pinned up hair.

"Good. Let us away," Giana said as she reached for Abbi, pulling her out of the room.

They silently walked to the dining room where Tom was impatiently waiting just outside in the hallway.

"What took so long?" Tom scolded.

Giana just rolled her eyes and walked in with Abigail.

"Mother, Father, this is my friend, Miss Abigail Taylor."

"A new acquaintance?" Katherine asked, looking Abigail up and down as Abbi scanned the table for where Tom was seated.

"We met in town," Giana answered.

"Very well. Take your seat, Giana. Miss Taylor, you can sit at the the other end by our eldest son. Henry usually sits there, but he's seems to be missing this evening."

Giana took her seat at the end of the table next to her mother. As per the customs of society, Abigail was not seated next to her. The guest was seated in the middle of the table to allow engagement in conversation. Fortunately, Tom was directly on Abigail's right. She let out a sigh of relief when she saw him there. But after the information overload from Giana upstairs, she wasn't sure how to feel.

Once everyone had taken their places, Tom leaned in and whispered in her ear, "How are you holding up? You look very pretty by the way."

She blushed just slightly and answered, "I have no idea how your mother and sisters wear these things every day! I'm hardly breathing! These are awful! But I'm doing alright even so. However, I don't think I can reasonably stomach any food."

He chuckled at her comment and replied, "It's probably for the best. Food from 2018 is much different than in this day."

Tom winked at her and gulped down what she was certain was homemade vodka from the kitchen. She shook her head at the sight, secretly admiring it. Under the table, she reached for his fingers, lightly grasping his in hers. At her touch, he pulled her hand up onto his lap, holding it firmly in his.

"Miss Taylor, tell us about your family," Katherine spoke up from the other end of the table.

At her words, Tom spoke into Abbi's mind giving her the exact things to say, *"Lie. Lie your heart out. Lie like you've never lied before. Say this …"*

"My father has passed on. My mother and I have taken up residency with another family member. I am only in this part of the country for a visit," Abigail told her at the demand of Tom.

"Then how did you meet Giana in town?" she persisted.

"I visited here last year and met her on my visit."

"Miss, might you have been at town last October? I think I remember meeting you," Tom interrupted, turning Katherine's attention elsewhere.

"Yes. As a matter of fact …" Abbi replied. But as soon as Abbi realized everyone's attention was off her, she whispered *thank you* to him and breathed a sigh of relief.

"When everyone is finished eating, they will retreat to their rooms. Giana's maid will show you to yours, but I will come to you soon after. Okay?"

Tom's father observed them whispering and asked, "What's that whispering happening over there?"

"Oh, uh … Miss Taylor saw the family portrait and noticed I am a twin. She hadn't realized before then, and I was merely pointing out to her that though I may have a twin, I'm still the far better looking one. Plus, she also needs to know that I have this obscenely charming personality," Tom remarked.

He flashed her a smile and Abbi smiled shyly back to him as everyone else laughed. That is, everyone except Lord Barclay, who didn't like the friendly playfulness that was happening between them and quickly put a stop to it.

"Well, Miss Taylor, what Lord Thomas forgot to point out is that while he might be the more charming of the two of them, those charms will never get put to the test because he is soon to be married. His marriage to Lady Harriet Loudgraves is soon to have a date set; the arrangements are already being planned."

Ferocity grew inside Tom faster than he could contain himself, and he quickly stood and exited the room. He spoke to Abigail's mind as he exited.

"Everything's fine. Meet me in my room when Giana excuses herself. You cannot leave the table until she does. Just come up to my room."

"Well Father, I think that you shouldn't bet too much on that marriage!" Giana laughed as she looked at Abbi.

"He's going to marry Lady Harriet whether he wants to or not! There is no negotiation!" Patrick grumbled.

The three-year-old version of Charlotte at the opposite end of the table remarked, "But he doesn't love her. Shouldn't everyone marry someone they love like in the fairy-tales?"

"Life is no storybook, Charlotte," Lord Barclay returned, "Thomas has been born into a privileged life. He must marry the woman who will best benefit the future of the estate."

"I think it's sad," their sister, Brielle, spoke up. "Lady Harriet has shown no courtesy or interest in Tom whatsoever. Whenever she's here, she has a haughty attitude and she parades around our house as though she already owns it. She only wants our brother because of who he is. She'll throw us all out as soon as she can! Come on, Gi. I don't want to think of some titled ninny moving in here and redecorating!"

Brielle and Giana stood to leave the table and motioned for Abigail to follow them.

✪✪✪

Tom had stormed up the hallway and into his room, remembering every reason why he hated life in this century and all the reasons he created such an independent and modern life for himself as a vampire.

"I didn't think you were ever going to come and see me again," said a voice from his bed as he opened the door to his chambers.

"No. You can't be here, not today," he told her and walked away into his changing room, but she followed.

"I don't understand. Why not? You're always up for surprise visits. Where's my dress? Who was it for?" she asked. He walked back out in only his breeches and untucked, loosened collared shirt, and spoke again.

"Look Scarlett, I needed that dress for a woman who is becoming very important to me and …"

"And?"

She walked over and started kissing him, wrapping her arms around his neck, and grabbing at his thick, dark hair. Tom savored it for a moment, but then pulled away. Something in him couldn't do these things with Scarlett, not anymore, and he wasn't even sure why.

"No. I need you to leave," he said and pointed to the window, knowing she'd climbed up the trellis.

"No way. I don't care who this woman is, but I only have you for a few more months until Lady Horseface steals you from me, and I'm not letting anyone take you. NO ONE."

She started unpinning the fasteners of her dress, and he started to walk to the door figuring that she wouldn't wait in there for him forever. But just as he reached for the latch, the door swung open.

"Tom, sorry I took so long. Giana—" Abbi said as she stepped inside and saw him standing there with Scarlett dropping her dress to the floor. Abbi let out a gasp as her heart flew from her chest, shattering on the floor right where Tom was standing.

"No, Abbi. This isn't what you think," Tom tried to explain, raising his hands.

"I don't … I don't care to know w-what it is … not a-anymore."

Abbi turned and walked out.

Scarlett laughed. "Is that the woman who's become so important to you? She's pathetic. Be serious, Tom."

His vampire rage was building up inside him like steam inside a pressure cooker. He couldn't hold it back any longer and he attacked, pummeling Scarlett onto the ground, fangs extended, eyes black and encircled in red.

"Leave!! I don't want you here. I don't want to see you *ever* again."

He stood, tossing her away from him. She stood and walked over to the window kicking her leg up and over. "You're obviously not yourself. But you'll come crawling back. You always do!" She yelled as she climbed out. He didn't say anything to her, threw her dress out after her.

He paced back and forth inside his room for a few minutes trying to think of what to say to Abigail and wondering on whether or not he should go talk to her— ultimately deciding that he should—and walked the long hallway to the end of the family wing where her room was located, being sure not to be seen. He quietly knocked.

"Hello?" she answered but didn't open the door.

"Abigail, it's me. May I come in? Please?" Tom asked. She didn't respond but opened the door and pulled him inside.

"I was wearing *her* dress, wasn't I?" she scolded. "Was I in your disgusting lover's dress? I feel so dirty! How could you do that to me?!" She started slapping at his arms and chest and began sobbing forcefully, so forcefully that she eventually collapsed into his arms against her will. Tom held her tightly against his chest.

"I'm sorry. I didn't think of it in that manner. I apologize for that."

He picked her up and sat on the bed, holding her on his lap. She sobbed a few more minutes before she sat up, wiped her eyes and asked, "Was that Scarlett? Do you love her?"

"What?" he responded, surprised by her question.

"That woman … do you love her, Tom?" Abbi moved off his lap and stretched out across the bed next to him, causing him to notice she was once again in only that chemise. Immediately, his senses became aroused.

"Scarlett? No … No. I don't love her. There was once a time I thought I might. But she was just entertainment for me—a beautiful image, a plaything. Why do you ask? How did you know her name?"

"Um … Well, I heard what your father said about you marrying that Lady Harriet woman, and I thought … and Giana said …" She sighed.

"Eh, I see. Don't let them get to you. He thinks every woman who walks by is after his money. By making him believe your father is dead, he thought you are another gold-digger, only after me for his money. Giana … well, she just likes to make sport of every woman I bring around because she gets bored. She has three-year-old Lottie steal my journal for her and then pays Lottie in candies, making a game of it. Had she known … never mind."

He moved and stretched out next to her.

"Oh … have you ever been in love?" she asked as she gazed up at him, twirling her finger through his hair.

He thought for a moment as he stared into her eyes and realized that the reason he didn't want Scarlett, that he was so worried about Satan's venom, and that Abigail was so important to him was not because he was hired to protect her, but it was all because he loved her. He was in love with Abigail Taylor. The answer was yes.

"Yes. I've been in love."

"Oh really?" she responded. "Tell me about her."

"She's the most beautiful woman I've ever seen. She's quite extraordinary, actually, unlike any other woman I've ever met. Her personality and charm took me by surprise because I was expecting to loathe her. However, just the exact opposite happened."

"How did you meet her? Why were you expecting to hate her?" she asked, growing interested but also a little jealous, moving her hand from his hair and resting her head against his chest, tucking her hand in close to her own chest.

"Well, she's very much the opposite of me and she just showed up one day and I never looked the other way after."

"Oh. So, love was never something you desired? Charlotte was wrong then."

"How do you mean?"

"Nothing."

Tom wanted to know if she'd ever been in love but was afraid she'd admit to feelings for that bloody sheriff. He didn't want to lose any chances of affection from the only woman he'd ever loved by going on an fit of rage and killing the only man she'd ever loved. He refrained from asking the question.

After a few moments of silence, she asked, "Tell me about your mind power. Downstairs you were talking to my mind as though it's nothing at all, like it comes so naturally."

"What would you like to know?"

"What do our minds look like to you, like how do you find one?" She glanced up at him.

"Well, your mind doesn't 'look' like anything. It's more like a frequency. I can't hear what you're thinking, but I know whose mind belongs to who. Your mind has its own wavelength and if I want to talk to it, I have to 'dial-in' so-to-speak," he shrugged as he tried to explain his great power to her.

"Wow, Tom … You are the most extraordinary man I've ever known. Tell me more."

She cuddled in closer, pulling the covers over them. But their position—bodies cuddled together under the blankets, her hands holding his face and stroking his hair, and his arms around her—was not only calming his vampire rage, but it was also igniting his passion and he wanted so much more from her than ever before.

"Well your mind is the easiest for me to find, for some reason. It's very pretty and has a calming effect on me. When I find it, I almost want to stay tuned-in. I've never had that happen before. It must be your Slayer power drawing me to you. But, generally speaking, the longer I've known someone, the easier it is for me to find their frequency. Like Lottie, for example, I know hers very well and I can shut her up without even trying."

Abbi laughed at that and then asked, "Oh? How so? What does it sound like?"

"Well, yours sounds like butterflies. Lottie's is more like an annoying buzzing bee," he explained.

"That's silly. Butterflies don't make noise."

"Their wings do. You forget that my hearing is much more advanced than yours and I pick up on noises that you cannot. I hear butterflies—like the Monarch butterfly—as they clap their wings together, and your mind sounds like the wings of butterflies. It's so beautiful."

He kissed her nose.

"That's amazing. So, if you can't hear what we are thinking, then how do you speak into our minds?"

"Well, once I find the mind and frequency I want, I find its rhythm. Each person speaks in a rhythm, which means they think in a rhythm. I just interrupt that pattern. I have to break it. It wasn't as easy for me to do when I first became a vampire, and it took a lot of practice. But now I can do it as easily as …"

"… I can speak. Do you see what I just did there? I waited for a break in the pattern of your butterfly thoughts and I broke it. Now that I'm in, you won't get me out."

"Stop it! Get out!" she energetically yelled at him.

But he started tickling her and planting kisses on her neck, enjoying listening to her giggle as he continued the mind control.

"Nope. You are mine, little temptress!"

"Tom?" she asked, pulling away.

"Yes?" he pulled her back to his lips.

She pulled back once more, "It doesn't bother you that my fate in life is to kill you?"

He let out a small laugh and ran his hand across her cheek. Then said, "Absolutely not. I'm a man who loves a challenge. You're my biggest conquer yet."

Abbi pulled away again and said, "Tell me more about the woman you loved."

"Oh, um …"

"It's okay. Never mind. I suppose it's not really any of my business," she said when she noticed the hesitation on his face.

"I'm just not ready to talk about it yet," he said, holding her face, kissing her cheek.

"I understand."

He began kissing down her neck, pausing where he could see the blood pulsing through the veins in her neck.

"You know, you have the most beautiful neck …"

"Oh?"

She leaned closer to him and willingly surrendered herself.

✪✪✪

While Tom was getting the better of the Slayer, Henry had other plans with his own lover. After what Henry thought was their usual routine of meeting in the woods, Claire surprised him.

"Don't go back to your mansion. Come somewhere else with me," she said as he moved to put on his breeches.

"Where do you want to go?" Henry asked.

Claire and Henry always parted ways once their time in the woods was finished. Sometimes he went to her window late at night, but he never accompanied her through town. Henry couldn't be seen accompanying a servant that wasn't his own family's.

"I was hoping you would come to my room for the night. I like it when you stay with me."

She leaned in and kissed him. As Henry savored the kiss, he moved her over onto his lap and nodded. Mumbling through their kiss, Henry said, "I'll come to your room."

Henry waited until Claire left and then followed her across town, being sure to give plenty of time between their journeys.

"Mr. Henry Barclay?"

"Do you have business with me?" Henry asked the dirty and portly man standing with his back against the wall just a few houses away from the house that Claire served.

"I do if you have ties to Claire Davenwell."

Henry's quick reaction and protective instinct was on alert. He reached in and gripped the man's throat, pushing him tightly up against the wall.

"What's your business with her?"

"Five shillings a word, gent."

Henry squeezed his throat tighter.

"You'll get nothing from me! Now, tell me your business with her!"

"If you want information about your whore, it'll cost you."

Henry reached into his waistcoat pocket and pulled out a few coins. "This is all I have on me. Now … TELL ME!!"

He shoved the man forcefully against the wall.

The man picked through the few shillings Henry had given him and put them in his own pocket.

"There were two gentlemen leaving her house just a few minutes ago that said if I were to see you that I should tell you to go to this address."

He handed Henry a wrinkled paper with an address on it.

"Thank you for the information."

Henry walked away from the man and searched for the address.

On the far opposite end of town, Henry found the house, which was far nicer than Claire's usual house. It was a rectangle shaped red brick house with white shutters.

"What is she doing here?"

He glanced up at all the windows and saw Claire peeking out one on the second floor. Henry hurried to the front door when he noticed her in the window. Standing at the front door, Henry was greeted by the footman.

"May I help you?"

"Is Miss Claire Davenwell here?"

"She's in the kitchen, sir. Please, do come in and have a seat. Should I let her know who has arrived?"

"Just say it's Henry."

A few minutes later, Claire emerged from the servants door.

"Henry," she whispered and motioned for him to join her behind the door.

"What are you doing here?" he asked, closing the door behind them.

"I work here now."

"What?!"

"I have to. My life is so different from yours, Henry."

He ran his fingers over his face for a few moments, contemplating what to do.

"I've not moved in here, yet."

"You're going to live here?!"

Claire nodded. "Eventually. It's more money."

"I'll give you money ..."

"Not if you marry."

Claire turned to walk down the long hallway.

"Claire!"

"Yes?"

She turned and gave Henry a smile.

"Will you be at your row home tonight?"

Claire nodded silently and continued walking down the long hallway.

✪✪✪

Henry went back into town and sat for a long while in the Brown Tree tavern.

"What'll it be for ya tonight, young lad? You're lookin' down trodden, like ya need a heavy one. A young woman stole your heart there, has she, lad?"

"I suppose."

"A broken heart calls for an ale on the house!"

The bartender turned to get Henry's drink as another man sat next to Henry.

"I have a solution to your problem."

Henry looked at the hooded figure. "Excuse me?"

"I'm Arlington." He extended his hand to Henry. "It's a pleasure."

Henry shook Arlington's hand. "You're Claire's father. She's spoken of you before."

"Yes, well, I hold a reputation."

"For what?"

"You decide."

A little confused, Henry returned to his previous comment. "You claimed to have a solution to my problem. I'm assuming, being that you are Claire's father, you are here concerning her."

"Come to her row home tonight and all will be revealed to you."

Without another word, Arlington slid out of the bar.

The bartender turned back around to Henry, handing him his drink. "An ale for the lovesick gent."

Henry consumed several ales before he walked to Claire's pale blue row home.

"Claire!" he hollered through her bedroom window as he tapped on the frame where the paint was chipping.

She hurried to open it for him and pulled him in by his arm.

"The hours were long without you," she said and pulled him in close, kissing him.

"I met your father today."

Upon hearing that, she quickly withdrew and gasped. "You did?!"

"He was very interesting."

Claire nodded. "He always makes an impression. What did he say to you?"

"That he had a solution to my problem."

"Oh?"

Claire pulled Henry over to her bed and started unbuttoning his waistcoat.

Henry nodded. "Do you know what he meant?" he mumbled as he began unfastening her dress.

Grateful that he was there and not wanting to ruin the mood, she replied, "No."

Several hours later, Delius paid Henry a visit while he was sleeping next to Claire in her room.

"Henry, we haven't been properly introduced. I'm Delius," he said, holding Henry by his hair and shoulder as he bit into Henry. Claire screamed out as she watched Henry react to the agonizing pain from Delius's powerful bite.

"Henry!" she cried. "I'm so sorry! Forgive me!"

Claire darted from the room as Delius nearly drained Henry dry. Leaving him weakened, Delius stared into his eyes and said, "This is it. This is the day you will remember as the day you and your family belonged to me." He bit into his finger and dribbled his blood into Henry's mouth.

Delius snapped Henry's neck—transforming his eternity.

✪✪✪

The next morning, Tom and Abigail were still cuddled close together. Tom was prepared to get intimate once again, but Abbi was very aware of her morning breath and felt shy.

"What did you do for bathrooms in this century, Tom? I have got to pee and my morning breath is kicking."

She covered her mouth. Tom kissed her neck and chuckled. "Human problems. You're really cute while you sleep, by the way."

"Did you watch me sleep?"

"All night."

They were interrupted by a knock at the door. Tom quickly covered Abbi with the sheets. Before Tom could protest the entry, the head maid came walking in.

"Hello Miss, I just wanted to inform you that …" she stopped her words at the sight of a shirtless Tom lying next to Abbi on the bed under the sheets.

"Oh sir! I apologize. I did not know you were here."

"Not a problem. Could you bring Miss Taylor a chamberpot and some necessities for her hygiene?"

The maid nodded and exited, closing the door behind herself.

Abigail turned to Tom, mortified, and said, "Now they're going to know for sure that I'm not here to see Giana! What will we do?"

He smirked and replied, "Don't be so sure. You're not my first. Why do you think my father was so concerned when he saw me whispering to you?"

"Tom, what's a chamber pot?"

He smirked. "It's a pot to piss in, Abigail."

"Gross."

Tom laughed. "It's 1787. What did you expect? You could get dressed and go to the privy behind the garden if you'd prefer…"

"No, thank you! What are those necessities you asked for?"

"We do have ways of brushing our teeth. Mrs.Johnson will bring that to you."

Tom kissed her cheek and put on his breeches to start pacing the room as Abbi laid thinking, once more, on how she wanted to tell him how she truly felt. She reached to the bite marks on her neck.

"What's the matter?" Abbi asked as she saw the concern on his face.

"This is the day Henry disappears. The day is soon approaching that everything for my family will change. I need to find a way to stop it. However, I don't know what to do to change it because I don't know how or why he disappears. If I don't stop this, then I don't know how to change what happens to you. I need to fix what happens to you."

There was a knock again at the door.

Tom answered and took the requested items from Mrs. Johnson. "Thank you."

He placed the toothbrush and a small circular bottle of what Abbi assumed was some kind of toothpaste on the table next to the bed.

"Just use a small amount and spit it into the pot when you're finished. I'll be in the hall. I'll ring for a servant."

"How did you get used to this?"

"What do you mean 'get used to this?' There was nothing to get used to. I was born into this life. I lived this way. It's all I knew. Do your business and come get me when you're finished."

She pulled on the chemise and looked at the pot and toothbrushing supplies as Tom walked out.

There's no toilet paper and this is tiny… like for babies.

She finished up and peeked her head out to see Tom.

"That's the most ridiculous and hardest thing I think I've ever done in my life. I miss 2018. I want to go back."

He smiled. "Two hundred years makes a huge difference?"

Abbi sighed. "You have no idea."

Tom rang the servant bell and walked back into the room with Abbi.

"Tom," she wrapped her arms around him. "I don't have bad human breath anymore. I can hug you now. So tell me, the issue with Henry and your father... I want to help."

He stood there wrapped in her arms, allowing himself to be overtaken by the beauty that was her as she kissed his cheek and said, "Tell me what happened, Tom."

"Henry disappeared. When he returned, he turned me ..."

"Wait, Tom. You can't change this. If you do, you'll erase your turning and then you won't be a vampire anymore. I don't want that. No one does. We can't truly change the past. Can we?"

"I suppose not."

"Perhaps there is another way to change what happens to your father without changing Henry's turning?" she suggested.

"I believe you are right. We need to allow Henry to be turned. We can't change that. I'm already turned, so we know that won't be changed. Now, we just need to figure out what to do about Delius."

"Delius?!" Abbi exclaimed.

"Yes. He is the reason my father is in Hell."

"Will Delius be involved in all of this then? Will he have suspicions of what is happening here?"

He glanced down to her for a moment and contemplated her words, a little concerned for what she was saying.

"Tom ..." she said as she looked up to his face. "Your eyes ... they're blue."

Upon hearing her words, he reached to his mouth, feeling his teeth. Then he took a breath and felt his urges were that of a human again. Immediately, he picked Abigail up in his arms and kissed her, but his strength was poor and he struggled to lift her tiny body.

"Tom?" she asked as he set her back down and pulled away from the kiss. He stepped a few feet away as Abbi repeated herself.

"Henry's been turned. I'm a human again. Everything that happens from this point forward is crucial to the future."

He rushed out of the room, Abigail following behind in a confused daze.

Fifteen

"I know where she is," Henry said as Delius played a hand of poker with a couple of no name vampires.

"My game!" he hollered out as he pulled the cigar from his mouth and moved the chips to his side of the table. Then he turned to face Henry.

"What in the devil's name are you talking about?" Delius asked as he flicked his cigar butt on Henry's shoe.

"Don't be an ass. I'm trying to help you."

"Out with it then," Delius said, picking up a new hand and putting on his poker face.

"He's got a full house," Henry said, snatching the cards from Delius's hands and laying them face up on the table. "Time to get serious. My sister took the Slayer back in time. I know it because Tom slipped up and I saw her, which changed history and …"

"Now she's in your 1787 memories," Delius said, finishing his sentence.

Henry grinned and Delius stood and turned to face everyone else.

"Finish the game without me, men. We have a Slayer to catch."

Tom searched through all the papers and stacks of books he had piled up all over his chambers. Abbi nervously sat on his bed wondering what he was up to.

"Tom? What are you doing?" she asked, sprawling across his bed on her stomach, gazing at him. She was trying to see if his human self appeared any different than his vampire self.

"I have to find it!"

"Find what?"

"My journal!"

"Please don't yell at me. I'm just curious. You're not very good at communicating."

He looked to her apologetically and continued in a softer tone, "I need to see what I wrote. I need to see the exact day that I left. If things don't take the precise course they did previously—"

"You won't get turned," she said, finishing his statement.

"Yes."

She walked over to where he was searching but went past him to look out the window at the trellis. As she was leaning out to look at it, his gaze wandered in her direction, and he realized that even his human eyes found her the most beautiful woman he'd ever seen.

"Tom?" she asked when she noticed his gazing.

"Yes?" His fingers grazed hers and he pulled her into his embrace. He began kissing around her neck, enjoying the delicateness of her earlobe down to her collarbone. He lifted her into his arms to continue, but she stopped him and persisted in questioning him.

"How many women have been up and down that trellis?" She pulled back to look in his sparkling blue eyes.

"That's not important." He began kissing her lips this time to keep her from speaking, also because he knew he didn't have the fangs to become a hindrance.

She pulled away and put her feet down. "It matters to me."

He sighed and spoke with his British accent coming out in his voice just slightly, "I didn't keep track. It's not like I kept a log, Abigail. I didn't love those women. It was just sex. Besides, I did it mostly to spite my father. He was set upon me marrying this terrible woman with no personality and who had the face of a horse!"

A smile crossed her face at the state of his exasperation and accent, and she held her finger up to his lips just then to quiet him.

"Well, I've heard of all these women and I'll admit that it makes me a little jealous."

He took the hint because he walked over to the door immediately, latching it shut.

"Do you want to be the last?"

She giggled enthusiastically and skipped over to his bed.

He started removing his shirt, and Abbi noticed that he was a lot hairier as a human than as a vampire, causing her to smile. When he approached, she ran her hand over his very dark chest hair, stirring quite a reaction from him.

"Mmm," he said as she ran her hand along his chest muscles, "That drives me crazy. Do you claim to know my weaknesses?" He smiled and climbed on top of her as she relaxed herself on his bed.

"Actually, I know all of your weaknesses," she said and kissed his cheek, reaching her arms around him to rub her hands up and down his back. Then she took her legs and wrapped them around his waist and cupped his face in her hands as she continued kissing him.

"Mmm ... Yes, I would say you do," he said as he lifted her up, shifting positions and moving her onto his lap. "I thought you enticing for me as a vampire, but it is possible that you are even more irresistible for me as a human."

"Show me what it's like," she said.

"What's that?" he asked as he lifted the chemise over her head and smiled satisfactorily at the sight of her.

"Show me what it's like to be with you without your god-like features," she asked as she began kissing around his earlobe.

"I won't say no to that," he readily agreed, laying her down, and her mind wandered to how much gentler he was as a human—his kisses, his touches, all of him—than as a vampire.

✪✪✪

"Mmm," she said a little while later.

"Yes." He agreed and looked over to her. "Well? Do you miss Hercules?"

Shaking her head, she replied, "No. It was a new experience, different than that first time, but I liked it. Honestly, Tom, I'll take you any way you are."

He laid down next to her and said, "Talk to me. No one ever does."

His comment pricked at her heart's strings and she thought for a moment about what Charlotte had told her.

"What do you want to talk about?"

"Anything. I haven't had a real conversation with a woman probably … ever."

"Oh. Well, then … Let's start with the basics. You know I'm Abigail Janette Taylor. Born September 12, 1996 to Janette Camille Taylor and Arlington Patrick Domitius …"

"Yes, he will be my demise," Tom groaned.

"I thought you weren't intimidated by him?" she teased.

"I never had been, but …"

"But?"

"Nothing. Let me hear about you."

She continued, "My favorite color is blue. I love pizza and french fries, sweat pants, and ice cream, but somehow, my most favorite thing in the whole world has become you." She moved closer and tapped his nose.

"Wow. I don't know about most of that. What are french fries or this pizza? Since when do women wear pants?"

"Stop teasing me," she giggled. "Tell me about you."

"Oh, uh … Where to begin?"

"Start with your human life," she said.

"When I was a human, I was dreadfully awful. I tormented my servants and stayed in bed every day until 10 or 11. I never did what I was told and was always giving everyone a hard time. My siblings would make bets with one another on how long it would be until I would be called into our father's study for a 'talk'."

Abigail laughed at his description of himself. "I find you charming. Tell me more."

"You're the first to think that. Lottie was my favorite person. Henry and I never got along, but we did help each other out when we needed to trick our parents into thinking one was the other." He chuckled slightly, as did Abbi.

"Tom! That's terrible! They couldn't tell?"

"Nah, I'm surprised that you can tell the difference between us so easily. Most cannot. Even our siblings confused us frequently. The only way they knew the difference was that Henry always had his hair parted to the side and mine was combed straight back. But if we wanted to trick someone, we'd switch."

Abbi laughed. "What was it like having 10 siblings? Was it always exciting?"

"Exciting? Maybe. Busy? Definitely. I had an equal mixture of brothers and sisters, which helped in the mischief making. But being the eldest, I didn't have anyone around when I was growing up, except Henry of course. Gi was five years my junior. But Henry and I were shipped off to Eton when we were only 10."

"How sad."

"Not exactly. I much preferred school to being here. Life here was intolerable at times."

"I cannot believe that at all," Abbi said, glancing around. "What a fabulous life this seemed to be. It had to be quite exciting to be the son of an Earl."

"Possibly. However, with that privileged life came a lot of sacrifices too."

"I bet you were lonely."

"At times."

He kissed her forehead, then her lips, again igniting a small passion inside himself. "But I'm not anymore."

"What was the hardest part for you back then?"

Tom leaned up on his elbows and thought on her question for a moment. He situated a pillow behind his back and leaned against his hands. "My parents had high expectations of me but not of my siblings. Henry ran around with your sister and our father knew it, yet he was never reprimanded for it. However …"

He paused and glanced to Abbi, cautious to reveal his past.

"It's okay. You can tell me."

"It's no secret I hold a reputation."

Abbi laughed. "Oh, really?"

"I was always getting into trouble over it. It didn't matter with what woman. Servant? I was in trouble. Lady of high standing? Trouble. My father was determined to make my life miserable."

"Tom … maybe, now this is just me going out on a limb here, but maybe he just didn't want you risking the chance of getting all those women pregnant?"

Tom gave her an annoyed expression. "I wasn't an idiot. I used protection."

"Protection fails, Tom. I don't want you upset, so let's change the subject. What was the best part about your life?"

"My siblings."

"What were their names?"

"Henry, Leonard, Giana, Brielle, Amelia, James, Edwin, Marie, George, and …"

"Charlotte," she finished.

"Yes," he smiled.

"I'm sorry you lost them."

"I'm glad I have you, Abbi."

"Tell me what happened to your family, Tom. I want to know," Abbi said, cuddling closer and wrapping her arms around Tom's, relaxing her head against his shoulder.

He leaned his head against hers. "I can't bring myself to discuss it."

"Is it really that terrible?"

"It is a tragedy that I never want to relive. The memory of it that I've had replaying in my mind for the past 231 years has haunted me."

"I'm sorry, Tom," she interrupted. "Tell me your good memories. What were they like?"

"My mother was pretty much like how she is now."

"Intense?"

"Yes. Also, very stubborn but kind and generous too."

"Hmm … I suppose the apple doesn't fall too far from the tree. That sounds like another Barclay I know."

"Tell me more about your siblings. I always wished I'd had siblings."

He just smiled slightly and continued. "My brother Leonard was quiet and shy. He was always jealous of the attention Henry and I got from the ladies because he wasn't brave when it came to the female species at all."

"What were your younger siblings like?"

"Lively and energetic. They kept the Barclay house full of life. Charlotte was very much like she is now. Intuitive and smart but she began to know her powers when she was only three."

"Amazing. To be so young and yet so powerful. Your life really is a fairy-tale."

He looked over to her. "It is now."

She smiled at him and cuddled closer. "Tell me about your father."

"He was serious and never gave us affection."

Pausing on his thoughts, not wanting to speak any more on his father, he decided to probe her mind. *"Abbi, what advice would you give my future vampire self?"*

"Hmm … That's a tough one."

She bit her lip and thought for a moment. "Just remember that you'll want to invest in Microsoft and Google, McDonald's and Starbucks. If anyone ever asks you to ride on the Titanic, don't do it. It's not unsinkable."

Tom laughed and said, "Thanks for the heads up."

"What was life like for you growing up?" he asked. "It had to have been a little strange having Arlington as a father."

"Well, he left when I was five years old, so I didn't have him around constantly. But he did show up a lot, which I now realize is because he was curious about this whole Slayer thing. Arlington doesn't care about anyone but himself."

"There was *never* a truer statement."

"He's embarrassing to go places with because he would curse people that upset him right to their faces. For the longest time I didn't know if he was just mentally unhinged or if he was actually cursing people."

Tom chuckled. "That is unusual, which says a lot because my mother and sister are witches."

"Tell me more about her."

"Who?" Tom asked.

"Your mom. She seems so interesting, especially to be married to such a—"

"Terrible man?" Tom interjected.

"What? Why?" Abbi asked.

"Nothing. My mom … She came from a noble family, as did my father. But from what I know, my father chose her specifically. Now, I know that he wanted her power. I always knew there was something interesting about her growing up. She was always saying and doing weird things and she frequently had headaches. But Henry and I never believed that they were headaches."

"Why? What were they?"

"Well, you know Lottie can warp and manipulate time. That's her witch power. My mother's is quite different."

"What is it?"

"She has visions of the future."

"Your father knew about her?"

"I believe so," Tom said. "He married her for that reason. It wasn't for love. Our house was happy but it was a typical noble family."

"What did you like about this life. There must be one thing you miss."

He thought for a moment. Tom sighed and said, "I miss my siblings. For the most part, other than Henry and me, we all got along."

"Some days I wish I had a brother or sister."

"You have Claire."

"She doesn't count."

"I suppose not."

"Tell me something most people don't know about you," Abbi said.

"I hate being a vampire."

"That's not fair. I already knew that!"

"But most people don't. Plus, I don't hate it as much anymore. Well, sometimes I don't," he added.

"Oh?" she asked, "Why's that?"

"You. You make life happy. Tell me one thing most people don't know about you."

"I'm a vampire Slayer."

"I already knew that," he said.

"Well, two can play at this game because most people don't know it and I hate it too."

"Touche."

"Had you ever seen me before the night we met?"

"You honestly took me by surprise that night in the alley. I didn't expect you." He began scratching his forehead and Abigail knew he was thinking heavily.

"How is it we spent my whole life in the same town but never met?"

"Fate was waiting for just the right moment I suppose."

"Tom? I don't want to return to 2018 and to the chaos that has erupted. I don't want to risk losing you. You've become the best part of my life. I don't like that Arlington said you're going to leave me."

"That's probably the nicest and kindest thing anyone has ever said to me. 231 years seems so long now," he said as he pulled her into his embrace.

"What do you mean?" She looked up at him, brushing her finger along his jawline, which wasn't as drastic and defined as it was in his vampire form, but it was still strong and masculine—still so handsome.

"If I miss the day for Henry to turn me … I have to find the journal. If I miss the day, you'll have to return with Charlotte without me and I will have to find a new way to be turned … reliving the last 231 years alone. History will forever be changed."

"Oh Tom. Don't say that! Everything is going to be just fine!" she said, teary-eyed. "Giana! She probably has it! She said something to me about having Charlotte steal it from your room."

Tom nodded knowing Giana and Charlotte probably had it. There was a knock at the door and Tom hurried to answer, where a man spoke to him. Unable to hear what was being said, Abbi maneuvered herself closer on the bed.

"Tell him I, uh …" Tom looked back at Abbi before continuing the conversation, "Tell him I can't entertain Lady Harriet at present."

"But sir …" the man said. Abbi lean forward, peeking her head around the door, where she saw a nicely dressed servant. The servant saw Abbi and looked over to her direction with a small smile, now understanding Tom's predicament.

"I see …" the servant said and looked away from her. "I will let Lord Barclay know you are otherwise engaged." He looked back to Abbi again, amused. "What shall I say in regards to the Countess?"

Tom looked back to Abbi, contemplated his words for a few moments, then he said, "Oh right, Mother … uh, tell her I would like to see her."

The servant nodded. Tom closed the door, latched it, and started pacing the room in his usual manner.

"Tom? What's going on?" she asked as she pulled the blankets up over herself, suddenly feeling very vulnerable.

"Do not be alarmed. That was mine and Henry's servant, Wellington. The Loudgraves are here. My father wants me to entertain Lady Harriet," he said and looked over to her but disgust crossed his face. Unknowing of what to say and feeling intrigued by this woman that Tom's father was set on him marrying, she blurted out, "I want to meet her!"

"No. I don't think that is a wise decision," he said sternly. He continued in his pacing. Upset she wasn't getting her way, Abbi crossed her arms and protested. But he only found satisfaction in her reaction and said, "You won't win. I've been around longer and am much more stubborn."

"Thomas Patrick!" His mother pounded on the door. Tom let out a groan and walked over to open it. Just before he did, he looked back to Abbi and said, "Do not be concerned."

"Yes?" he opened the door and leaned on it in a relaxed, lackadaisical manner.

"Why are you not showing yourself to Lady Harriet? And why are you dressed like that? It is the middle of the day! Honestly, you are my eldest child; I …"

"Mother, calm yourself," he interrupted and looked back to Abbi, winking. Katherine stepped inside the room.

Startled at the sight of Abbi on Tom's bed, she hollered out, "Oh! Goodness me!" and closed the door. Eyes wide, she spat, "Explain yourself!"

"Really, Mother? Don't be so naïve; I'm 27 years old."

He looked over to Abbi and smiled, motioning for her to stand, which she felt awkward doing— as she was only in just that chemise—but obeyed nonetheless. She bit her bottom lip to hide her growing smirk and closed her eyes out of embarrassment, thinking, *"He really is too much sometimes!"*

"Hello, young lady," Katherine said coldly.

"Hello," Abbi replied, unsure of what else to say.

"Well, I suppose we will have to marry you, now," Katherine said.

"That won't be possible, Mother."

"What?! Why not?" she demanded "You're not a servant, are you? Thomas! Tell me you didn't throw your engagement to Lady Harriet away on some servant!"

Tom interjected and yelled, "Mother, please! Calm yourself! She is not a servant. Look at her face! It's the woman Giana brought to supper last evening."

"Oh, yes. I do suppose you are correct. I did not recognize her with her hair down and all fussed up. What type of income does your family have?" Katherine asked Abbi. Tom rolled his eyes, but Katherine continued. "No matter. Lord Thomas will have enough from this estate. Are you titled? No. I would suppose you are not. We will have to make do as you are—"

"Enough!" Tom yelled and grabbed her arm, ushering Katherine out. "Just get out! Soon enough you will see why I won't be marrying anyone!" He moved her through the doorway and locked the door behind her.

"Tom?" Abbi called for him as she watched him pace frustratedly across the length of his room. After several minutes of watching, she called for him again. "Tom?"

"I'm sorry I got angry like that. Life for me in these times was always full of demands from them. It was always, 'Lord Thomas be here … Lord Thomas meet this woman … Lord Thomas show yourself to her … Lord Thomas you were born to privilege …' I didn't want that life, though Abigail. I just … I don't even know … Had Henry been born a few minutes before, it would have been him, not me."

"Come sit," she said, patting her hand on the bed, motioning for him to join her there. He sat down next to her and but she could tell he was still tense, so she began rubbing her hands up and down his back to calm him and she asked, "If you knew she would react that way, why did you ask to see her?"

"I thought it might help stir her power."

"Her power?" Abbi asked.

Before he could answer, he jumped up and raced to the window in a panic.

"I have to go!" he exclaimed. "Stay here in my room. Do NOT leave. I will return tonight."

Frightened, she followed after him. "Tom?! Where are you going? Don't leave me here!"

"I have to go! Henry turns me today!" He climbed down the window trellis and jumped onto the grass below, taking off toward the stables.

Abigail's mind was fretting. *"What am I going to do for a whole day locked inside his room?"* She wondered. *"Should I stay in there? Should I wander the house?"*

She thought about possibly following after him, and ultimately decided that was the best solution to her problem. Throwing her leg up and over the window, she carefully climbed down.

With absolutely no horse-riding skills whatsoever, she had to hoof it in her bare feet. Immediately regretting this decision, she looked back up to the high window and realized there was no way she was climbing back up there. Onward she went as she tried to follow the horseshoe prints in the mud and grass.

Several hours later, she sat down and cried when she lost sight of the horseshoe prints and saw that the sun was starting to dip down behind the horizon. Feeling exhausted, she laid down on a soft spot of grass under a tree near the brush line. But as soon as she did that, she heard voices in the far distance. Not wanting to be seen, she hid herself behind the tree and listened closer.

"It's Tom!" Though unable to discern what was being said, she was certain it was his deep, sultry voice. She tried to make out the other voice.

"NO! I can't hear this!"

She sat and covered her ears, beginning to cry, knowing that Henry was killing Tom. Many minutes later, she uncovered her ears slightly, hoping that Henry was gone. When she stood to look around, she saw that Henry was no longer there and she walked closer. The image before her, however, was brutal. Tom's body was lying there bloody and lifeless.

"No!" she cried out and ran over to him. Kneeling down, she held his wobbly head in her hands. Panicking and looking around frantically, she struggled to move his body onto her lap, cradling his head onto her arm, pulling him carefully on her.

"Tom!" she sobbed. "Wake up!"

But his neck was broken; he was dead. Her sobs were irrepressible. "Tom! Come back to me!" She cried even harder. "You can't just leave me here! I'm so afraid!" She looked around, unknowing of what to do. "Please come back!" she pleaded and laid down in the grass with him, wrapping his arms around her, waiting for him to wake.

✪✪✪

"Henry!"

Tom hollered out in a deep, low growl as he jumped up many hours later that evening, knocking Abigail away.

"Tom!" she shouted, surprised at how happy she was to see those deep rings of crimson and long, extended teeth. "You're okay!"

But his look was fierce, intense, and ravenous. "Henry!" he growled again.

"Tom? It's me, Abigail," she said.

He knocked her back again and sped off into the darkness.

Devastated, Abbi became like an overflowing fountain of tears once more. But the more she cried, the more tired she felt, and she laid down in the grass to sleep.

Already on his third victim, Tom was starting to regain some sort of composure and he paused to think for a moment as he wiped the blood from his chin, trying to recall events before his new turning. He tossed the last man's body to the side of the back street and suddenly remembered Abigail.

"I've got to get back to her!" he thought as he sped back through the woods to return to Greenvalley. He hurried up the trellis and into the window, but Abigail was nowhere to be found. Frantically, he quickly inspected other rooms, asked Giana, checked with his servant … nothing. He went into a panic.

"Where the hell is she?!" He wondered, not remembering having woken up next to her in the field a few hours prior.

"Tom!" Charlotte opened his door just then.

"What is it?" he spun around, surprised to see her back in 1787 so soon.

"It's Abigail! Delius has her in 2018!! Let's go!"

Sixteen

"Do you think he'll come for you?" One of the vampires mocked Abigail while they downed shots of vodka in the corner of the room of Delius's old castle where she was tied, arms behind her back and legs tied together.

She didn't respond, not wanting to think about that, as she looked around at the room, watching them where they sat on the couches, tables and chairs and the wooden floor.

"How did you know where I was?" Abigail asked Henry, who was standing nearby.

"You're not playing with fools, Abs," Henry replied. "This is why you shouldn't mess with my sister's amazing skills. Time manipulation is a great power, but it comes with serious consequences."

"What do you mean?"

"I mean that when my brother took you into the past, he changed that past."

Abbi looked at Henry, bewildered.

"Let me put it simply for you … you know, you're just like your sister …" He paused and rolled his eyes, then he continued. "When I saw you in my dressing chambers—"

Abbi interrupted, "I was now in your future memories because your past had been changed."

"Exactly. The life I was living in 2018 was automatically renewed with the new memories and I was able to tell Delius exactly where to find you."

She let out an exasperated sigh.

"What do you want with me?" she asked as he stood and walked over to her.

"Don't you get it at all?" he asked, stroking her face with his thumb.

Moving away from him, she replied, "Get what?"

"We need *him*. We don't want you. You're just the lure," he said.

"What?! I don't understand."

Delius strolled in and spoke, "Abigail, let me make it very clear to you." He approached her, knelt down, and grabbed her chin between his thumb and index finger. Then he continued, "One stake from you and any vampire is put away in Hell for all of eternity. This is especially problematic for me, however, because you're the only one who can stake me. No one else holds that power. But you see, my dear Slayer, you are just a pebble in the path until I can get you away from the one I really want."

"Who is that?" she asked.

"We knew you were coming. You were predicted. But we never imagined we'd be betrayed by our most powerful weapon! In order to destroy you, I need to destroy him!"

"Tom!" she shrieked.

"Yes," he whispered in her ear. But she spit at him, so he smacked her.

"The longer we keep you alive, the more of a chance we have at gaining his attention," he said, running his fingers again along the side of her jaw. "Your touch is very enticing. I can see why Barclay likes you so much. I see those marks on your neck. I take it you've surrendered to his dark side?" He smirked.

Embarrassed, Abbi quickly turned away. "It's not what you think!"

"Come now, we know that Barclay holds a reputation."

The vampires in the room cackled as Henry leaned in.

"You know, Abs, I'm his identical twin brother. How about a comparison?" He knelt down and ran his finger along her collarbone.

"You are nothing like him!" she yelled.

But Henry laughed. "You're right! I'm far better because I don't live a lie! My brother is a vampire but tries to live the life of a human!"

"Oh, shut it, Henry. We have business to take care of," Delius snapped. "He hasn't arrived yet and until he does, we cannot—"

"You cannot what? Delius," Tom said, walking into the room. He used his mind to move everyone to one side of the room while taking his time to walk towards Abigail to untie her.

"I knew you'd figure it out sooner or later," Delius said, "When Henry told me how you'd rewritten history—"

"What?!" Abigail and Tom said together.

"Taking her back to 1787 with you changed the entire course of events for the last 231 years." Henry said.

"Explain yourself," Tom glared at Henry, who was unnervingly satisfied with himself.

"Well dear brother, because I saw her when I was a human and I already knew her sister ..."

Tom didn't let him finish his sentence before he pummeled Henry to the floor.

"What did you do?!"

Henry shrugged. "Nothing much. I just made sure history didn't veer too much off course. You should really make sure that girl is better clothed, she's practically naked under that 18th century chemise, Tom. It's really an enjoyable sight to the male eye."

"Henry, quit playing games with me! What do you mean?!" Tom shouted. He stood up and walked over to Abigail, lifting her up from the chair she'd been tied to.

"Are you okay, Abbi? I'm sorry you're dressed in only this. I promise we'll fix it soon." he said to her, removing his black, long-sleeved shirt for her to cover herself with it. Abbi nodded, wrapping herself in his shirt, then climbed into his arms, tightly gripping her body around him. The vampires in the room had regained their composure, so Tom grabbed the stake from his belt and inconspicuously handed it to Abbi.

"Just in case, go for Henry first."

Abbi gave him a small nod.

Henry smiled and continued, watching Abbi and Tom. "I just mean that our mother also saw her which changed the course of many things. You do know of a man named Patrick, do you not?"

"What does our father have to do with anything?" Tom asked.

"I guess you'll just have wait and see. Besides, Scarlett needs to stake you and send you to Hell. Don't you remember? If you would've stayed in 1787, that wouldn't have happened. Don't you remember how things took course before?" Henry asked. "You really should get along with others better."

Tom scratched his forehead for a moment and suddenly recalled a memory.

"Yes! I was in Hell. Scarlett had staked me. Delius was there and memory controlled my previous life as a vampire and made me unleash the Beast, but now that my mind is healing itself."

"Henry! Tell me all!! Tell me what you know!" Tom demanded as he put Abigail down, looking around for Delius but not seeing him.

"Okay … Let's see now …" Henry chuckled. Tom refused to indulge his antics and motioned to Abbi.

"You can't rewrite history, Barclay," Delius chimed in as he entered the room with Scarlett, grabbing hold of Abbi's arm. In a flash, Tom had him pinned against a wall in an instant and pulled Abbi away.

"Keep away from her!" Tom yelled.

"Tom," Scarlett said approaching him, "I said it to you in 1787 and I will say it to you now. Be serious, because you hardly can be. This little human girl is a pathetic joke!"

At Scarlett's words, Tom's fury exploded and he leapt toward her, crashing into her. But just as he did, she pulled out a stake from her side. Abbi saw her quick motion and she cried out.

"Tom! Look out!" Abbi shrieked.

"See you there, Tom," Scarlett said and plunged the stake into Tom's heart. Immediately Abbi's shock caused her to run over to him.

Abbi looked down at Tom's body as his heart beat its last, and she reached for his hand as the reality of the last few moments overwhelmed her own heart. Just before his body began to shrivel up and disintegrate, he looked up to her as she reached for the stake and whispered, "No, Abbi. Don't do it. Rewrite history."

Tom shriveled up and was gone.

Abbi dropped to the floor in grief and despair, reaching her hands out to touch the spots of blood splatter where his body has been. She grabbed his cell phone and wallet which had fallen out of his pocket, noticing that only his clothes were transported with him. Meanwhile, Scarlett was laughing a few paces away. The sound of her laughter was all that was needed to ignite the flame of anger inside Abbi.

"Scarlett … he never loved you," Abbi growled as she stood and dove to knock Scarlett onto the floor, pinning her with her knee to chest and her hand gripped firmly to her throat, being certain she was touching her skin. Scarlett had no choice but to lie there as Abbi drove the stake into her heart.

Scarlett only snickered as she reacted from the piercing blow to her heart. Abbi didn't move quickly enough to move out of the way of the blood spatter and was left to be drenched in the nasty mess of it. Once Scarlett was gone, Abbi shifted to focus on Henry, thinking about her memory of Tom lying dead on the grass and how painful it was to see him that way.

She looked to the far corner of the room and saw that he was the only one left in the room. She lunged and grabbed ahold of his arm, pushing him against the wall.

"Henry, you might look like Tom, but you are *not* Tom. Goodbye, Henry. Go to Hell."

Deciding to give him the fiercest stabbing she'd ever done, she switched positions and tossed him to the floor.

"Do it, Slayer, come on down here." Henry motioned with his hand for her to sit on him.

When he did that, she took a few steps back, feeling very cautious about his intentions.

"I'll say hello to Tom for you."

Henry's words it reminded Abbi of every reason why he deserved to be staked. She straddled his waist, gripped the stake with both hands and raised it high above her head as he nonchalantly laid there with his hands behind his head waiting to die. His egotistical attitude made her plunge that stake as hard as she could, giving him no mercy, splashing blood into her face, as he cried out in agony, louder than anyone had previously.

"That's for everything you *ever* did to him. It's for my mother. It's for my sister. It's for me," she said. She closed her eyes because it was hard for her to look at his face, feeling as though she were seeing Tom. She stood up off of him, grabbed the stake from his chest, then Henry Barclay was dust. Abbi thought she would have a more satisfied feeling from staking Henry, but surprisingly, she didn't. Somehow, it didn't heal the wound from losing Tom.

She looked around for Delius too, but he was nowhere to be found, having obviously run off out of fear that Abigail would send him to Hell for all of eternity. She suddenly had an idea. If this was Delius's castle, then he must be keeping that Beast here! Tom said she was the only one who could bring it down.

She began running through the massive castle searching for anything she felt might lead to the creature, though she had no idea what she was searching for.

After running the stone halls for many minutes, she heard voices coming from a dark staircase with a heavy, medieval-looking, wooden door. As she approached, she immediately regretted her decision as the door started to creak open and she recognized Delius's voice.

"The situation is far worse than we could've predicted. Her power is greater than the eternal world has ever seen and I'm not sure that any force stands a chance against her. Even Barclay has been brought down by her. I've never seen him in the company of a human ever. But there are bite marks on her neck. And you saw what her blood is doing to Satan."

Abbi wondered what could've happened to Satan and why her blood was so unique. Tom drank her blood and she'd seen no reaction in him, although he was a vampire and was supposed to be drinking blood. Satan was a completely different creature. Her thoughts were curious as she listened further. She held her breath and listened to a second voice she didn't recognize.

"We have to be the key decision makers from this point forward. We can't allow these games to screw up anything else! My son and daughter are experienced in manipulation of the underworld, which is why he needs to be taken out of the picture before it's too late."

"Patrick Barclay!!??" Abbi thought.

"Yes. Their little interlude into the past has created quite a problem for me. Now I've got to figure out how to get the Beast back once again. I fear that this Slayer's power is too unpredictable."

"Well, her power is too unpredictable for you because you are not me. I knew she was coming and I've known it from the moment my wife saw her in my son's future which is why I changed hers! Now, let us see how well she fares against her greatest adversary … ME!"

"*You* might not be her greatest adversary," Delius said.

"What do you mean? Of course I am!"

"Do you forget that there are other eternal creatures who have power in the underworld, especially when it comes to humans?"

"Are you talking about Satan?"

"No. I'm speaking about her soul, which is something neither you nor I have known for a long time, Patrick."

Patrick paused on that topic for a moment and realized it actually held value.

"I do believe you are correct in this. The Guardian of dead souls could be a great asset to us," Patrick Barclay replied. "Let me think on this and see how he might be of use."

"Perhaps you did change her future, but you missed one key component," Delius said.

"Which is?"

"Your son has feelings."

"I now see that, which is why I will do away with him, too."

Hearing that, Abigail gasped and backed away from the stairwell. Patrick Barclay stood from where he was sitting in Delius's dungeon and approached the stairwell when he'd heard the door creaking from Abigail's movements.

Hearing him speak of "her greatest adversary" frightened her, and she now realized that Tom's warning of his father escaping from Hell could've been true. She wondered about what Henry had said about her trip to 1787 and if it was true that her being there really had changed the course of history forever. As she hurried down the hallway to find an exit, away from Patrick, she also couldn't help wondering about why Tom had been staked.

Abbi decided she needed a plan. First priority was to figure out a way to get in touch with Katherine or Charlotte to tell them about Tom and about Patrick. Running as fast as her legs would carry her, she hurried through the castle and away from her threat, so she thought.

✪✪✪

In the meantime, back in Grundy, Arlington had exhausted *all* his resources to track down Janette. Spells, vampires, werewolves, and sorcerers. When he finally found her, the sight was shocking.

"Janette!" he yelled as he watched her drain a young woman's blood. Janette used her flame power to light up the woman's body and toss her to the side once she was finished. Janette looked up to him, smirking, knowing why he was there and sauntered over to him where he was on the far end of the woods.

"I know why you're here, Arlington. I'm not going to give in."

"Janette!" he yelled, as he crashed her into a tree using the force of his magic, the tree buckled from the blow.

"I know that Satan has you under his control. Now, tell me everything I need to know. Abigail is *our* daughter! She is in great danger!"

"I will tell you NOTHING!!" she yelled, torching a few trees as she did. Arlington quickly reacted and used a cooling spell to put out the flames.

"Quilaciem!" he yelled and ice flew from his hands to put out the fire she had lit up around them.

"You ruin everything!"

Arlington patiently walked over to her, grabbed her up by the throat, cooling her by the touch of his hand as he spoke.

"If you tell me nothing, you die. If you tell me everything … you die. Either way, you die. One way just helps our daughter to live. Which way do you choose?"

She was quiet for a long moment before she said, "There is a man who is working with Delius who wants Abigail—"

"What's his name?" Arlington interrupted.

"Barclay something … I don't remember. He wants Abigail because her powers can destroy Satan."

"How can she destroy Satan?" he asked.

"With her blood."

Arlington nodded, satisfied with her response.

"Now you die."

He pierced her heart with the branch of a nearby tree and tossed her onto the remains of the burning woman. Arlington walked away from Janette's corpse. He needed to find Patrick Barclay.

Seventeen

"Katherine! Tom is gone!" Abigail cried into the cell phone she'd grabbed from Tom while looking behind herself and trying to run as far away from that castle as quickly as possible.

"I know," she responded.

"Wait. What? How do you know?" Abbi asked breathlessly, running through the woods.

"Abigail, slow down and stop running. I'm going to put a spell on you to transport you to me where I am in my estate."

"How did you know about Tom?" Abigail asked again, once she stopped running and sat on a fallen tree. She tucked herself inside Tom's shirt as she wrapped it around herself, seeking comfort.

"Henry," she replied.

"Henry?!" Abigail asked, confused. She didn't have the opportunity to continue the discussion further because she was soon hearing whispering inside her head.

"Abigail, this is a highly anticipated moment."

She spun around, looking for the man who was speaking to her.

"Who's there?! Where are you?!" she yelled out, as she frantically looked around in every direction.

"Abigail, I think the question on your mind should be, 'What do you want with me?'" he hissed as he slithered up the ground next to her feet, looping and entangling his thick body around her feet.

"Ah!" she shrieked. "What are you?!"

"Some like to call me a serpent. Some call me the Wicked One or Lucifer. I've also been known as the ruler of the underworld … But I'm best known as …"

"Satan!" Abigail called out as she stumbled backwards, kicking him off her. "Get away from me!"

"Most certainly not. I've won you. You're my prize," he said as his sheen black serpent's body transformed up and into a handsome man's physique right before her eyes. He reached for her and ran his finger over her nose and then down her jawline, his blue eyes turning yellow, then green as his tongue shot out, hissing at her.

"Get away!" she reached for his skin, hoping it would hurt him.

He laughed at her. "Your power doesn't work the same way on me, Slayer. Just watch and see. Go ahead. Touch me. Give me life."

As Abbi reached for his arm, a black cloud of smoke surrounded them and they disappeared.

✪✪✪

"How did your father get out of Hell?" Katherine asked Henry while she lit a few candles, preparing to resurrect Tom.

"I'm not certain. But as soon as I'd realized I wasn't working only with Delius anymore, I knew it was time to come here. Delius doesn't know what he's working against … or with… I don't know at this point, but Patrick can't be stopped by anyone other than Tom, of this I'm sure. He needs to be resurrected," Henry said, motioning to Katherine's oils and supplies.

After grabbing Tom's hair from his comb, the sheets from his bed, and an old shirt of his in his old chambers, Katherine laid it all in the center of a circle, dousing the pile with oils and enclosing herself in a circle with the lit candles.

"Reperio vir cui non sunt investigatione. Et perducunt illum in potestate nostra, non tenetur habere inferos."

Once Katherine's words were spoken, the pile ignited into flames. Katherine continued on with the spell.

"Et invenerunt eum in conspectu nostro. Omnes virtutes rerum resurrectionem iam!"

The flames extinguished and the candles burned up; Katherine collapsed to the floor. Henry felt Tom had been resurrected and he walked over to help his mother.

"Katherine," Henry said, extending his hand, "That's the fastest you've ever pulled his ass out of there!"

She took hold of Henry's hand and pulled herself to stand. "Well, this time he wasn't being punished for misbehavior, so he wasn't down there too long. However fast it might've seemed, it still takes effort. I cannot keep track of how many times he's been staked. For some reason, people don't like him."

Katherine looked to Henry and brushed the dust off his shirt and ran her fingers through his hair. "For the life of me, you two can't keep yourselves out of trouble."

"Let's clean this mess up," he said, and motioned to her candles and Tom's burned up sheets and clothes. They began cleaning up the different items as they heard footsteps. Katherine glanced to the door.

"We have work to do," Tom said, walking in. "Let's go."

"Bringing you back is getting more and more difficult, Thomas," Katherine said as she stood back up, "Don't get staked anymore."

"It's not like I do it on purpose! Believe me, it isn't something I enjoy."

Tom and Henry immediately headed for the nearest airport. Tom quickly arranged for his private jet to transport them back to the States.

"How did you get out of Hell, Henry?" Tom asked, once seated in his favorite spot in the first row of seats at the front of the jet. Henry chose the seat next to his brother, just to aggravate him.

"I have resources just as you do."

"Your lover's father, I assume?" Tom responded.

"Also the father of your lover, Tom. The secret of my escape will remain safe with me," Henry smirked. Tom sighed, frustrated, and turned on the TV. He mentally prepared himself for a long and irritating flight.

"So, brother, what is it about that Slayer has got you so intrigued?" Henry asked a little while later, after Tom had helped himself to vodka and blood.

"What makes you believe that I have any kind of feelings for Abigail?" he responded.

"I didn't for sure. But your response just confirmed it for me."

"How?"

"Because you called her Abigail. That shows me how connected she is to you. I called her the Slayer, but you replied by using her name."

Tom made no reply but stood to get another vodka.

✪✪✪

Upon their arrival to New York, Tom was summoned to meet at the Café Du Paradis by an anonymous text.

< Messages   **Unknown**   Details

Barclay, meet me upon your arrival to the city at your restaurant. We have some matters to discuss.

Curious about the negotiations, he walked into his private meeting room of the Café Du Paradis expecting to see Delius, but who he saw was someone far bigger than he'd anticipated.

"Good of you to meet me, Barclay. This is quite the place you've established for yourself here."

"Why are you here?! Where is she?!" Tom asked, eyes reddening as he sat down across from Satan.

"I have a deal to make with you over that Slayer," Satan said, leaning forward onto the table, rubbing his chin with his thumb and index finger. His eyes narrowed deceitfully.

"I'm not making any deals. You tell me where she is."

"That won't be happening. You've got a good thing, Barclay. She's … so yummy. Her blood is so lifegiving that I've never felt more powerful."

Tom lunged up, grabbing Satan by the throat, pinning him against the wall by his strength and his mind power, threatening him, "Tell me, Satan. Swear you haven't touched her!!"

"I might've had a taste."

Tom extended his fangs to bite, unsure of what to do, knowing that he couldn't kill Satan, at least he didn't think he could.

"I wouldn't if I were you …" Satan said.

Tom relaxed his stance, calming himself in order to hear what was happening with Abigail.

"Glad you're coming to your senses because there's one other creature in this underworld I want more than her."

"Who's that?"

"You."

"Why do you want me?! What've I got to do with anything?"

"See, she won't cooperate with me as long as you're out and walking about. My little Slayer has developed quite a liking for you."

"Why would you need her cooperation?"

"I don't, not really. But she's kind of getting on my nerves with her whining and her crying …" Satan let out an annoyed sigh and rolled his eyes.

"What's your point?" Tom asked.

"Hand yourself over so I can move on with my plans!"

"What exactly do you want from me?" Tom asked.

"I want your power. Your power is even greater than mine. You can influence anyone, anything, any creature. Even I can't do that. You've had such a great impact on her. You've made the most powerful Slayer to ever exist fall in love with you—a vampire. Work for me."

"Fall in love with me?"

"She's so smitten with you that she hardly knows what to do with herself down in my lair. She keeps crying and pleading for you, asking if she can see you, wanting to know that you're alright— you know, all that love nonsense—I could vomit at the thought of it, really."

"Please just let me see him … I won't do what you say until I know he's okay," Satan said, mocking Abigail's voice. "It's pathetic."

"Could it be possible? Could she really be in love with me?"

"And Abigail? What will become of her? I want to see her before I make any sort of deal with you. How can I even be certain she is alive and well?" Tom asked.

"I will take you to her. Follow me," Satan said, standing and walking to the hallway directly behind them, where he quickly disappeared into a black cloud of smoke, taking Tom with him. Satan and Tom were transported directly into Satan's lair, right into the black depths of Hell.

"She's right over there. See, she's alive. She is well," he said, pointing to Abigail, who was sitting in a cage, leaning against the silver bars, with her arms chained overhead.

"What is this?!" Tom shouted, hurrying over to her but quickly being blocked by the demon guards. Tom paused and scanned for their minds and Abbi's.

"Abbi, are you hurt?"

She shook her head, looking over to him, breathing a sigh of relief at his presence, mouthing, "I'm so scared."

"It's going to be alright. I'm going to figure something out."

"Now you've seen her, Barclay. Do we have a deal? You, for her. Her blood made me strong, but you will complete the picture."

"What's he talking about, Tom?" Abbi yelled from where she was chained inside the cage, leaning forward as best she could to grip ahold of the silver bars, watching Tom walk toward Satan.

Tom looked over to her and thought about how the fate of the world was really resting in her hands. But then he looked at her arms clasped in the shackles and his heart dropped in his chest at the sight of the only woman he'd ever loved being trapped in such a state. He felt desperate to do anything he could to release her from those binds.

"How do I know you'll keep your word?"

At Tom's question, Satan motioned for the guard to bring Abigail over to them. "You give me the word and not only will I release her, but she will also—from this moment forward—be broken of the binds of my venom."

The demon dropped Abigail on the floor at Satan's feet, where she reached out and gripped Tom's ankle before Tom kneeled down, scooping her up, whispering, "I don't know what to do. You make feel so helpless."

Wrapping her arms tightly around him, she whispered, "Just do what you think is best. I trust you. I love you."

After hearing her words, now knowing someone in his life loved him, he made his decision. "I'll take your deal, Satan. You took what you wanted from her. You have her blood in you. You're powerful, full of life, strong, and you don't need her. Let her go. Spare her. Use me."

"What?! No, Tom!" Abbi shrieked.

"Done," Satan said, and before she could protest any more, Abbi was out of Tom's arms and disappearing into a black cloud of smoke.

"Thomas Barclay …" Satan said.

Tom turned to Satan as he sat alone in the darkness, anticipating his first job as one of Satan's demons.

"What am I to do?" he replied.

"Destroy her."

✪✪✪

"Tom?" Abigail yelled out as she stood, looking around herself.

"Tom?!" she yelled out once more, panicking, realizing he was nowhere in sight. She realized she was now standing all alone in his Grundy house.

Nervously, she ran through the house, calling his name, searching for any signs that he might be there but found nothing.

Eighteen

"He's going to head straight for her. She needs protected," Henry said to Katherine as he rushed down the halls to the main entrance, Charlotte and Katherine quickly following behind.

"Henry!" Charlotte yelled, "Why should we believe that you are suddenly concerned for Abigail's safety? You've been on Delius's side this whole time. Why are you against him now?" she demanded, causing Henry to stop and face her, eyes reddened.

"Because I didn't know that Delius was working with our father. I hate our father and I will do anything I can in order to be certain that he doesn't succeed. By the end of today, that Slayer is going to be so in love with me she won't know who Tom ever was!"

"Henry, wait!" Katherine yelled.

"What?"

"Whose side are you on? Delius and Patrick want her away from Satan in order to gain control of the Beast and open Hell once more. Satan wants her destroyed because of her blood. Tom is now under control of Satan. Then there's you. Where do you stand?" she asked, unbelieving of his intentions.

"I stand alone."

Henry exited the house, leaving Katherine and Charlotte in a mind-frazzled daze and headed straight to Grundy, where he knew Abigail would be mourning the loss of Tom.

Abigail was sleeping peacefully in Tom's Grundy house, unaware of what was coming to her as Satan's instructions were coming into fruition.

"You said you want her, that she's valuable to you," Tom questioned, hopeful to spare himself of killing the only woman he'd ever loved.

"It is true. But you see, what was valuable for me is no longer useful, as now I have become bored and I shall play a different game," Satan taunted, spinning his glowing rod, balancing it with one hand.

"A different game?" Tom asked.

"Yes. *Kill* her. I want to see the second most powerful creature in the eternal world crumble. Once you see her die by your hands, you *will* fall. And then the god will be in his heaven and all will be well and right with the world."

He laughed wickedly at himself, eyes turning yellow, jumping down off his throne, walking over to Tom. "You and your father have ruled this underworld for FAR too long. It is I who should be most powerful … I! Not you, not him, not even that beautiful little Slayer who is going to be the destruction of you. I am the god of this underworld!!! Today will be the day that you remember as the day Lucifer regained control of the under realm!" he yelled as he dropped the rod at his feet, transforming into a serpent as he did. When he slithered away, he whispered into Tom's mind, *"Destroy her and you will see how quickly the heart destroys you."*

Before Tom could react, he disappeared into a black cloud of smoke, being transported right outside his Grundy house to see Abigail sleeping peacefully inside.

"I can't …" he whispered when he saw her lying on his bed wrapped up in his blankets.

"Oh … but you must," Satan said, appearing behind him.

"And if I don't? What then? What if I decide not to participate in your games? What's the worst that will happen to me?!" he yelled.

"Nothing, which is the beauty of it all. Everything will happen to *her*. Because the quickest way to destroy a man is to attack his heart," Satan said, reaching around and tracing the shape of a heart on Tom's chest, where the tattoo of the sun was still burned on him. "That is why you wanted the ability to walk in the sun, now, wasn't it? Everything you've done since leaving Hell has been for the heart. Let's see how quickly it destroys you." Satan vanished.

Tom jumped down off the house and sped quickly away, trying to escape the relentless noise of Satan's attempts to torment him—even for only a few brief moments—when he found himself at Arlington's house.

"Arlington!" he called out, stepping inside, looking for any signs that he might be there.

"I can't help you," Arlington answered from where he was sitting on the sofa.

Tom walked into the living room and responded, "How is it you even know what I want?"

"I know much more than for what I am given credit, Barclay. And this is the very reason I told my daughter not to become attached to you. She is crying herself to sleep in your house because she loves you and you've sold your soul to Satan. Oh, what wicked tangled webs we do weave."

"Are you going to help me or are you going to sit there ridiculing me like the bloody son of a bitch you are?!"

"Son of a bitch ... while technically a true statement, that's still an insult, even for me. As I already said, I cannot. There is nothing I can do. My suggestion would be to ask your sister."

"Charlotte?"

"I've found time manipulation to be a very successful tool for getting myself out of sticky situations. She's the most resourceful time traveler there is. Goodbye now," Arlington waved him out.

He knew that Arlington was probably right and sped away to search for Charlotte.

In the meantime, there were bigger plans in the making.

✪✪✪

"Tell me again, Henry, why are you helping this Slayer whom I call sister?" Claire asked.

"I told you what my father said. I'm not actually helping her. We just need to keep her away from Tom. If we keep her away from Tom, then they can follow through with all the plans. Satan wants to destroy her. My father doesn't want to do that because he says there is value in her."

"What value is there in her?"

"She can destroy Satan if he uses too much of her blood."

"Oh. I suppose he would want that since they're enemies," Claire reasoned. "I understand. That makes sense. Well, you'd better get to it then. Go get some Slayer lovin'. Just be sure to save some time for me," she said and winked.

"Of course," he replied with a kiss to her cheek. "But you get rewarded with good behavior."

Henry left and strolled over to Tom's house only to be interrupted with a surprise in his plans.

"Tom!" Henry exclaimed when he saw Tom sitting on the porch roof, staring into his bedroom window.

"Why are you here, Henry?"

"Just checking and making rounds."

"I want the truth!" Tom yelled, jumping off the porch roof, pummeling Henry to the ground.

"That's the truth," he stated.

Tom stood, holding out his hand, helping Henry to a stand.

"Why do I not want to believe you?" Tom asked.

Henry shrugged and said, "Probably because you shouldn't."

"You're an ass."

"I know."

"Charlotte is dead," Tom said.

"Our sister?" Henry asked.

"No, the other mutual Charlotte we know. Yes, our sister!" Tom said.

"What … why … how?" Henry replied, seeming actually regretful.

"Satan. Because I haven't killed Abigail yet. He's going after things Abbi cares about. He'll keep it up, until I kill her," Tom said, pointing up to his window and then started pacing frustratedly, running his hands through his hair.

"I can't do it, Henry. I can't kill her."

"Want me to do it? I can kill her," Henry shrugged.

Tom flashed his fangs, growling. "Touch her and you lose your life."

Henry put his hands up passively, "Just a suggestion. But, whatever … You know, I bet our mother could resurrect her or even Arlington, you know, if you killed her." He shrugged.

"That is true … you're right," Tom responded.

"I thought you didn't have feelings for the Slayer?" Henry asked, trying to provoke his brother.

Tom began pacing back and forth, not knowing how to respond, until he finally said, "She told me she loves me."

"Love? Do we even know how to love?" Henry asked.

Tom stopped his pacing and looked over, shrugged and said, "I'm not sure, but I know whatever I'm feeling is enough that I can't kill her."

"Wait. How did you know about Charlotte?" Henry asked and followed Tom onto the porch roof.

"I contacted Katherine hoping that Lottie could reverse time and erase everything that's happened. She told me that Lottie was casting a spell using fire and the flames got out of control and Lottie couldn't bring the spell back into her command. They overtook her and …"

"That doesn't sound like her at all. She's no amateur," Henry pointed out.

"I know. This is definitely the work of Satan," Tom agreed. "But I don't know what to do. Would you kill Claire?"

"Maybe. She's kind of an annoyance sometimes. Although, I might miss her. I like having her around because she's not a normal human and she's better company than vampire women, who are dreadfully annoying, which is why I assume you're so infatuated with that Slayer. I've kept her around a long time. On second thought, no. I wouldn't kill Claire. I don't think I could. I guess that's the human still in me." Henry shrugged again. "But any other chick? Yep, in a heartbeat."

"Barclay …" Tom heard Satan whispering. "Go upstairs right now and kill her or I will have my next victim …"

"Who will Satan choose next do you think?" Tom asked Henry.

"Who does the Slayer love?" Henry asked.

"She has a friend …"

"Nah, that wouldn't be useful to Satan. It's got to be someone of use to you but also that the Slayer cares about …"

"Arlington?" Henry asked.

"No. I don't think Abbi really cares that much for him."

"Hmm …" Henry thought for a moment, then said, "Why did he pick Lottie?"

"Satan said something about attacking her by attacking my heart."

"Well, think about the next best person he'd be able to do that …"

"Katherine!" Tom yelled out.

Tom panicked, knowing Satan would follow through, and Tom didn't want to lose his most trusted and valuable resource. So, he quickly raced inside and leapt onto the bed, eyes reddened, fangs extended, hovering over Abigail.

"Please forgive me …" he said before grabbing her head in his hands, ready to bite, startling her from sleep.

"Tom?!" she cried out when she saw the red in his eyes. "What are you doing?!"

Looking at the fear and terror in her eyes, and hearing the tremor beating from her beautiful heart, he leaned in to kiss her forehead and said, "I can't do it. You're still you. I might be different now, but you'll always be you. I'll accept my fate, whatever that might be. But this … I just can't. I could never hurt you. I love you, Abigail."

Tom jumped off of her and opened the bedroom window and quickly exited.

With her mind in a whirlwind, she sat up, wondering what had just happened *You're still you … I could never hurt you …*

She paused on his last words to her.

I love you.

Unbelieving of what she heard and thinking that Satan must've sent him there to hurt her, she felt sickened at the thought. She was also shocked to hear those words coming from him. Reality hit her fiercely and she laid back down to cry.

"Tom …" she sobbed. "How could you do this? How could you leave me to deal with this chaos? I'm so afraid."

"I'm here," said a voice from the corner.

"Who's there?!" she yelled out, "Show yourself!"

Henry emerged from the far corner of the room and walked over to where Abigail was on the bed as she cautiously stared at him.

"You're not Tom. I know you're not."

"This is true. Don't be afraid of me. I'm here to help you."

"Help me? Why would you want to help me?" she asked.

"Because I know of what you're up against," he leaned in closer, running his index finger along her arm.

"I don't trust you." She yanked her arm away and moved back in the bed.

"It isn't me you should be cautious of, not anymore. Charlotte is dead and it is all Tom's fault!" Henry yelled, spreading his arms out angrily as Abigail let out a horrified gasp.

"He killed her?! What?! Why? How …" she asked, beginning to cry, knowing that the man she loved was no longer who she thought he was.

"That's a complicated question," Henry responded, not wanting to answer with the whole truth, wanting to proceed with his plan.

"He was here. Where did he go?" she asked, moving closer, resting her head on his chest, trying to soothe her sadness from the loss of Charlotte.

Feeling hopeful, like he was one step closer to seducing Abigail and ruining his brother, he wrapped his arms around her and replied, "I haven't a clue."

"Oh. Is he going to kill me? Is he coming back?" she asked, wiping the tears from her eyes, looking up to his face, understanding it was Henry but seeing the face of Tom.

"Yes, I believe he will. He's not who he was, which is why I'm here. I came for your protection."

"But he said …"

"He is under Satan's control now. I am certain that he will say whatever he needs in order to make you believe what needs to be done. Delius and my father want you away from Satan and my job is to keep you away from them."

"What do they want with me?" she asked, burying her head in his chest once again, forgetting he wasn't Tom.

"Many things, but they know your value, and they know that Satan wants you destroyed."

"Is there anything we can do? Anything at all?"

Concerned that she was focusing too much on Tom, Henry hurried around to the other side of the bed and laid down next to her. "No. I don't think there is."

"But what about Adelemar? I think I'm going to ask Arlington …"

"Abigail," Henry grabbed her hand, pulling it to his lips. "There's nothing you can do. But I'm here now."

"No!" she snatched her hand away, "I don't believe it! I won't accept it!"

She stood and walked to the closet, where she emerged a few minutes later in Tom's sweats. "I'm going to see Arlington. He will figure something out." Then she walked out and drove Tom's Aston Martin straight to Arlington's house.

"Arlington!!" she banged on his front door a few times before realizing it was unlocked and she walked inside.

"Arlington, wake up!" she said after walking into his bedroom and seeing he was passed out in boxer shorts on his bed with his TV playing.

"Abigail?" he answered groggily.

She walked over and turned off his rotary dial TV, then she stood at the foot of his bed with her arms crossed, impatiently tapping her foot.

"It's like five a.m. What do you want?" he asked, sitting up.

"I need your help. You need to fix this! This is all your fault!" she yelled.

"I assume you are speaking of that vampire …" he groaned, rolling his eyes, moving his legs to the side of the bed, putting on a green robe as he stood.

"Ugh!" she huffed. "You *will* fix this! I know you have powers that I have not even witnessed and I know that you can reverse time and teleport … or whatever … you have to do *something!*" she continued shouting at him.

"Number one," he said, exiting into the hallway and descending down the stairs where she hurriedly followed after. "This is not my fault and I am not obliged to help at all. Number two," he paused and walked into the kitchen and began brewing a pot of tea in order to aggravate her.

Abigail spat, "Number two?! What's number two, Arlington?!"

"Right … I told you not to fall in love with that vampire. I warned you. So, technically this would be *your* fault."

"Ugh!! I can't stand you! So, are you not going to help me?!"

After a few moments, he sighed and picked up his cup of tea and headed into the living room where he sat on the green sofa.

"While I would really *love* to assist you in your relationship problems, I'll tell you what I told him when he was here yesterday."

"Tom was here?"

"Yes, asking the same favor that you are."

"And?"

"I cannot," he said, "The only way to undo any of this would be to reverse time. I told him to ask his sister."

"Sadly, Charlotte is dead," Abbi said.

"I see. Well, Satan must've known Tom would go to her for help."

"What do you mean?" she asked.

"Well, I know that if he doesn't kill you, which he is currently refusing to do, Satan is going to dispose of all that he needs or cares for. Charlotte is one of his most trusted and valuable resources. The witch community needs her, as does your lover boy. I'm assuming Katherine will be soon to follow," he stated passively.

"But you *won't* help me?" she pleaded.

"I can't."

"You can reverse time. Tom told me you took him back in time."

"I can travel in time, not reverse time. There is a very big difference."

"Oh. What am I to do now? Can't you bring her back from the dead or do *anything*?" she asked, wiping tears from her eyes, feeling as though there was not one bit of hope left.

"I cannot help you. There is one, however, who can."

Nineteen

"Why can't we just travel to places like normal people do?" she complained as Arlington ushered her onto the private jet.

"You weren't complaining when you were flying around in luxury on that vampire's private airplane."

"Well, his plane wasn't owned by ..." she paused and looked around at the men wearing a variety of different colored cloaks, "His plane wasn't owned by the wizard mafia."

"There's no such thing of what you speak. Besides, you're safer with me than you ever were with not-so-Prince Charming."

Ignoring his remark, she asked, "What's he like?"

"Well, he's nothing like your lover boy, so get that idea out of your head. But he is the most powerful being you'll ever encounter, which is why your Barclay is the way he is, and also his sister and brother—"

"What is he?" she interrupted. "Is he a god?"

"No. I suppose you could think of him as the designated authority of all the underworld."

"You mean, that's not who Satan is?"

"No. Satan is a very powerful demon and he reigns in Hell. But there is a larger underworld than just Hell. That's where Patrick comes in."

"Oh, what's he called? Like, you're a ..."

"Warlock."

"Right ... He's a ... ?"

"They call him the Ascendant."

"What?"

"He's unlike anything else, Abigail. There is no other creature like him. He holds dominion."

"And Tom?"

"I would assume, had Tom not been turned into a vampire, that he would've tapped into skills and powers much like his father's, eventually."

"What does he do?" she asked, taking her seat on the plane next to Arlington, feeling nervous to meet Tom's father. She kept wondering why it was that he was being kept in secret and what about him was so powerful.

"You'll see," Arlington replied.

✪✪✪

When they arrived to England, Adelemar arranged to have them taken straight to Gwarenmogt—far removed from any city life—where Abigail would be training to fight.

"Welcome … Welcome to a place where only the true sorcerers leave," Adelemar said as they entered. "You've arrived just in time. Quickly now! There's not a moment to spare."

"But … I'm not a sorcerer. What is going on?" Abigail asked as she was ushered down a dark stairwell and into a large room with swords and knives, daggers, and bows and arrows hanging all along the walls.

"We are training you. The Beast will soon be released out of Hell. You are the only one capable of stopping it. No spells will work directly on the creature, but indirectly, yes. However, your power will work. You can contain the creature and bring it down. You have to get to it before it destroys all of mankind," Adelemar explained, handing her a silver sword.

"She ready?" Henry asked coming into view.

"Why is *he* here?" Abigail asked.

"Fight him. Give him all you've got," Arlington ordered.

"You can't be serious!"

"We very much are. There is no way we are sending you out into the unknown to battle not only the elder Barclay, but also this creature without at least having some necessary battle skills. Now, fight!"

At Adelemar's command, she ran full-speed into Henry, crashing into him, but he had her pinned on her back by her throat faster than she could blink. He was wearing gloves, so her power didn't affect him, not this time.

"Abigail, pay attention!" Arlington hollered to her as she stood back up. "You need to concentrate. Use your abilities! Look for skin; let your emotions take you over."

"I am!" she cried, wiping tears from her eyes as one of Adelemar's adjunct wizards handed her sword back to her and she approached Henry once more.

"Have another go?" he asked.

She nodded and walked back over to where she'd been before, resuming her fighting stance.

At Adelemar's command, they lunged at each other—Henry knocking her back, pinning her down once more—until she reached her hand around and pulled on his ear.

"I'm not going to let you take me down, Henry."

Abbi quickly turned the tables, holding him by the throat, straddling his waist, and looked to one of the wizards to throw her a stake. As she did that, Henry took his advantage and tossed her onto her back, holding her hands above her head.

"You're mine, Slayer," he taunted. "Did you play these games with my lookalike? I bet Tom loved games like this. It's kind of a turn on."

"Ugh!" she spewed, standing back up, walking away from him to grab a different weapon off the wall near the wizards-in-training.

"Which one will it be?" a young, girl wizard asked.

"The silver dagger, please," she said and smiled slightly, looking over to Henry.

The wizard girl giggled and handed her the dagger, whispering, "Go for the left ribs; he's been protecting his right side."

"Huh, thanks." Abbi took the dagger, re-centering herself across the room from Henry as he crouched down in his fight stance, extending his teeth, ready to attack.

"Show me what you've got!" he hollered, taunting her, flashing his fangs.

She slid the dagger up her arm, slipping it underneath her sweater to conceal it from his view but still holding it firmly in her grasp. Then she took off at him, just as he dove at her, full force, knocking her back. But just as he did, she took that dagger, and plunged it into his side, watching him groan, and she reached her hand up, grabbing his throat, spinning him around, landing on top of him instead.

"Gotcha," she said, as she straddled his waist, yanking the dagger out from his side, watching him moan in pain.

"Damnit, Abigail. That hurts," he grimaced.

"I know," she replied and playfully smacked his cheek then stood up, while he laid there waiting for his stab wound to heal. "That was the point, Henry."

"Oh really?" he asked, raising his eyebrows, watching her walk away, now understanding his brother's fixation on her.

They repeated this process about six or seven times until she'd about given up, and then Adelemar ordered Henry to remove the gloves.

"Now, Henry. Remove the gloves. Let her have the advantage," Adelemar said.

"Now, Slayer!" Henry said. "Come at me once more," he incited, motioning for her to attack him.

She breathed heavily, looking to Arlington, then to Adelemar, who both nodded at her to proceed, and immediately she lunged at Henry, dagger extended. But he had her pinned to the floor by her neck.

"Gotcha!" he laughed.

Abbi's adrenaline was high and Henry was soon being controlled by her touch. His canines retracted and the redness around his eyes faded. She moved her arm out to the side of where she was laying and grabbed the silver dagger to pull it towards her, grasping it in both hands and pushing it against his neck.

"You …" he said, staring into her eyes, stroking her jawline with his thumb, while he held her jaw in his hand. "This power you have over me is … gaining my attention."

He stood and held out his hand to assist her in standing.

She let out a disgusted groan. "Knock it off, Henry. I know what you're trying to do. It won't work." She shook herself off and walked over to Arlington.

"You're looking better," he said as she approached. "Keep using that power to your advantage. No one will gain authority over you; well, no one other than … you know. We just need to work on your slow reflexes." He looked to Adelemar. "No one stands a chance against her once she gets them in her grasp."

"I agree," Adelemar said. "But we need to be sure they don't kill you before you're able to do that," he said to Abigail.

"What about a protection spell?" Henry suggested.

"I can do that," Adelemar agreed. "That should be easy enough."

Adelemar jumped down off his marble pillar and walked over to Abigail, placing his hands on her shoulders. As he closed his eyes and said "Intrusidoros," a green sphere of light enclosed around her, knocking his hands away. As that happened, he said, "Finis!" and the sphere vanished and Abigail was thrown to the floor.

"Oh my!" she hollered out as she pounded onto the hard marble floor. "What did you just do?!"

"I protected you from all intruding hands. It's very simple really. Your body's power will know when to use it." He walked away and hopped onto the pillar once more.

"I don't understand."

"I tapped into the force of your Slayer energy. I used its power to help shield you from those who shouldn't be touching you. Your Slayer instincts are smart and will know when to put the shield up. Go ahead. Try it." He motioned for Henry.

"Give it a go, Slayer. What's the worst that could happen?" he teased.

Her heart beat a little faster as she ran full speed at Henry, while he sped lightning fast towards her, claiming her in his grasp and pinning her once again. But as soon as he did, her defense went up and he was knocked back at least 20 yards away and into the far wall.

"What the hell was that?!" he yelled out while he gained his composure and she stood to look at him.

"She is now able to use her naturally given forces to her full advantage," Adelemar said.

"You just cheated the system!" Henry yelled. "I want a redo!"

"Who's running this show now?" Abigail laughed, sticking out her tongue at Henry.

"Enough flirting," Arlington said, walking over. "You have bigger problems to worry about."

"I can't do it. I can't …"

"I know. But we won't worry about that problem until we face it," he replied as they continued walking towards Adelemar.

"Let's get her going. We need her to see Katherine," Arlington said to Adelemar.

"I'll arrange for it immediately," he responded.

"This all sounds wonderful, but …" Abigail interrupted.

"But?" Adelemar questioned.

"You're all forgetting one vital and very crucial piece to all of this."

"What's that?" Henry shrugged.

"I won't kill Tom."

"I'll do it," Henry said. "I'll kill Tom."

"No one is killing Tom!" she yelled, walking out. "Let's go Arlington. We have a lot to accomplish."

✪✪✪

"I don't feel ready," Abbi said to Arlington as they exited the plane and entered the airport terminal.

"There's no turning back now. You're going to be fine. No one else can do this. It's your destiny. It's what you've been chosen to do."

"That doesn't make me *ready* for it, Arlington."

"But you must be! This isn't a choice. That fate of the world is resting in your hands." He put his hand on her back and hurried her

261

along through the terminal towards the exit, much to Abigail's dismay.

Abigail watched out the window the entire drive, counting the trees as they passed by her window, recalling the time she'd had to go into hiding because of very similar reasons—her powers and Slayer abilities—and she thought about Tom.

"Where do you think he is?" she looked over to Arlington as he concentrated on driving.

"I would surmise that he's watching your every move. I'm sure he's somewhere nearby."

"Do you really believe so?" she replied somewhat hopefully, looking back to the window.

"He no longer belongs to himself, Abigail. He must do as commanded."

"Can you stop at that convenience store right there? I need to pee." She pointed to the lit-up signs across the road and gave a pleading look to Arlington, letting him know she desperately needed to go.

"Fine," he grumbled. "But be quick."

"Give me some money. I want some food." She held out her hand like a teenager with an allowance.

He handed her ten dollars from his wallet. "Be quick, Abigail."

After using the restrooms, she took her time browsing the aisles in the shop for something to snack on. But she started feeling anxious when she felt as though someone was following her, and several times she turned around to look for the suspect, finding no one.

She hurried to buy a bag of chips and a Coke and exited out the front, but a quick figure snatched her up, speeding to the back of the building. Abigail dropped her drink and chips to the ground when she saw who it was.

"Tom!" she yelled out almost cheerfully but still frightened as he held her shoulders against the wall, bracing his arm across her chest. He reached his other hand around her neck, pulling firmly against her head by her hair, being careful not to touch her skin.

"Hello, Abigail," he growled, "I've missed you."

"You're going to kill me."

"You didn't state that as a question," he smirked.

"No. Because I know that's why you're here."

He extended his fangs and moved in to bite.

"I want you to know that I've thought about you every day and that I haven't stopped loving you. You've meant so much to me, even in all of this. I truly loved you."

He backed away, looked her in the eyes, allowed himself to feel her emotions as she cried, and placed her hand on his cheek.

"I can still feel this, Abigail. I feel your hurt. Satan didn't take that away from me, which is making it all the more difficult. I never told you, but you're the woman—the one I told you about in 1787—the one I loved, which is why …" he stepped away and looked to a nearby tree, snapping off a branch with his mind and gave it to her. "Do it. Kill me. Lock me away."

"No!" she yelled.

"Abigail, you don't understand. Satan isn't going to stop. This is the only way! Stake me! Only you can make all of this go away!"

"No, Tom!"

"Abigail …"

He looked at her intensely, scanning for her butterfly thoughts. Once he found them, he mentally commanded, *"Abigail, stake me,"* and she had no choice. She walked over, held the branch up as he laid on the ground, and she forcefully plunged it into his heart. Then he was dust, again.

Inundated by a mixture of emotions, she just sat there staring at the blood saturating her shirt and pants and the tree branch she was still holding.

Arlington ran up. "Abigail?! What's taking so long? What are you doing out here and why are you covered in blood?"

She looked up to him, tossed the branch away, and began to cry, unable to answer.

"Abigail, tell me what happened." He pulled her to stand.

"It's … Tom …" she sobbed.

"You mean?" He pointed to the bloody stake questioningly.

"Uh huh," Abbi nodded, sniffling.

"Right. Well, then I suppose that's all settled. He's safely locked in eternity for all time."

"What?!" she yelped.

"Well, once a vampire is staked by the Slayer, there's no escaping."

"We need to get to Katherine! Hurry!" She took Arlington's hand and pulled him along to the car.

"What's Katherine going to do?"

"There is much to be done."

Epilogue

"Welcome back," Satan said as Tom paced the length of the darkness, realizing that he was now trapped down there for all of eternity.

"It isn't as terrible down here as you believe it to be," Satan continued. "And considering that now you're no longer one of my demons, you're free to roam about with the rest of the condemned. You might as well make the best of it."

He motioned around to everyone else, and Tom looked around suddenly realizing …

Charlotte.

✪✪✪

"We cannot leave Charlotte down there," Henry said to Delius as he downed a shot of vodka, leaning back in the leather chair as he sat in Delius's conference room.

"Of this, I am aware. However, I cannot risk exposing either of them to Arlington or Abigail yet. We are in the midst of a very critical time," Delius responded.

"Can't you just resurrect her and bring her here?" Claire asked.

Henry laughed to mock Claire. Then he said, "My sweet, you underestimate my sister's powers. If we resurrect her, there is no way we'll ever be able to contain her here. She'll either put us all under a spell or she'll be transporting us all through time."

"Henry is correct. Charlotte is too powerful a creature for us to contain. We need to seek out higher intelligences," Delius said.

"If she is so powerful, then can't she just resurrect herself?" she asked.

"This is also true, which is why I want him summoned before she brings him out. I want him for myself!" Delius said, slamming his fists.

"C'mon, Delius. I don't want to get involved with him again," Henry said. "Besides, who's to say he would even cooperate with us? Only a few weeks ago he was making googly eyes at Arlington's favorite offspring."

"Hey!" Claire exclaimed.

Delius turned around in his chair, and resting his elbow on the table, he placed his chin on his hands before he spoke. "Claire, it's no secret that Arlington prefers the Slayer, and for good reason too. Now that Tom is in the picture, there is a lot to risk. There might be reason to believe that she is more valuable than *he* is, and he is *our* most valuable resource."

"I wouldn't say he is our *most* valuable," Henry scoffed. "He's only the second most powerful creature."

"Do be quiet, Henry. Your jealousy of your brother is very evident 99% of the time," Patrick Barclay said, walking into the room.

Henry glared at his father and said, "Patrick, you've always had a certain fondness for that son. What was it about him? Perhaps his ability to pay particularly close attention to every woman he wasn't supposed to? No. Though that sounds like Tom, it usually just pissed you off! Or maybe it was his ability to disregard his duties as eldest son? Nope. Wasn't that one either. Maybe it was just the special resemblance he bore to you? Wait … no … not that one either! I think that's *both* of us! Could it have been that he was the one who gave up his love and was agreeing to marry the woman of your choice? No? Wrong again? Was that me, you say?" he said and looked to Claire, who saddened her eyes, knowing that Henry gave up marrying her and would have married the woman of Patrick's choice had he not been turned.

"Could it be that he was the one who just happened to do every little thing that you wanted? That was me too!" Henry yelled, lunging across the table toward Patrick. But as he did, Patrick motioned with his hand and picked Henry up with his mind, spinning him around, causing Henry to disappear into thin air.

"Henry?!" Claire exclaimed, "Where did he go? What did you do?!"

"He will return. I'm putting him in time out. The next 10 minutes of his life will be spent as though he never existed," Patrick said.

"What?!" she exclaimed as Delius laughed.

"I transformed his current reality. He needs taught a lesson."

"Can we all just get down to business here?" Delius asked.

"Absolutely, Delius," Patrick said, "You want my son out of Hell and you don't want Katherine or Arlington to know about it, yet you also want to keep him away from the Slayer and Charlotte," Patrick said, picking Henry's vodka bottle up from the table and taking a swig, leaning back in his chair. "I understand all of that, but you certainly don't need Tom out of Hell now because I'm here. Remember, he is only the *second* most powerful creature in the underworld. I am the first."

"In spite of that fact, we know eventually Katherine or Arlington will resurrect him," Delius said. "We cannot let him into the path of either of them. Together they will destroy the Beast!"

"Why are you so certain that Arlington wants anything to do with Tom?" Claire asked, wondering why her father wanted involved with her lover's twin when he'd never mentioned or cared about him before.

"Claire, you innocent child," Delius said, "You see, Arlington doesn't care about Tom. Arlington cares about your sister. Your sister is in love with Tom. Therefore, Arlington is now vested into the world's most powerful vampire. You see, dear, the way the system works is: a woman falls in love and it controls everything and everyone around her. Your sister is currently the most wanted being in the above and in the underworld; therefore, so is Tom."

"Why?" she asked.

Patrick chuckled for a moment before he responded, "Because there is nothing else like her … yet."

"Yet?" she asked, but neither Patrick nor Delius responded as Claire stared at Patrick for a moment. Claire observed how much Henry looked like Patrick with his dark hair, masculine features, and strong chin. She noticed, however, that Patrick's eyes were a bright, brilliant blue, and she found herself missing Henry's human color as she stared at his father.

"Claire!" Delius yelled, snapping her from her daydreaming.

"Yes?" she asked.

"Henry is going to return here. You need to be here to wait for him. I'm going to see Ingrid and figure out a way to …"

"You're going about this all wrong, Delius," Patrick said.

"Why?" he asked.

"Tom isn't in Hell. He's in Grundy Hill."

About the Author

Meg Sechrest knew she wanted to write since she was a teenager. As a teen, she received a scholarship from the American Cancer Society for an article she wrote about her struggles with brain cancer. After rotating through several majors at Ohio University Eastern, she realized this writing thing might turn into a career. She's an avid fan of classic literature (Shakespeare, Dickens, Austen) and considers Jane Austen the most influential person in her life.

Follow Meg:
Twitter: @Meg_Sechrest
Instagram: @Meg_Sechrest
Facebook: @MegSechrestWrites

Follow The Slayer Series (@Slayer_series) on Twitter for updates!